DARE TO SURVIVE

By

Carolyn V. Hamilton

Based on a true story.

ISBN 978-0-9909664-9-4
Trade Paper Edition

Cover Design by Swift House Press

www.carolynvhamilton.com

DEDICATION

This novel is dedicated to every woman worldwide who in her struggle for survival finds herself in such a desperate situation that she feels helpless and compelled to mule illegal drugs from one country to another.

Chapter 1

At Lima's airport security check-point Cathryn Prentis's life changed forever. Dragging the wheeled scuba case across the scarred linoleum, she shifted her backpack on her shoulder and headed for security. An attendant with a wordless half-smile placed the case and backpack on the conveyor belt.

Cathryn had arrived early—three hours before her scheduled Aero Mexico flight—and found Lima's international airport almost empty. Her watch read 8:10 p.m. Dom wouldn't arrive for another half-hour. She would get the x-ray part of check-in out of the way, find a place to sit in this lifeless, shoebox of an airport, and wait for him and the Aero Mexico desk people to arrive. Darkness outside and the humid October night air in 2003 made the airport chilly, and her feet in their stylish, strappy, high-heeled sandals were cold.

She thought of the warmth of her recent days at Machu Picchu, the surreal spirituality of the famous Inca ruins, the kindness of her guide, Hector, and hot coca tea. She thought about how fortunate she was that her dear friend, Dom, had gifted her with this amazing trip. For so many years she'd dreamed of Machu Picchu and she was so grateful that Dom had made it possible for her to realize that dream.

Minutes passed. The x-ray attendant asked her something in Spanish. All she understood was her name. *"Kath-rrreen Prrrentees."*

"No habla Español."

He rolled over the scuba case. *"Escuba?"*

"Sí. Scuba tank. There's no pressure." Cathryn smiled and opened the case so he could see for himself.

He removed the tank's valve and sent the tank back through the x-ray machine without the case.

"Something wrong?"

He didn't look at her when he answered. "No."

Cathryn figured he didn't speak much, if any, English. She shifted her weight from one foot to the other. What had she been thinking when she put on high-heeled sandals? She spotted a nearby row of chairs and tottered towards them.

The Peruvian x-ray attendant exploded in a loud barrage of Spanish. Who was he yelling at? Cathryn looked around, saw people staring at her. She stopped, perplexed, looked back at the x-ray guy. How military he looked in his brown airport uniform.

In broken English he cried, "No move."

She pointed to the chairs. "I just want to sit down, okay?"

This time he screamed. "No move!"

Cathryn saw the Aero Mexico people getting ready to open their check-in desk. Two of them raised their heads to look at her.

"It's just scuba gear. I checked it myself before I left the hotel. How much longer do I have to wait?"

The way the x-ray guy stared at her made her skin flush, her neck blossom. His face had contorted, reminding her of a horror movie opening scene. If nothing was wrong, why was he yelling at her? A helpless feeling swirled around her, linking arms with unease.

"You – no – move." His words were a low growl that nibbled at the back of her neck.

Other airport people joined the x-ray attendant. None of them spoke English. Cathryn could tell they were talking about her from the way they looked at her while they spoke to each other.

Other travelers were now presenting their luggage for x-ray. Where was Dom? He should have been here by now. Why was everyone staring at her like she was a tall, high-heeled, alien? Cathryn saw a cockroach scuttle under the x-ray machine. She shuddered. She hated cockroaches.

A new group of airport personnel arrived to look at the scuba tank and babble in Spanish and stare at the tall *gringa*. The airport spun in a haze of other-world activity. Cathryn felt like the only person in the whole galaxy who spoke English.

Where had the two men come from who grabbed her from

behind? They pushed her into a small office where the only thing that looked inviting was a chair. She began to talk, to explain, as though if she said enough words, they'd suddenly understand English.

"The scuba case belongs to my friend. I'm carrying it because he's over the weight limit. You need to find him. His name is Domingo Ramos. He's probably here by now. You need to go look for him. D-o-m-i-n-g-o-R-a-m-o-s. We're from San Francisco. He's my friend. This is his scuba case..." The men, with their stern expressions, frightened her. "He's Peruvian, speaks fluent Spanish. He can answer all your questions." Then she thought, *oh, I know what must be wrong...* "You think the scuba tank is a bomb?"

That's it—they thought she was a terrorist planning to blow up the airplane. That made sense! Dom would come and explain to them she was not a danger to Peruvian skies. That she'd figured out on her own what was wrong gave her a false high of elation.

One of the men produced a mechanical gadget and used it to drill a hole into the bottom of the scuba tank.

They can't do that, Cathryn thought. *I didn't give them permission. How can they do that without asking?* The sound ground in her ears like giant dental drills. When it stopped the area erupted with commotion and loud voices.

The only word Cathryn understood stabbed her—*cocaína.*

Chapter 2

After the commotion Cathryn was taken to a windowless upstairs office.

There they opened her fanny-pack and backpack and spread out on a wide table her tee shirts, skirt, souvenirs, panties, camera, walking shoes, socks, toiletries, money, passport, California drivers' license, notebook and pens. Strangers pawed her personal things, and she could do nothing to stop them. They gathered everything into piles and took it all into another room and closed the door. Most of it she never saw again, including $1,600 American dollars.

How can this be happening? she wondered. *Dom and I have to work tomorrow. We can't miss our flight. We don't have time for this.*

In a slow, methodical tone that sounded far away Cathryn repeated, "Domingo Ramos. That's my friend. Find him. Page him."

Other people came into the room and spoke to her, but she couldn't understand what they were asking. It was as if she wasn't there, as if she was in another dimension, as if she was floating through another plane of time.

A woman handed her a phone. "Hello?" A man's voice, a native English speaker! But a new fear edged her relief. He identified himself as a United States DEA agent. With one hand she held her stomach as if that would help to keep her voice steady, to tell him about her situation in a rational manner. She explained to him why they had to find Dom.

"Let me speak to the woman again," he said.

The woman listened while the DEA agent repeated her story in Spanish. She handed the phone back to Cathryn and left the office.

"I have to work tomorrow," Cathryn told him. "You have to call my employer and explain this. People depend on me. You have to call my parents..." Her shocked senses blocked any memory of phone numbers she'd known for years. "Call information for the

11

number." How stupid she must have sounded, to not be able to say the telephone number of her own parents.

Cathryn felt a surge of encouragement when he said, "I'm going to dispatch someone to the airport to help you."

How much time passed, she didn't know. A Peruvian national who worked in Lima for the DEA arrived, introduced himself as Mr. Vargas. She was relieved that he spoke good English. At last she was in the presence of someone who could understand her. She babbled to him how scared she was.

The woman returned. More conversation in Spanish. Vargas said, "The airline says Domingo Ramos has canceled his ticket."

Everyone in the room seemed to close in on her, steaming with menace, like a surreal dream where she needed to run, but was feet-in-cement paralyzed.

Vargas asked her to come with him to another part of the airport. He was polite, but she knew that not going with him was not a choice.

In this area there were a lot of mechanics. One of them made motions indicating they wanted to drill off the bottom of the scuba tank. More abrasive dental drills assaulting her ears. More Spanish, low, ominous. Fear flushed her cheeks, her neck, her armpits.

Her eyes hurt from the brightness of the white powder they poured from the tank.

Back to the upstairs office. Long periods of silence broken by spells of loud Spanish. The room swam around her. When had the air become so hot? When would they let her go to the bathroom?

Mr. Vargas: "Miss Prentis. You need to sign these documents."

"If you say it's okay. You're the only person here I feel I can trust."

Vargas began to translate the first document in a voice that sounded like schoolroom chanting. Cathryn couldn't focus on the words. She decided it must be okay if *he* had read and understood it. She signed.

Vargas folded the papers. "We have 15 days to catch this guy."

What did that mean?

He assured her they would "do everything in our power to apprehend" Dom. He advised her not to sign any more documents without an attorney.

Cathryn thanked him and he left. She never saw Mr. Vargas again.

Now she sat in a car...the driver obnoxious with bad teeth. They arrived at another building where he wanted her to sign something. She refused, remembering Vargas' instructions. Mr. Obnoxious screamed at her, his face warped in anger. "*Cocaina*," he spit. When he spoke bits of phlegm sprayed from his mouth. Back in the car...driving for a long time. They stopped. In a raggedy office with beat-up furniture that made her think of a third-rate thrift store, they made her pee in a bottle.

When did they put me in handcuffs? Her mouth tasted dry, metallic. Her body, cold lead. *This is not real...it's happening to someone else...I am just a movie camera eavesdropping into someone else's life.* Her feet were no longer cold...she felt nothing. Outside the window she noticed the first rays of morning sun.

Chapter 3

Much of the day after Cathryn's arrest was a blur. In another office she was handed a telephone, and on the other end was the U.S. Consul, David Ryan. He told her he would "come by" the next day. Come by where? Where was she? How could she bear to wait twenty-four hours to see him? When would they let her sleep?

She was taken below this office to a basement where a cellblock housed both men and women. Now she sat in a chilly concrete cell, just big enough for one person, with a concrete bench. With no toilet, the cell reeked of so much urine Cathryn's eyes burned. A guard gave her a lice-filled blanket that smelled like a combination of human grease and resin, all she had in the dampness to keep her warm. She hugged it around her shoulders. If only she could stop her body from shaking…

Cathryn's arrival awakened a Peruvian woman sleeping on the floor.

"*Como esta usted?*" the woman asked, her voice soft. When Cathryn didn't answer, she spoke more Spanish.

Cathryn's voice trembled as she breathed the words, "American. Where am I?"

"*Dinandro.*" The woman made a limp gesture with thin brown arms and repeated the word. "*Dinandro.*"

They tried to communicate, and all Cathryn understood was that "Dinandro" was the name of this dungeon and her cellmate's name was Jenny. The woman had just found out she was pregnant. After that there was not much more to say.

Jenny dozed and Cathryn stared at the scribbling on each wall, the handwriting of former occupants, most of it in languages she didn't understand. The metallic taste in her throat had turned to bitter bile. What was Dom doing right now? Was he still in Peru? Would he go back to San Francisco? Probably not—what could he say had happened to her?

As Cathryn looked around this cold cement box—the opposite of the cocooning comfort of that Lima hotel room—she thought of her older brother, Mark. When they were children he would lock her in the basement "with the bogeyman", or have one of his friends howl like a wolf outside her bedroom window while he told her in gory detail how the werewolf was going to break in and rip her face off. Such terrible teasing. How silly—that was nothing compared to this. Thinking of Mark made her think of her parents, and she began to cry.

Her father, a retired plasterer, had joined the Navy as a teenager and fought in the South Pacific against "the Japs" as he and his war buddies called them. This cement wall with its foreign scratched words and hatch marks that counted days made her wonder, *was this what it had been like for prisoners of war?*

Her parents—well-loved by friends, the king and queen of their cocktail set. Always with great lounge music on the hi-fi—Sinatra, Martin, Bacharach—"The Look of Love" and "The Girl From Ipanema." Good jazz and swing, too—Sergio Mendez and Benny Goodman and Sarah Vaughn and Nat King Cole. Cathryn had been the only kid in her elementary school who could recite the lyrics of Cole Porter *and* Jimi Hendrix. Would she ever hear those songs again? Would she ever hear her mother's voice again?

To distract herself she thought of her favorite lyrics from those great songs, and was disturbed to discover she couldn't remember any of them. It was as if all the good things in her life had been wiped out by Dom's betrayal. When she thought she had no more tears, more came. Great wracking sobs over which she had no control. Crying that left her sinuses bloated, her eyes burning, her ribs aching, her body weak.

During the day the cells were unlocked. On the other side of an open area, a women's restroom contained toilets, none of which worked. The door, old and broken, never closed. The powerful odor of feces made Cathryn thankful her cell wasn't next to it.

There was no hot water, no place to bathe. One morning she

found a dirty plastic bucket she could fill with water to try to clean herself. The next day she was happy to see the bucket, her new best friend, was still there. But the water was turned on in the mornings and turned off for the rest of the day.

Days later the U.S. Consul came to see her. Sandy-haired David Ryan, shorter than Cathryn, wore a wrinkled suit. Cathryn learned that Dinandro was the Anti-Drug Directorate of the Peruvian National Police, around which all counter-narcotics law enforcement efforts were structured.

Her mother had wired fifty dollars to the embassy, and David Ryan had purchased and brought with him one towel and bottled water. He handed her photocopied papers—the standard handout for U.S. citizens who find themselves in prison in a foreign country. After reading them, Cathryn concluded that basically it said, "You're fucked."

"You need to get a good attorney." In a businesslike manner the Consul pointed to names listed in the handout. Cathryn got the impression that she was just another case in an already busy load…nothing immediate…nothing unusual…nothing important.

"I'll call them," she mumbled, having no idea how she would do this from a concrete cell.

He handed her forms to sign—a power of attorney to her mother, and a confidentiality form. This latter covered the U.S. embassy's legal position in case a journalist contacted them asking questions about Cathryn Prentis. Did she authorize them to release information?

"I guess."

The Consul frowned. "It's not in your best interest to do that. Though of course, I can't advise you."

So Cathryn checked, "No."

As he turned to leave Cathryn remembered her needs. "There's no toilet paper. And I need a toothbrush and toothpaste."

His assistant delivered the items three days later—no rush for the imprisoned American, who sat most of the time in her cell, huddled in her infested blanket, crying.

Food was brought twice a day in a plastic container, but Cathryn feared to eat it. This place had cockroaches, lice, fleas, insects she couldn't identify. How clean could the kitchen be? What if she got sick? Mind over stomach—Cathryn steeled herself so that she almost never felt a pang of hunger. Surely she wouldn't be here long enough to starve to death...

One morning a guard came and took Jenny away. She didn't say good-bye, and Cathryn felt surprised by a deeper loneliness.

Chapter 4

Domingo Ramos did not look Latin. When Angela, Cathryn's employer, had introduced her to him in the summer of 1999 she had been surprised by this. Dom, about her height—five foot ten—sported ash blond hair and a fair complexion. *We could have been brother and sister,* Cathryn thought. Almost always in good humor, his intense green eyes crinkled at the corners.

"Dom owns Security Shipments," Angela said. "He picks up and delivers furniture for us."

With his bulky, muscular physique, Dom looked the part. Though he was the company owner, he often took an active part in the moves, lifting things himself.

"Pleased to meet you," Dom said. Perfect English. Another surprise. No hint of any Latin accent.

That summer four years ago Cathryn had just begun work as a sales associate for Petrocelli Antiques in San Francisco. Angela Petrocelli specialized in high-end retail for the interior design industry. Cathryn felt she had landed the perfect job, in a delightful environment of *objets d'art* and exquisite classical furniture.

She and Dom worked well together. In the course of a day they would have interesting conversations about heavy subjects like politics, religion, the Iraq war. They would swap stories about the "wealthy but cheap" people they came in contact with in the antiques business, and laugh at their quirks. Dom reminded Cathryn of a younger version of Mark.

Besides sales, Cathryn conducted inventories and cost analyses, designed marketing strategies and coordinated shipments via air and ocean freight. Almost daily she dealt with Dom and Security Shipments.

One afternoon Dom arrived to pick up a large, 18th century Chippendale writing table that had been sold to a decorator for a home in Pacific Heights. She hadn't had time for lunch and was pleased to discover he'd brought *dim sum* and soft drinks for himself, his worker, and Cathryn.

"How much do I owe you?" she asked.

Dom made a dismissive gesture. "Nothing. A girl's gotta eat." His smile made Cathryn feel like his big sister.

After that, knowing she liked dim sum, he often brought it by, and he'd never let her reimburse him.

One afternoon Angela went to see a client in Nob Hill. Cathryn, alone in the showroom, focused on a marketing strategy to introduce a new shipment of fine Dutch paintings to their designer clients.

The Tibetan bells hanging on the front door jangled.

Cathryn saw Dom enter bearing two large paper cups of lemonade. She hadn't realized she needed a break until he handed her one and she took her first refreshing sip.

"Thanks. This is great."

He sat down on a folding chair next to her desk.

"Angela said to come by to talk about picking up the paintings from the dock."

Once a container of antiques arrived, it was allowed to sit on the dock for eight hours before hefty storage fees began. The ship could arrive at any time and they had to be ready at a moment's notice for the pickup.

Cathryn told Dom that Angela had gone to Nob Hill and would be back soon. Dom said he could wait, and they began to talk about our families. Cathryn told him she had a brother and a sister, and that her parents were in their seventies. He asked after their health, and she was happy to be able to say they were fine.

"I envy you that," he said. "I never knew my biological father. I was adopted by an uncle, and my mother has a lot of problems."

Cathryn thought her family seemed so normal and couldn't imagine what it must be like to have a family like his.

"Where does your mother live?" she asked.

"In Peru. I lived with her there for awhile, but I hated it."

"What did you hate about it?"

Dom swirled the melting ice in his lemonade cup. "Mostly my mother. She's high-strung, quite the hypochondriac. She had me when she was seventeen, after a brief affair with an Italian tourist." He made this announcement about his mother's affair in an offhand way, giving Cathryn the impression that if he'd been bothered by it, he'd gotten over it. He sipped his lemonade.

"Anyway, because I'm German and Italian, I was able to get the documents to move to Germany."

"How'd you like Germany?"

"It was different from Peru."

"But you said you grew up in Peru. Didn't you miss it?"

"I loved all those old ruins of ancient civilizations—Moche temples, the Nazca lines, and Chan Chan, the world's largest mud-brick citadel. All those pre-Hispanic artifacts in the Museo Arqueológico in Lima, and the ruined fortresses of the Incas, like Sacsayhuaman—"

"I've heard of that."

"It's right near Cusco and Machu Picchu. Cusco was the heart of the Inca empire. Fabulous colonial architecture."

Probably why Dom's so successful with Security Shipments, Cathryn thought. He had an appreciation for antique furniture not found in the average furniture-moving guy.

Dom took a long gulp of his lemonade and said, "Cusco's the oldest inhabited city in the Western Hemisphere, you know."

Cathryn had never been to South America. "Someday I'd like to see Machu Picchu."

"Did you know there used to be dinosaurs in Peru? They found engraved stones with pictures, I think in the thirties. In old tombs."

Cathryn rattled the ice in the bottom of her paper cup. "I'd like to see that."

"The Andes is a cradle of old civilizations. Thinking about it, it was cool growing up around all that stuff."

"Sounds like you miss it."

"Long time ago." He shrugged. "I'm an American, now. My life's here."

About seven months later Cathryn fell in love with a mahogany game table from the mid-eighteenth century, with carved shell motifs and ball-and-claw feet.

Cathryn just had to have it, but how could she afford it? She wasn't in the same antique-playing league as the Pacific Heights and Nob Hill ladies. Angela saw that she lusted after the expensive piece of furniture and agreed to barter. Cathryn could have it for extra overtime without pay. Now, how to get it to her apartment? Dom became her delivery angel, offering to move it free of charge. Cathryn thought he took as much pleasure as Angela did in seeing the games table go to an appreciative owner.

Cathryn borrowed an altar table from Angela for about three months to see if it would fit with her décor—it didn't—and again Dom never charged her to drop it off or return it. He was generous that way.

Six months later Dom began dating a Peruvian girl, Cristina.

"She's terrific, Cathryn. You'd like her. She's got a great job in a law firm up in Marin, and—"

His enthusiasm was infectious. Cathryn laughed at his smitten-with-love grin. "I know. She's the most gorgeous girl you've ever seen."

"Well, yeah, but I mean she's nice, too."

Dom had spent a bundle taking Cristina to dinner at an upscale French restaurant, and she thought his eyes still bubbled from the champagne. Afterwards he'd whisked Cristina off for a weekend at Ventana Inn & Spa in Big Sur. When he wasn't wining and dining her here and there, he was buying her expensive little gifts.

"What do you think of this, Cathryn?" he asked, pointing to a gold ankle bracelet in a catalog from a Beverly Hills jeweler.

"They'll engrave it for free."

"At that price I should hope so," she murmured.

Head tilted at the catalog, his blond hair tousled over the side of his face. "But do you like it? Do you think she'll like it? I'll have our names and the date engraved on it."

"I don't see why she wouldn't like it." Cathryn had begun to get the impression Cristina had a highly-developed taste for nice things.

Dom announced that he planned to marry Cristina. Every day he walked around with a Brad Pitt grin.

"Wow," Cathryn said to Angela. "This is serious."

What is it about a man in love that makes us all feel happy? Cathryn pondered. *It's endearing in a way that reminds us both men and women share the same humanity. No matter what other differences our genders entail, we both want the same things: to be appreciated, respected, loved, to feel in control of our own lives and to be treated fairly.*

"You should see the engagement ring." Angela shook her head. "Four carats. Humongous. And he's looking at pricy Honeymoon packages to Hawaii. I told him he'd be better off putting all that money on a down payment for a house."

Cathryn told him the same thing, but he didn't listen to either of them. After Dom and Cristina got married—only family attended but they heard it was a fabulous wedding—he approached Angela with a business idea. He wanted to import antiques from South America. Would she be interested in a new business partnership?

"He's got a sound business plan," Angela said. "I think we could make money. Security Shipments is established, it's solid. It's a good idea for him to diversify. And he knows the South American market."

"Are you going to do it?" Cathryn asked.

"I'm considering it. But I've got this Asian thing I'd need to get out of. I don't have the money to invest in both directions."

One night Cathryn's car was identified as having been used in a deadly crime. Witnesses had positively identified it, according to the SFPD detective who came to her apartment. "Witnesses say a Hispanic man was driving it," he said.

"That's impossible. I was working."

How could this have happened to her? She'd been at the showroom. "Got to be a hoax, or a case of mistaken identity."

Why did freaky things like this always have to happen to her? For a long time she'd been fighting to get past what she felt to be a well-established persecution complex. Before her current position, she'd worked in the office of a psychiatrist. That night she didn't sleep, tangled in the sheets as she tossed about. She couldn't get comfortable. She couldn't relax. She couldn't shake off the swirling thoughts of people coming to arrest her for something she didn't do. Something she didn't know about, couldn't identify.

Nobody's out to get you, she told herself.

The next day Cathryn forced herself to focus on her work, made more arduous by her lack of sleep. In the afternoon Dom came to the showroom with another one of his wonderful dim sum deliveries. She told him what had happened with her car.

"Bummer," he said. "It's so classy here, you forget there's so much crime."

It felt good to be able to talk to someone who listened, who empathized with her troubles, who cared what happened to her. Cathryn felt calmed, knew somehow she'd be cleared.

Later in the week Angela decided "the timing was wrong" and told Dom she couldn't go into the South American furniture-import business. She said she couldn't finance her part in it. Dom responded with his usual healthy moving-forward attitude. He had a happy personal life. He had Cristina, Security Shipments continued to do well, life was good.

They'd found a great apartment and spent their spare time scouting high-end stores for contemporary furniture. Dom preferred antiques, but Cristina wanted everything new and modern, so new and modern it was. Together they went to movies and gourmet-food shopping. When Dom began scuba diving lessons, Cristina refused. Her idea of an outdoor activity was walking all day Saturday from one exclusive shop to another.

All of this he shared with Cathryn over dim sum or lemonade in the summers, and cappuccinos he brought for her and Angela in the winters.

When Dom arrived at Petrocelli Antiques in late September Cathryn was relieved to see him. She always knew that if his company handled a delivery, her job would be easier. In the five-plus years he'd worked for Angela, he'd never blown a delivery.

"Do you know anyone who might want to use a ticket to Peru?" he asked. "We planned this scuba trip, and now my buddy can't go."

Cathryn had no interest. "Sorry. I don't scuba dive."

Two weeks later he mentioned it again. He explained that a sales girl at another store he delivered for had committed to take the ticket, but at the last minute she couldn't go.

"Didn't you say you'd never been to South America? You'd love Peru. It's a beautiful, friendly country full of incredible history. And there's Machu Picchu—"

A Technicolor picture burst into Cathryn's mind. Machu Picchu. A magical mystical place like the Great Pyramid in Egypt and the Taj Mahal. Now that Dom had planted the idea that she might actually see it, she couldn't get that beautiful green, mountainous image out of her mind.

"But what about Cristina? Doesn't she want to go?"

Dom laughed. "There'd be no high-end shops for her. Besides, she has to work."

That was Dom, so generous to give away a round-trip ticket. If she went, she'd pay for the Machu Picchu leg of the journey. Such an incredible opportunity, just like when Angela couldn't use her timeshare in Los Cabos, and Cathryn got it for free.

In addition to being happily married and running a successful delivery company, Dom never oversold himself; one of the reasons everyone liked and trusted him.

Cathryn accepted the round-trip ticket to Peru. They would depart the following Saturday.

On Wednesday Dom called Cathryn in the showroom.

"What are you taking?" he asked.

"Just a backpack, since I'm not staying a long time."

He said he was over the weight limit with his scuba stuff. Would she mind taking two suitcases of clothes that he'd bought for Cristina's family?

"Of course." For a free airline ticket, how could she refuse to help out?

Friday morning before the departure he brought to her apartment two big suitcases and handed her the airline tickets. Cathryn noticed that the flight to Lima flew direct, but the return trip changed planes in Mexico City.

"Why not fly back direct?" she asked.

"We planned to fly from Mexico City to Cancun to dive," he said.

Cathryn smiled. "Hey, thank you for the chance to see Machu Picchu."

On the telephone Friday evening Cathryn told her girlfriend Marge how excited she was to be leaving the next day to see Machu Picchu.

"Cathryn, how can you agree to carry luggage for somebody without knowing what's inside it?" Marge demanded. "I'm coming right over. We're going to open those suitcases."

As awkward as Cathryn felt, she knew Marge was right. Yet the idea discomforted her. Here was her good friend Dom, buying clothes for his wife's family, and she was going to be pawing through them like an ungrateful stranger.

Marge arrived at her apartment, her tone serious. "Where are they?"

Cathryn gestured towards the two suitcases. They spread them out on her living room carpet and opened them. There were tee shirts, button-front shirts, baseball caps. Removing those, they found jeans, shorts, tennis shoes.

"These are just clothes you'd buy at Wal-Mart," Cathryn said.

"I guess in Peru they can't get things like this," Marge speculated. "I'm sorry I pressed, Cathryn, but it's better to know for sure."

They made tea in her kitchen and spent the rest of the evening talking about Peru and Machu Picchu, how lucky Cathryn was to be going, and how nice it was of Dom to buy all those things for the less fortunate people in Cristina's family.

Chapter 5

Dom didn't want to be away from Security Shipments too long, so he'd designed the trip to Peru to be short. Their flight arrived in Lima late Saturday night. Cathryn couldn't get a flight to Cusco until early Monday morning.

Dom said, "Hey, why hang at the airport? Stay in my hotel room. I'm going to go hang with friends tonight and won't even be there."

At dawn Monday morning Dom and his cousin, Luis, arrived at the hotel and drove Cathryn back to the airport to fly to Cusco. Dom had made reservations for her at the Cusco Hotel Novotel and with a Cusco tour sales representative. She was waiting for Cathryn with a sign bearing her name, and drove her to the tour office to complete paperwork before taking her to check into the hotel.

"I want to see as much as I can, because I don't have a lot of time here," Cathryn told her.

The tour sales rep agreed to arrange for a private guide to show Cathryn Cusco and the outlying areas, including the ruins at Sacseyhuamon. She would arrange to get her train and entrance tickets to Machu Picchu. Total cost, $235. US. Cathryn laid two one-hundred-dollar bills between them on the desk and, since she'd kept her hundreds separate from her smaller bills, opened a different purse for the thirty-five dollars.

She heard the sales representative say, "You need another hundred dollars here."

Cathryn couldn't believe what she now saw. Only one hundred dollar bill lay on the desk.

"I put two bills right there," she said.

"No no," the woman insisted. "One bill."

"I know I put two bills there." A chill from the air conditioner made goose bumps rise on Cathryn's arms. "You took it."

The woman assumed an indignant air, took out her own wallet, spread the pockets to demonstrate that it was empty, insisted Cathryn was wrong.

Could she have been wrong? Was it her imagination that she'd put two bills on the desk? Had she falsely accused her? Cathryn counted what was left in her wallet. No, she hadn't had that much to begin with, so the count was easy. Less two bills. She wasn't wrong.

Cathryn could do nothing if she wanted her tours. She handed the woman another hundred dollars.

Later she would learn that ripping off tourists is quite common in Peru. Another girl sat nearby whom the tour sales rep could have passed a bill to, or she could have dropped it to the floor and placed her foot on top of it. In this con, both methods are common.

At the hotel Cathryn sipped coca tea—whole leaves floating in hot water—served to guests to alleviate sickness from the 11,000-foot altitude. Fifteen minutes later Hector, her private guide appeared, driving his own car. They rode around Cusco, Hector pointing out the sights—Spanish colonial architecture with white walls and orange tiled roofs, Quechua people in colorful native costumes, postcard perfection. All around the Cathedral and Plaza Los Armas they sold jewelry, bags, blankets, embroidered dolls, baby alpaca sweaters and other souvenirs. Outside the city Hector drove to a higher point of ground where the view made Cathryn hold her breath. Below her lay mountainous terrain and a series of roads.

In the rural setting a Quechua farmer tended a herd of llamas through the large carved square stone ruins of Sacseyhuamon. On flat ground at Sacseyhuamon Cathryn stood on one stone in the center of a circle of square stones, about twelve inches high. When she spoke she heard the echo. In this spot Shirley McLain had slept all night outdoors as she describes in her book, *Out On A Limb*. Hector told her they don't know the meaning in Inca history of this site. His pronunciation made the name sound like "sexy woman."

Sunday evening Hector recommended a restaurant and Cathryn paid for his dinner because he refused to accept a tip for the day's tour. When she told him about the incident with the tour saleswoman, how she had been conned out of a hundred dollars, he seemed embarrassed. During dinner Hector told her about his family. Cathryn liked Hector and felt lucky that she had gotten him as her guide.

At first light the next morning the tour woman arrived at the hotel to give Cathryn her tickets and drive her to the train station. As a precaution Cathryn left most of her money in the safe in her hotel room.

The early train would to the most famous site in Peru. Machu Picchu. Cathryn refused to let the incident with the tour woman spoil what she knew would be an unforgettable experience. She inhaled the sights as the train rattled along the Rio Urubamba, a tributary of the upper Amazon. One side yellow with scotch broom, the other side churning river rapids. Sheer rock walls rose from one side of the tracks, creviced with mist-shrouded ferns and bromeliads. The almost four-hour train ride became a hypnotic experience.

At the village of Aguas Calientes Cathryn left the train and boarded a bus that would take her up the Hiram Bingham Road to the entrance to Machu Picchu, a thirty-minute ride on a harrowing, hairpin one-lane road full of bumps and holes. Twice the bus had to stop and back up to make room for buses coming down the mountain. According to the rules of this road, they had priority. Cathryn sweated with terror. Each time the bus backed up she could see over the edge of the road into space.

She tried to imagine American archeologist Hiram Bingham stumbling into Machu Picchu in 1911, when it'd been covered with huge trees and dense tropical cloud forest vegetation. Bingham had been supported by the National Geographic Society in his search for the Lost City of Vilcabamba, the final refuge of the Incas fleeing the Spanish conquistadors; he thought this was it.

Cathryn fled from the bus. She breathed the crisp air of Machu Picchu, where eight Inca roads had converged, now a UNESCO World Heritage Site and a Peruvian State Park complete with entrance fee and covered turnstile. Among the ruins of stone architecture grew bromeliads and begonias and three hundred species of orchids. She marveled at several natural waterways and one of the most important structures in the ruins, the Temple of the Three Windows. She poked her head through one of the windows to look down onto the central plaza of this ancient city and out across the Urubamba Valley.

Cathryn learned that the famous mountain in all the travel posters is Wayna Picchu, the photo taken from a high point in the Machu Picchu ruins. She learned that in the Quechua language, the words *wayna picchu* mean "new mountain" and *machu picchu* mean "old mountain." The latter is pronounced, "ma-chew-*peek*-chew." She was told that if you pronounce it "ma-chew-*pee*-chew" you are saying, "old man's penis." She wondered if that was really true or a Peruvian joke for the tourists.

In cool, cloudy, mystical weather Cathryn wandered among ancient Inca ruins along gravel paths and stone steps and imagined what it must have been like hundreds of years ago to live on those green terraces. Would she have been a woman who gardened and bartered food? Or would she have been a woman who wove cloth? What kind of work would her husband do? How any children would she have had? So many wonderful nooks and crannies here for a child to explore. Cathryn could have stayed at Machu Picchu for a week, just walking and meditating, high in the Urubamba Gorge.

Into the high mountain air she whispered, "Thank you, Dom."

The last train arrived back in Cusco at nine p.m. Cathryn collapsed on the bed, weeping from exhaustion. When the phone rang, she found a tissue and blew her nose before answering. It was Dom.

How had she liked Machu Picchu? She told him what a long, emotional day it had been. "Four hours on a mountain train each way." Although she felt profoundly moved by the experience of being in those ancient Inca ruins, she also felt vulnerable. "On the way back I fell asleep on the train and money was stolen out of my fanny-pack. And a tour guide here conned me out of $100." As sorry for herself as she felt, the sound of Dom's voice made her feel less scared and alone.

But Dom had bad news. He had gone to Pisco to visit relatives. "I'm worn out, Cathryn," he said. "My family argued the whole time I was there. Anyway there's one last thing I need to do, so I'm not going to be able to take you to dinner tomorrow tonight like we planned. I hope you understand. I'll meet you at the gate. Since I'll still be in Pisco tonight, use my hotel room in Lima. I've already paid for the taxi to the airport."

"I understand. Do what you have to do. How was the scuba diving?"

"Didn't get to do it because of the family thing," he said. "Oh, and my cousin Luis will bring my scuba case to the hotel. Could you bring it to the airport and check it for me? I'm afraid I'm going to be overweight again going back. I'm bringing sweaters and blankets in the two suitcases."

She agreed. The suitcases were large and unwieldy, but his scuba case had power wheels that made it easy to pull.

"What about the pressure in the tank?" she asked.

"The tank has a valve that moves. There's no problem if it's open. Don't worry, Luis will show you."

"Okay. Hope you get your family business cleared up. We'll catch up on things on the plane."

Before she went to sleep Cathryn went downstairs and paid the hotel bill so that in the morning she could leave with no delay.

The next morning Cathryn flew from Cusco back to Lima. Waiting for her at the airport was Luis. He took her on a pleasant drive by the sea, happy to be able to practice his English. Two hours later he dropped her off at Dom's hotel.

Still tired but exhilarated from her long day at Machu Picchu, Cathryn looked forward to being able to relax before the flight home to San Francisco. She grabbed her backpack out of the back seat of the car. Luis opened the hatchback and pulled out Dom's shiny metal scuba case with the power wheels, the same one she'd seen him bring to Lima.

Cathryn had brought an old pair of raggedy sneakers that she could toss if needed to make room for souvenirs, and she left them in the back of the car and told Luis to pass them on to someone who could use them. From where Luis parked the car they walked a short way to the hotel. She carried her backpack, and he rolled the case, *ca-chunk, ca-chunk,* across uneven pavestones.

In the hotel the concierge smiled in recognition and handed Cathryn the room keys. "The taxi to the airport has already been paid for. What time do you want him to come?"

"Eight o'clock tonight. Can you give me a wake-up call at seven? I'll probably take a nap."

She called a bellhop who took the scuba case from Luis. The three of them went to the room in the elevator.

In the room Luis said, "I must show you the valve on the tank," unlocking the scuba case. He opened it and handed her the key. Inside the case she saw bathing suits, flippers, a wet suit, face mask, snorkel, and the cylindrical air tank with a black valve. Luis moved it back and forth.

"Dom told me the airport people will check that to make sure there isn't any pressure in the tank," she said. She didn't touch any of the things in the case or take any of it out.

On his way out of the room, Luis paused in the doorway, an odd expression on his face. Later Cathryn wondered, *Was I seeing pity? Guilt? Was Luis in on the set-up?*

Luis nodded, not looking at her. "Dom will meet you at the gate."

Chapter 6

Again and again authorities summoned Cathryn from her dungeon cell in Dinandro. More questioning. She gave numerous statements to both Peruvian authorities and the American DEA.

Several times she was introduced and asked to sign documents to retain this or that Peruvian attorney. Some of them spoke a little English, but she felt they just wanted money. She hadn't forgotten what Vargas had said, and she refused to even touch a pen. The captain at Dinandro pressured her to sign with one of them and became more threatening each time she refused. Later she learned that if she retained one of his chosen lawyers he would get a kickback.

Every time Cathryn was taken out of the dungeon—in handcuffs and to different places for things like urine tests, dental ID's, Interpol questioning—other prisoners would rifle through her things and steal whatever they wanted. How could she complain? She didn't speak the language of the guards and they didn't speak hers. She felt weak, isolated, vulnerable.

After her bottled water was stolen she had to drink the weak tea served in a communal bucket. With dread she dipped her cup and drank. Two days later her throat was raw, and she shivered with all the symptoms of a terrible cold.

Other prisoners began to come to her cell to share their stories and to encourage her to eat. A German man had served in Croatia with UN troops and had been dishonorably discharged. He'd been carrying drugs for years before he'd been caught. A short, Spanish lesbian talked constantly, and Cathryn always felt relieved when she went back to her own cell. Later a sweet, overweight Spanish woman arrived. About thirty, in broken English she told Cathryn that, unable to live on her wages as a teacher's aid, she'd agreed to carry drugs in her vagina. She encouraged Cathryn to eat to survive.

The majority of Dinandro's prisoners were Peruvian. A young man taught her several useful Spanish words—*toalla* and *agua* and *papel higenico*. He'd been arrested for having a hit of ecstasy, and later released. A Peruvian couple shared another cell. The husband had immigrated illegally to New Jersey where he'd learned a little English before being deported by the INS. His wife, who seemed to be emotionally unstable, was pregnant.

A tall, heavy Canadian woman who had arrived at Dinandro the day after Cathryn introduced herself as Kate. She said she was a professional mule and as a result of her arrest was "going through a lot of changes." Kate worked for a Nigerian in Amsterdam, and this was the first time she'd been caught. What a comfort—to speak fluent English with her.

Cathryn's cold developed into a chronic, miserable cough, which made her feel more despondent. By now the guards had figured out that she hadn't been eating and had told the DEA agents.

"Why don't you eat?" Mr. Estrada asked, his expression quizzical.

Mr. Tjon said, "You must eat. Your health will deteriorate if you don't."

Their concern seemed automatic, as if encouraging her to eat was just another part of their job. Cathryn told them the truth. "The food is horrible, and I'm too upset to eat." In anger she found energy to talk. "How can anyone enveloped in the stench of piss and shit have an appetite?"

Cathryn found it impossible to close her nostrils to the smells, the air like living in a bathroom where someone had constant diarrhea. The rank air became so overpowering that the idea of food nauseated her. When she told Tjon and Estrada this, they shook their heads and said nothing.

In a defeated monotone, she told them the other prisoners were stealing what little she had. "Every time you call me up here, when I go back, one more thing has been stolen." She told them the

Peruvians had advised her to plead guilty because "no one is ever found innocent."

The vision of a cold, miserable death, coughing in pain, all alone in a concrete box, overwhelmed her. She would never see her parents, her sister, her brother again. She would never again hear music or laugh with her friends or debate with Angela over the placement of antique pieces in the showroom. This tiny cell would be her final coffin.

Cathryn felt so demoralized she said, "I'm never going to survive this."

Estrada wrote in a notebook, giving her the false impression that something might be done about it. The two DEA agents left, and she wondered, would they do anything? Would she ever see them again?

When someone went free it was customary to leave things behind. The only clothes Cathryn had were the jeans, panties, shirt and high-heeled sandals she had been wearing when she had left for the airport, plus one other shirt and a second pair of panties. So when a British girl left her two tee shirts and a skirt, they were welcome.

The guards changed daily. One night Cathryn was awakened by a guard who gave her an extra blanket. This gesture surprised her. The rest of the night she slept without waking from the chill of the cell. The next night a different guard snatched it away. The cells were locked at night, so if she had to use the bathroom, she had to wake the guard to let her out. One night she awoke in urgent need and called out, but the guard slept on.

"Help! I need to go to the bathroom!" Cathryn yelled louder, waking other prisoners who became angry at her for disturbing their precious sleep. She waited, coughed, and tightened her legs as the pressure in her abdomen increased. She called and called and called to a guard who never came. When she could no longer stand the pain in her bladder, she urinated on herself. In the inky blackness of the cold concrete cell she cried and coughed and tried to clean herself with a corner of her shirt. She recognized a different smell and, though she couldn't see in the dark, she felt the blood on her hands. Such an awful mess—she had started her period.

Chapter 7

Two weeks passed. Cathryn learned that the Peruvian authorities planned to transfer her to a permanent accommodation, the Santa Monica Women's Prison at Chorillos, on the outskirts of Lima.

When Cathryn was brought from her dungeon to the offices to receive a telephone call, she discovered the U.S. Consul, David Ryan, had arranged to patch through a call from her sister, Dierdre.

"Look, we're flying to San Francisco and we're going to empty out your apartment, put your stuff in storage," Dierdre said.

"What? Why would you do that?"

"Well, it's obvious you're not coming home."

This, from her own sister! How could she think this? A numbing sensation choked Cathryn's throat.

"If you do that, I'll give up. I won't put up a fight. There'll be no point. I'll just lay down and die here." Cathryn could hear hysteria in her own voice. "Because I'm getting out of here, and I'm coming back to that apartment!" When she paused, the silence on the other end made her think the connection had been broken.

Dierdre made a noncommittal response. "Okay, we'll see."

Cathryn still had not found an attorney she felt she could trust. One attorney told her that if she paid him $10,000, he could get her out in nine months. Cathryn concluded that most attorneys in Peru were shysters. Peruvians seemed to have the idea that all foreigners are rich—especially Americans—and would pay lots of money upfront. Later she would be told—from Peruvians—that attorneys would say anything you wanted to hear to get you to give them money. Once you paid a hefty retainer, the attorney would disappear—with your money. And what recourse would you have? Ask your brother to drop by their office? Your family is on another continent, and so are all your friends. You don't know the terms of the legal document you signed to hire him/her—it wasn't in your language. Scores of foreigners in Santa Monica Women's Prison had been financially raped by Peruvian attorneys.

Again Cathryn was summoned from the dungeon. This time to meet Cesar Xavier, who introduced himself as one of the lawyers called for her by the American embassy. Right away Cathryn noted a difference in Cesar Xavier—he wore a suit that fit and spoke excellent English. He acted like a professional attorney, asking her questions none of the others had asked.

"Can you get copies of your tax filings and bank statements?"

"Yes."

"Can you get employment documents and a letter of reference from your employer?"

"I'm sure that wouldn't be a problem."

Xavier asked to see the scuba tank that had been kept at Dinandro as evidence. The other attorneys had asked only how many kilos she had been arrested with.

The captain stood at the side of the room. From the look of aggravation on his face, Cathryn deduced that his English was too limited and he had no idea what she and Xavier were talking about. He was also aggravated, she was sure, from fear that she would retain this attorney he didn't know, and who therefore wouldn't give him a kickback.

Cesar Xavier made notes. As he put them away in preparation to leave he said, "If you hire me, we will have to work hard to get the judges and prosecutors to read the book, not the page. You are in a corrupt place. It's best you don't trust anyone or say anything to the captain."

He handed her his business card. Though Cesar Xavier impressed Cathryn, she explained that she couldn't hire anyone without first talking to her sister. "I need her to wire me the money."

Days passed and Santa Monica Women's Prison loomed closer. When Cathryn hadn't heard from her sister, she decided to go ahead and try to hire Cesar Xavier. With no access to a telephone, she asked Ruben, the Peruvian detective who worked with the captain, to call Xavier for her. A day passed and Cathryn was told nothing. She asked again. Another day passed. She couldn't understand the problem. Next time she saw the captain she insisted he telephone Xavier. Again, nothing happened.

The U.S. Consul's Peruvian assistant, a handsome woman named Bianca, came by to check on her. Now less embarrassed by her appearance and smell in front of well-groomed people, Cathryn poured out her frustration.

"I've been trying for days to get someone to call Cesar Xavier for me," she said. "I want to retain him as my lawyer."

Bianca went to the captain's office to find out what was going on. When she returned she announced, "No one has called Xavier. The captain has scheduled Juanita Tomas to meet with you as your attorney."

Anger made Cathryn's voice hard. "You call her directly, and tell her I never hired her. Tell her the captain did this. Tell her I don't want to see her, and tell her I definitely do not want her to represent me."

Bianca went to the office and found the detective, Ruben. She brought him back and spoke to him sternly in Spanish. With reluctance he allowed Cathryn to make the call to Cesar Xavier on his personal cell phone. The captain would not be happy with her for foiling his game, but he could do nothing about it with US Embassy personnel present.

Cesar Xavier let Cathryn hire him without paying a retainer. She had eight thousand dollars in her checking account in San Francisco, and she could ask her parents to wire money from it.

Every day in Dinandro brought new danger. Cathryn went to another prisoner's cell to borrow a book to read. When she picked it up, she noticed a fine coat of powder on it. No surprise—Dinandro was a filthy place. Whatever it was got all over her hands. She wiped them on her jeans, went back to her cell and began to read.

The next day she learned that prisoners had been snorting lines of coke off the cover of the book. Cathryn now saw that prisoners seemed to have ample access to drugs. She began to imagine all the things that could have gone bad for her just for borrowing the wrong book. Periodically she had to give a urine test for cocaine. Her hands and cuticles were also swabbed for it. She was told this process picked up even minute traces of the substance. If she'd been tested after she'd touched that book, how could she have explained that? Who would believe her?

The three disposable cameras she had had with her in Peru— filled with fun shots of her in Cusco and at Sacseyhuamon and Macchu Picchu—worried her. They'd been confiscated as "evidence" because the Peruvian detectives suspected they held photos of Dom and drug contacts. When she denied this the detectives were disbelieving and insolent.

Had she snapped a photo of Hector, her wonderful tour guide? If he were identified would they arrest him, thinking he was connected to drugs?

Might a damaging photo be planted with a developed roll of film? Cathryn explained all this to Cesar Xavier and asked him to watch for the processed photos. Tears of frustration and fear exploded when in one interview Xavier asked her, "Did you know you were carrying a counterfeit $100 bill?"

"No. All the money I brought with me came from US banks."

"You are also being charged with being in possession of counterfeit money, a crime in Peru."

Someone had planted it with her money, but Cathryn didn't yet understand why.

She felt so grateful for Cesar. He translated all her statements to the prosecutor and police. No interpreters were provided, and she couldn't imagine how her statements would have turned out otherwise. But Cesar Xavier couldn't prevent her transfer to Santa Monica Women's Prison.

Chapter 8

Petrified layers of panic, grief, and shock distorted Cathryn's days. The way the detectives in Dinandro acted toward the DEA amazed her. Each time the agents came to interrogate her it was as if the pope himself had dropped in for biscotti and cappuccino. Tjon and Estrada were greeted with smiles and handshakes and back slaps and head nods from an aloha-style welcoming committee.

Tjon and Estrada would fire questions at her, repeating them over and over. They would stop—out of breath?—and in the silence just stare at her. Another barrage of questions would follow. She felt like a wooden duck at an amusement park that twirls in circles after being hit by an air gun. She never stopped spinning because she was the target of sharpshooters.

Tjon stood up, opened his coat, and unhooked a hidden microphone. It signified that the interrogation was over, at least for the time being. Cathryn would go back to her cell to discover she'd been cleaned out of another roll of toilet paper or another irreplaceable commodity.

At last, in one interview, after an onslaught of questions, she found the courage to ask a few of her own.

"Why haven't you caught Dom? Did you check the last address he gave on his 1099?"

Tjon said, "It was the address of an abandoned warehouse."

"Did anyone bother to look for him the night of my arrest?"

"Mr. Vargas found him," Tjon said, "but he'd rescheduled his flight and had already boarded a plane for Mexico City."

"So, why didn't Vargas pull him off the plane?"

As if it were the most obvious thing in the world, Estrada said, "Mr. Vargas doesn't have the authority. Once Dom boarded, he came under the jurisdiction of Mexico, and the Mexican airlines don't want flight delays, let alone scandals. If Dom wouldn't get off on his own, there's nothing we can do."

She couldn't believe what she was hearing. They'd found him and done nothing!

"Couldn't you arrest him when the plane landed?"

"We don't have the authority to arrest a person in a foreign country," Tjon said.

"How could you let him get away?" she wailed. "How could you let him slip right through your fingers?"

Their faces remained blank and businesslike. The last time she saw Tjon and Estrada at Dinandro they brought her candy, toilet paper, toothpaste, old *Time* and *Newsweek* magazines—and bad news.

"The DEA has done everything within our power to find and apprehend Dom. He's still in Mexico," Estrada said. "We believe you, but no one in the Peruvian justice system will."

Therefore, Cathryn would be transferred to Santa Monica Women's Prison. She thought she saw a tiny trace of pity in Tjon's eyes. "It's time for you to throw out all the American ideals of justice that are instilled in us as kids," he said. "That kind of thinking won't serve you in Peru. In fact, it will hurt you. If you plead innocent, it will just inflame the prosecutors and judges, and they'll give you an even longer sentence."

Feeling shell-shocked, Cathryn whispered, "What are you saying?"

"Plead guilty, serve your jail time, and when you're released on parole, escape the country."

Telling her to plead guilty to a crime she didn't knowingly commit made her think of riddling a dead body with bullets just for cinematic effect.

Cesar Xavier arrived. While he talked to Estrada, Tjon pulled Cathryn aside.

"Have you seen the movie about the two girls in Thailand who were arrested for drugs?"

"No—I don't know what you're talking about."

"*Brokedown Palace.* It's a true film with similarities to your situation. It shows that it's better for you to plead guilty and serve your time."

Because Cathryn hadn't seen it she couldn't get the connection. Later she would learn that *Brokedown Palace,* while well-researched, was not a true story but a fiction created by its writers.

Survival at any cost wasn't part of who she was. Cathryn found enough of her voice to whisper, "There's no way I can survive prison for two or three years." She thought of the pregnant Peruvian woman in Dinandro who drank poisonous cleaning fluid to kill herself and only lost her baby. With the horror of sudden understanding Cathryn saw her fate, heard an iron door close behind her.

When they rose to leave, Estrada said solemnly, "What we're offering is just advice. You don't have to take it."

Cathryn said, "I'm never going to see you guys again, am I?"

With no change of expression Tjon said, "No. You won't see us again."

Cathryn didn't think he understood the significance of her question, or, maybe he did. She had meant, "I'm gonna die, aren't I?"

Cesar gave her a bottle of water. He sat down beside her, but in her paralyzed state she couldn't speak. He told her that he'd cancelled their appointment later in the day with the prosecutor.

"Today's not the day to give your statement to him," he said. He took her hand, and the tears she'd been holding back erupted. He said no more, held her hand and watched her cry. After awhile he slipped a blue pill into her palm. "Take it," he said. She swallowed it with a sip of the bottled water—not too much as the water was too precious. Cesar walked her to the stairs and watched her descend back into the dungeon.

Without any food in her system for almost two weeks, the Valium took immediate effect.

Chapter 9

Cathryn stopped thinking that her dear friend, Dom, would come forward and explain. Now she prayed that the DEA would find him and just get a confession out of him.

Meanwhile, from her fellow prisoners she got quite the drug trafficking education.

"It's common for traffickers to set up a *burrier* to be arrested," explained a Bahamian man with dirty dreads, "so a much larger amount of drugs can get through while the authorities are busy."

"How does that work?" she asked.

"There are always people working at the airport who've been paid well to wait for the right time to move the drugs out. So, for example, if your friend had eight kilos in his scuba tank, he may have moved out at least a hundred somewhere else that night." What an amazing idea that never would have occurred to her. "Probably more," he added.

However, the Canadian mule, Kate, told her it wasn't common to use someone who didn't know they were carrying drugs. In professional drug trafficking circles, this was frowned upon.

"He must have been mighty desperate to use you that way," she said. "The fact that you didn't know you were transporting drugs saved your life. Because you were duped, who could blame you for telling the truth?" She said that if Cathryn had been a real *burrier* who flipped and blew the whistle, she would be killed in jail or right after her release.

"It's the best thing that he got away," Kate added.

"How can that be?"

"Well, because if he was caught, do you think he would tell the truth?"

"Why not?"

"Cathryn, you're so naïve." Kate laughed and scratched her armpit. "Drug people always lie. They lie to save themselves, to save the people above them. If he was caught, he'd lie about you. Everybody would know he's lying, but it'd be your word against his."

Cesar Xavier arranged for Cathryn to call Dom's cell phone number. She didn't expect him to answer, but she was surprised to hear the voice on the recording had been changed—it wasn't Dom's. She left a message anyway.

"How could you do this to me?" she pleaded. "My parents are old. They depend on me. If anything happens to them because of this, I'll never forgive you." As if her forgiveness meant anything to him. She continued to babble into the phone, not knowing who on the other end would hear her desperate words. "How can you sleep at night knowing what you did to me? If you're too afraid to come back and take responsibility for this, the least you can do is wire me money. The attorneys here are asking for ten grand!"

Three days later Cesar received a call from a man named "Roberto" who said he wanted to send a wire transfer for Cathryn. Xavier took the information and turned everything over to the DEA. Cathryn never heard if anything came of it, but the money never arrived.

When Cathryn wasn't fantasizing about confronting Dom, she worried about her family, her health, the counterfeit $100 bill, and what would happen when her film was developed.

She worried for Hector, who had been so pleasant and helpful. Between Hector's historic tales of the sites, he'd told her he had a wife and three children in Cusco. He hoped he could save enough money to send his oldest son to college in Lima. Had she taken a picture of him, smiling into her camera? Was he standing in the corner of a picture she'd taken of the circle of ancient Inca stones at Sacseyhuamon? She couldn't remember. She worried that if he were in one of the photos he could be identified and arrested. Even with no proof against him, he could be detained for an indefinite length of time, separating him from his family and their means of support.

There was also the matter of the counterfeit $100 bill. Peru, a poor country, had a rampant counterfeit problem. In the Peruvian economy, they used the US dollar as well as Peruvian *soles*. Plenty of counterfeit bills floated around. The most common were the $100 bill and the 20 *soles* note.

Cathryn now believed that when she had been arrested, one of the officials or clerks took the $100 bill she had in her fanny pack and replaced it with a counterfeit. She had no way to prove this, but no one was surprised to hear that it might have happened.

All of this shadowed her thoughts as she waited for her now-certain transfer to Santa Monica Women's Prison.

Chapter 10

Cathryn awoke with her heart pounding, her mouth dry. She reached out her hand for the alarm clock next to her bed, and remembered where she was. Enveloped in the darkness that was Dinandro at night, all sounds of activity stilled in a false respite from reality.

A familiar pressure in her belly told her she wouldn't be able to go back to sleep without first relieving herself. She shoved back the rough blanket, sat up, and twisted her body to set her bare feet on the cold cement floor. She rubbed her upper arms, aching from an awkward sleep position. With no thought of what might be lurking there, she leaned down in the inky blackness and reached underneath the bed. When she found what she was looking for she positioned it on the floor between her feet and stood up. She slid down her jeans and panties and squatted, feeling for the water bottle on the ground between her feet. A guard had cut its top off so she could use it at night to pee in.

This must be what it's like to be blind, she thought. Feeling your way for things you expect to find in a certain place, arranging things in a blackness so complete there's not an outline of shape. Using the other senses to determine physical texture, telling sounds, the smell that says you're in Dinandro.

The plastic container now had greater value than it had as a water bottle. It meant she no longer had to wait in the middle of the night in agony for a guard who would take his time to come and let her out so she could stumble to the latrine.

When she finished she bounced on her feet, and rubbed the edge of the bottle against herself in an effort to catch last drips. With no toilet paper or rag, it was the best she could do before pulling up her jeans. Alone in the cell, it no longer mattered to her if anyone heard her pee or not. She crawled back onto the bed and thought about what, besides this, had awakened her.

It had been a powerful dream: *She was being chased. She ran until, trapped at the edge of a steep cliff, she had no choice but to jump. She leaped off the edge of the cliff to escape her pursuers, but instead of falling to her death she found that by controlling her breathing she could balance herself in an upright position. She could control the rate at which she fell. She learned to float. By just breathing she could float downward while she gazed at images in the side of the mountain.*

Lying on her cell bed staring with open eyes upward into darkness, she couldn't remember what the images were. But the feeling of their importance stayed with her.

She landed on her feet safely at the bottom of the cliff. When she raised her face she saw the people who had been chasing her standing on the edge, staring down in disbelief. They didn't try to come after her, and she saw awe in their expressions.

In the dungeon it was hard to distinguish time. Tiny openings at the top of a wall in the main room allowed air to circulate. Cathryn avoided the area because unsavory people hung out there.

One day Cesar, who had been watching out for her developed film, arrived with news.

"The photos are just as you said they were. There's no problem."

Cathryn in the pre-Columbian ruins, smiling and waving. She hadn't taken a photo of Hector.

Cesar reminded her that Tjon had said they wanted her to stay at least fifteen days at Dinandro in case they were able to capture Dom. She suspected that they didn't want to go through the expense and paperwork involved to transfer her.

For several days Kate had been saying, "Today they're transferring me to Santa Monica."

"What about me? Have you heard anything about me?"

Kate's look said she had no idea. There were always rumors and anticipation about something about to happen, and then it didn't.

When something did happen, it would be without warning. Men and women would just disappear, and if someone asked, they were told the person had been transferred to the prison system.

Days later Cesar informed Cathryn, "Your legal process is on hold. The courts are on strike."

On strike—meaning while court workers picketed and demonstrated, all scheduled cases were cancelled, creating a huge backlog. Everything stopped.

At first Cesar and Cathryn cursed it, but the strike turned out to be a good thing. It took longer than they had anticipated to get all of Cathryn's documents received and notarized and certified in the US and Peru. The strike lasted four weeks, during which time Cesar was able to prepare her employment 1099's, bank statements and tax records to present to the judge and prosecutor of the lower court.

Before Cathryn could leave Dinandro she had to give an official statement to the Peruvian detectives and to the prosecutor. Cesar was present to translate. The translating and typing of the "official statement" took an hour and a half, during which Cathryn worried about which of her belongings would be gone when she returned to the dungeon.

During the testimony, U.S. Consul David Ryan called. Cathryn told him the captain had been punishing her for not hiring any of "his" lawyers. Two different times she'd been ordered to strip, a humiliating experience. The reason for this, she had been told, was to see if she had identifying marks or if she was carrying a weapon. Another prisoner, an Australian girl, told Cathryn that she didn't have to strip—they just asked her if she had any scars or tattoos.

"When are you being transferred?" David asked.

"Soon I think, because I'm giving my statement now."

"Your sister's been calling here, and she hasn't found an attorney yet."

Dierdre had a neighbor, a federal prosecutor, who had agreed to try to find Cathryn a Peruvian attorney.

"That's okay, I've already found an attorney and I need her to wire me money to hire him."

"She'll want to check him out, first."

"It's too late. I've hired him and time is running out."

Chapter 11

Mid-morning on the fifteenth day after Cathryn's arrest the guard came for her and Kate. They would go to the more permanent Santa Monica Women's Prison, in the Chorrillos district of Lima.

Cathryn had little time to collect her things. They had given her the rest of her clothes—two shirts, a pair of jeans and a skirt. The tee shirts and alpaca socks she'd bought for souvenirs had been stolen either by people at the airport or at Dinandro. The piece of clothing she knew for sure had been stolen in Dinandro was a pair of dirty panties. She had her backpack and a belt—the rest had been looted.

Her things were given to Cesar for safekeeping during her transfer, to be returned to her when she arrived at Santa Monica.

Weakened and in deteriorating health, she had mixed feelings about leaving Dinandro. Here she knew her cell, she knew the toilet facility, she knew the guards and prisoners, she knew what was what. What lay ahead for her at Santa Monica? She'd heard the usual rumors about corruption, so that wouldn't be surprising, but she knew nothing about the facilities. Would they be better? Could they be worse? She didn't even know where Chorrillos was, though she knew it was on the outskirts of Lima.

At the entrance to Dinandro Cathryn and Kate were handcuffed and handed off to two detectives in street clothes. Kate tried to give her a reassuring smile, but she felt anxious, too. In the detectives' car, they snaked through the crowded streets of Lima.

These might have been welcome sights for Cathryn after being incarcerated for two weeks in rooms without a view, but they passed in a colorless blur. She took no interest in Peruvians walking or driving to their shopping or appointments, people for whom buying simple things like soap and toilet paper was a mindless errand. They passed at the Palacio de Justicia a demonstration of picketing court workers, screaming on the steps of the building.

Cathryn had thought that a transfer to a jail in the same city would be just a ride across town with armed guards. Not in Peru. Again and again, the car stopped. Each time she expected they had arrived at the prison, but nothing she saw from the car looked like one. The driver or one of the detectives would get out of the car, be gone for a time, get back in the car and drive again.

Another stop. This time the doors were opened, Cathryn and Kate pulled out. Cathryn would never have thought how awkward it would be to get in and out of a car with your hands in handcuffs. Both she and Kate were tall women, and she felt embarrassed, ungainly and helpless.

They were taken into a building, into what looked like a waiting room, and seated in plastic chairs. Kate's handcuffs were removed, and a man took her into another room while the detectives stayed with Cathryn. She thought of the magazines she would be perusing in any waiting room in America, but here there was nothing to do but go mindless and wait for time to pass.

Kate came out, and the same man motioned to Cathryn. She stood and one of the detectives unlocked her handcuffs. When she hesitated, he gave her a shove in the direction of the doorway. Awaiting her in the room were a woman and a man in a soiled, white jacket. The room reminded Cathryn of a shabby version of a movie set for a medical clinic. Neither the man nor the woman spoke English, but their meaning was clear. They wanted her to take off her clothes.

Cathryn shook her head, *no*. The doctor repeated his instructions, and the woman moved to help her. Without thinking, Cathryn made a sudden turn, deflecting the woman's hand with her arm.

"No way," she said. "I'm not taking off my clothes."

The woman and the doctor looked at each other, spoke more Spanish, scribbled notes, and ushered her back to the waiting room. Back in the car with the two detectives, Kate, who spoke Spanish, said the people at the clinic had wanted to see if they had any bruises or marks that would indicate they'd been physically abused.

At dusk, when colors recede into indiscriminate shades of gray, Cathryn and Kate were taken from the car and into a building in Callao, a town adjacent to Lima.

Before leaving Dinandro, there had been papers to sign, at the clinic there had been papers to sign and now they were asked to sign more papers. Caesar had prepared Cathryn for this; he had explained what she would be signing and what it meant. At Callao he was waiting for her to help with the paperwork. One of the documents she was asked to sign said that she was well taken care of, housed in proper facilities, not mistreated.

What an outrageous joke, she thought.

"It's in your best interest to sign," Cesar said gently. "Telling the truth will just cause ill will with people whose help we might need later." He explained that human rights are pushed on the Third World by a First World mentality that doesn't have a clue. In the Third World where corruption and constant fear of reprisal are the norm, it's impossible to tell the truth. There were procedural documents because some organization had donated money or products for the care of inmates. These goods, offered in such innocent American good faith, were regularly looted by the people who worked in the prison system.

When Cathryn objected, Cesar said, "The only way to tell the truth in this circumstance is to first dare to survive it, and speak later when there is no chance of retaliation."

Cathryn hated the idea, but understood what he meant, so she signed.

The two women were then taken to a cell with no windows. No furniture, no running water, not even a cement bench to sit on. A filthy, thin mattress lay on the ground. In the back a small open space with a hole in the floor accommodated bathroom needs. An overpowering stench, like a combination of toxic mold and twenty years of feces and nicotine residue made Cathryn's eyes began to burn. She found it painful to breathe. The stink was so intense it activated a gagging response.

A hole had been smashed through the wood of the main cell door, and they discovered that by sticking their heads through it they could get better air. They took turns doing this until they got so tired they abandoned the effort.

A chill night cold set in. In order to stay warm, all night they sat huddled together on the cement floor. Without being able to see outside it was impossible to know the time. Cathryn shivered and dozed, mind numb. There seemed no point in thinking—that way led to more depression. They were zoo animals without food or water in an ancient cage, nowhere to go, no will to fight, no reason to live beyond the moment.

It might have been the following day when Cathryn saw Cesar again.

"Why are we still here?" she pleaded. "What are they doing? I thought we were going to Santa Monica!"

Cesar had no answers for her. His face sagged with pity.

When she had left the cell to see him it had been such a relief to leave that stink, but after he left she had to return to it.

Cathryn's life had become a series of surreal moments haphazardly linked together. She had achieved the Zen ability to live just in the moment. She had abandoned thoughts of the past and the future was too uncertain to contemplate.

Again armed guards in bulletproof vests moved Cathryn and Kate.

At the next place, a woman in street clothes frisked them. Peru is too poor a country to hand out uniforms to every level of government worker. Just the army, police and guards working within the prisons wore uniforms. Her lack of uniform made Cathryn suspect this was not Santa Monica Women's Prison.

Kate and a guard watched as Cathryn stood with her arms straight out, towering over the Peruvian woman as she ran her hands over her body. She hadn't been allowed to take any personal items when she left Dinandro and had been under constant guard, so what was the point of this? No one else had bothered.

When the woman fondled her breasts, Cathryn twisted away, and slapped her hands. The woman said something in Spanish. Cathryn stared at the picture of the Virgin Mary on the wall. Religious icons did nothing to stop the people who worked in these places from thievery and debauchery.

Because no one from Kate's embassy was there to take it, when they had left Dinandro Kate had been given her purse, but at Callao she had to turn it over to her consulate representative for safekeeping. Now in her purse, she discovered keys. The guards in Dinandro had rifled through their things and mistakenly put Cathryn's keys back in Kate's purse. It was arranged that the Canadian Consul would give the keys to Cesar. Before that could happen Cathryn's keys disappeared—lust for her Sharper Image/LCD flashlight key chain? Since the time of her arrest, everything Cathryn had was up for grabs, and there was nothing she could do about it. Pissed that they didn't leave the keys, she understood that that would have left evidence of a theft—better to steal the whole thing and pretend it was never there.

The next cell where the women found themselves in had bunk beds. Cathryn lost track of time. Were they there one night, two nights? They were moved again. Cathryn tried to count the days since they had left Dinandro, but her mind wouldn't cooperate. They had not been given food or drink since. When Cesar brought Cathryn a bottle of water she took sips and clutched the plastic bottle to her body like a mother animal protecting her child. She had been without food so long that her hunger pangs had disappeared.

Kate suffered, complaining of recurring stomach pains. She would scrunch her eyes, moan, and shift her body in an effort to relieve her plight. Finally she made such a fuss in her broken

Spanish that she got to a pay phone and was able to call her embassy. They delivered to her a meal from a restaurant. She encouraged Cathryn to eat. Cathryn took a bite, but found she had no appetite or interest.

The last holding cell was under the Palacio de Justicia. A huge room with an open toilet in the center. Cathryn felt grateful that she hadn't eaten so she wouldn't have to shit in front of people.

At first the two women were alone in this cold cell. It was never quiet because in the corridor they could hear guards and staff who worked at the Palacio de Justicia. Later that night two Peruvian girls were brought in. They had alpaca blankets, which they offered to share. Cathryn so appreciated this a small act of kindness. They coaxed her to eat a cracker, but it made her thirsty, and she needed to conserve her water.

Now when she stood, her vision dizzied. When had the color of her urine turned dark brown? It had been a steady change, but she had been so despondent that she had paid little attention. Now she regarded it in detached amazement...so many changes in her body...what else must be going on inside her that she couldn't know until some new symptom presented itself?

At least once every day Cesar came to check on Cathryn. Without running water, soap, toilet paper and a toothbrush/toothpaste for more than three days, she felt almost too dehumanized and humiliated to talk to him. She felt embarrassed by her strong bodily smell and tried not to stand too close to him.

Desperate for this ordeal to end she wailed, "Why is it taking so long to get to the Santa Monica prison?"

Cesar said, "Because this is Peru."

Cesar said not to worry because her things were safe with him, and he would bring them to her as soon as she got to the prison.

"But here, for you."

He handed her a plastic bag. Inside she found a small package of tissue, a toothbrush, and a travel-sized tube of toothpaste. Cathryn suspected he must have bribed someone to be able to give her these things.

At nightfall the women in the cell were gathered with men who must have been held in another part of the building. They were put in contraptions that bound the hands and feet together, making it difficult to walk. Seeing that, Cathryn and Kate were grateful to have only handcuffs.

Again they were being transported. Cathryn's mind went to a different place—a place where nothing else existed but the rub of metal on her wrists, the stiffness of her filthy jeans, the smarting where the elastic leg band of her panties chafed, the sight of her dirty feet, the effort of climbing into the vehicle in her grimy slip-on high-heeled sandals.

Inside the enclosed truck forty-three filthy bodies were seated in a circle so each could be cuffed by the wrist to the person on each side. Small openings at the top of the enclosure allowed air to circulate, but they were too high to be able to see out. A small window looked into the cab where, if Cathryn positioned herself just right, she could see the armed guards and the road ahead. In the back of the truck in a barred off section two guards in fatigue uniforms and bulletproof vests sat with M16's to provide protection from behind.

Now it was dark outside. Drivers honked in the slow, congested traffic. In the street, people yelled above the noise. Each time the truck braked or accelerated Cathryn was thrust into the person sitting next to her. Her handcuffs made it impossible to brace herself.

The truck stopped to admit more women, two of whom were pregnant. They had to stand cuffed to each other. When the truck swerved or braked to a sudden stop, they fell onto the seated prisoners—a jumble of arms and legs, foreign cries and mutterings, sudden jerks of handcuffs, pain coursing through Cathryn's wrists.

With her hands cuffed, she couldn't protect her arms, her face or her breasts from sudden thrusts and accidental punches from moving body parts. Cathryn thought, *we're being thrown around like pieces of garbage being tossed by the wind...* A child's voice in the back of her mind whimpered, *I give up.*

Cathryn and Kate were the only *gringas* in the truck. Kate could communicate in broken Spanish with the other women...rumors...complaints...anger...despair...no one knew anything. This was Cathryn's life now; the truck, her world; Kate, her sister. Did someone pee? Or did the truck smell like this when they got in? Nothing existed beyond the moving walls of this world.

Brakes screeched and the truck stopped. Cathryn heard sudden yelling. The rear door was thrown open and several women were forced out of the wagon. Cathryn took a deep breath, but the air was no better with less bodies. The door slammed closed and the truck lurched to a start. A short drive—maybe a block? Another screeching stop.

The rear door opened again and all the remaining women were taken out.

One guard, an older man, put his hand out to help Cathryn off the truck. This unexpected courtesy surprised her.

She stepped into a horrible, barbed wire place...everything shabby, dirty, broken or obsolete...except for the barbed wire not much different from Dinandro...it felt normal...*it's what I'm used to now*...her high-heeled sandals were just as shabby. Cathryn felt no emotion, that it would be whatever it would be.

Que sera, sera.

Chapter 12

Cathryn caught the name from a Peruvian woman's conversation. *Santa Monica Women's Prison.*

One group of women from the truck were housed in the terrorist side of the prison. Peru had suffered a long history of terrorism by the Shining Path, brought to an end under Fujimori's presidency. Still, they kept the terrorists separate from the general inmate population.

Cathryn and Kate and the rest of the women were ushered into a large cement room with broken ceiling fans and weathered wooden tables. Several prison guards positioned around the room. One spoke in Spanish, and with rough gestures made Cathryn surrender her four personal items: water bottle, toothpaste, white toothbrush, and a writing pen Kate had smuggled to her. The only item she ever saw again was her white toothbrush.

A female guard took Cathryn and Kate into a separate room and made them remove their clothes. They stood naked, shivering in the chill room, while the guard took her time examining each item. Though their smelly clothes had been worn and unwashed for weeks, the woman turned them in and out until she was satisfied that there was nothing hidden.

When they were dressed again and allowed to claim their things—for Cathryn her lone toothbrush—Kate discovered that many of her items had disappeared. One was a writing pad containing valuable information. Her temper boiled over in Spanish. Big-boned and heavy, Kate towered over the guards, even the men. She exuded an attitude that she would not be pushed around.

After much yelling and gesticulating on Kate's part, the guards handed back some—but not all—of her things. Kate snatched her writing pad out of the hand of one of the female guards, but by that time the woman had already thrown away the top pages that held all Kate's important information—the phone numbers of her son and friends back home, the number for the Canadian embassy in Lima. Cathryn suspected the guard did this in an effort to hide the fact that she stole the writing pad, much like the person who had stolen her keys and key chain. Kate was devastated, but like Cathryn she was powerless to do anything about it.

Cathryn vowed to herself that if she ever got out, she would use any means necessary to never return.

Thoughts of Dom turned into fantasies with all the violence of a Hollywood mob film: DEA agents beat the shit out him until his face was deformed and bloody, her sister blew his head off with a shotgun. He would be hacked to death with machetes. But those deaths were too fast. Torture would be better—a thousand little cuts so he'd bleed to death in pain, hearing him scream while salt was thrown on his wounds. But that reminded Cathryn too much of the slugs she killed when she was a kid in the Pacific Northwest, running over the lawn after it rained with saltshakers burning the poor things to death. She still felt guilty over killing a bunch of slugs when she was a kid!

Cathryn realized she didn't have a stomach for revenge. Whenever she thought about revenge against Dom, it was always someone else who delivered the fatal blow, never her. She struggled to turn her anger over to the universe. This would be Dom's fate or destiny or karma or whatever you wanted to call it. He had to deal with it, not her.

This understanding forced her to look inward at herself: She saw herself as a pussy who did things she didn't want to do because she didn't want to argue with people. A pussy easily manipulated by guilt and other people's needs and wants. Because it was easier to just do what other people asked. Because she wanted people to like her. Because she wanted to be politically correct. Because she didn't want to hurt people's feelings. Blah, blah, blah.

Cathryn had turned her anger inward: she decided that she had been too much of a fucking wussy to say no to people. *I should've been born a bitch,* she thought. If they're not born, could real bitches be made? Maybe one day she could learn to tell people to go fuck themselves.

Because she saw herself as such a trusting wimp, Cathryn blamed herself for her predicament.

It had been dark when Cathryn and Kate arrived at Santa Monica Women's Prison. After the examination of their clothes and naked bodies, they were marched through another pair of barred doors into the prison proper. They passed through two more sets of bars before they got to where they would sleep.

This area of the prison was called Prevención, a place were prisoners stayed before they were assigned to a cellblock. In this small room bunk beds lined end to end against all four walls. Though the width of a bunk bed was a single bed size, two women slept in each one. High on a shelf between bunks sat an old black and white television.

To the side of this holding area were two other rooms, reserved for inmates who'd gotten trapped in the Montesinos/Fujimori corruption scandal. These were prisoners whose families had political pull, and terrorists who'd testified against inmates on the other side of the prison. They were kept separate from the general population, and though they got an entire bunk to themselves, they had to share the one toilet and shower. Again no windows, but near the ceiling on one side of the room were little vents where the girls in the upper bunks had hung clothes to dry.

All the bunks were full, but Cathryn didn't have time to wonder where she and Kate would sleep because they and the two pregnant Peruvians were taken to the prison clinic.

This room looked like a war zone that had survived a bombing raid. They sat in unstable metal chairs and waited. Cathryn huddled her arms and rocked forward and backward, afraid of everyone except Kate. A Cuban inmate in a wheelchair, also waiting, blabbed incessantly. She peered at Cathryn with frank curiosity. *"Gringa? Americana?"*

Cathryn nodded. The Cuban uttered a long statement in Spanish, shaking her head. Kate translated: "She says it will be worse for you because your embassy does nothing for its inmates. She says I'm lucky to be Canadian because Canadians get transferred back to Canada and get embassy assistance in the meantime. She says Peruvian girls have family on the outside to get them whatever they need, but you're American, so you're on your own."

A male doctor entered. One by one he took the four women into another room, even smaller and dirtier than the waiting room, with two chairs and an obsolete examining table. In the harsh light of the florescent ceiling tube, the doctor motioned for Cathryn to take off her clothes.

She stared into his face. "No," she said, surprised at the strength of her voice. She would not take off her clothes again for anyone.

He asked questions in Spanish. She had no idea what he asked. Five minutes later he motioned her to leave. His face and attitude were so expressionless that Cathryn felt like a piece of meat being passed by an inspector.

Two female guards entered the waiting room. Words were spoken. The two Peruvians and Kate lifted their shirts to expose their breasts to the guards. Cathryn had no choice but to do the same. None of the women wore bras. Cathryn hated bras and never wore them and Kate felt the same. Cathryn didn't know if the Peruvians took off their bras earlier when they came into the prison since they had all been strip-searched separately.

They stood with their shirts raised while these female guards ogled their breasts. Cathryn sensed feelings of power and lewdness in the guards, like they could make the prisoners do whatever they wanted. Not understanding anything that had been said, Cathryn lowered her shirt only when she saw the other women did.

They were escorted back to Prevención. An hour later Kate received a package that had arrived from her embassy: Sheets, pillow, a blanket, toilet paper, plastic Tupperware and eating utensils, plastic cup, packaged food. Kate would be allowed a stipend if her family was unable to send money to help her; her embassy made this available for her to purchase the items they knew no one is given in prison.

That first night, the women slept on the floor on grimy lengths of foam infested with lice. Cathryn had no blanket, no sheets, no pillow, but Kate shared her new sheet and blanket.

Over the next weeks more women arrived. At night they were lined on the floor like the proverbial canned sardines. Cathryn counted fifty-six women in this room, with one bathroom and one shower. When more bodies couldn't fit into Prevención, newcomers had to sleep in the hallway.

Cathryn asked Cesar, "Do you know how horrible this place is?"

"Yes, I know, but you're in a paradise compared to what the men's prison is like." This was supposed to make her feel better? What did she care about the men's prison?

"I can't stay here. Can't I get out on bail?"

Her lawyer shook his head. "No, they won't consider it. Foreign prisoners are a flight risk."

Chapter 13

Nights were noisy as well as chilly. Snoring and farting made it near impossible for Cathryn to sleep. When she rose in the middle of the night to go to the bathroom, she tripped over a woman's leg and stepped on another woman's hand. The sound of angry Spanish mutterings accompanied her to the bathroom.

So much unwashed humanity crammed into one small cement space made the smell overwhelming—an acrid body odor combined with the constant sour smells of urine and feces.

The next day several girls were allowed to go out into the courtyard, but not Cathryn. She envied them the air that they were able to breathe there—not fresh air by any means—but air less cloying. When an Israeli girl arrived, immediately she was allowed out of Prevención and into the courtyard. In the following days everyone was allowed to roam the courtyard, except the *Americana*.

Cathryn began to suspect that she was the last to be allowed out because the *directora* of the prison hated Americans. It was an act of power, an authority the *directora* would never know elsewhere and an authority everyone could see she had over a rich American. When Cathryn was finally let out, she realized the courtyard was so dreary and depressing that what she had come to envy was not much better than the room she had been confined in.

She had lost weight, and her jeans hung loose at her hips. Her body felt heavy and listless, and it took effort to raise it from the floor. Too sudden a movement and her head swirled in dizzying waves.

Most nights she lay on the floor praying for the cockroaches to leave her alone and the blessing of sleep that wouldn't come. After she was allowed out into the courtyard during the day, she found she preferred to stay in the room and try to sleep. The television ran all day with strident music videos and soap operas, and sleep was uneasy. Anyway, what did it matter if she was in the room or in the courtyard? What did any of it matter?

Guards with clipboards came each morning and each evening to take roll call. The women answered with their names, and Cathryn began to know her fellow inmates. After roll call they had to clean the prison. They were given ragtag equipment—brooms worn down to the bottom bristles, mops with heads worn away and wrapped in dirty rags, filthy recycled paint cans to use for buckets, and no soap or cleanser of any kind.

Cathryn, who never liked the smell of Pinesol, now would have relished it. "Cleaning" the prison seemed to just move the grime around. She heard that an organization donated cleaning stuff in gallon bottles, which never got dispensed and was forgotten. When an inspection by a VIP was scheduled, the *directora* brought out the cleaning fluid and used it all on the concrete pathway where the bigwig would walk.

The stocky little Peruvian women in their guard uniforms took special delight in separating Cathryn from the rest of the group and assigning her to the most repulsive tasks. One morning a little pinch-faced woman wanted her to clean toilets without gloves or a brush. Cathryn looked down at her and found the strength to say, "No way."

The guard's mouth tightened and she made a sound of disgust. Cathryn stood her ground, thinking, *what's she going to do, beat me?* Cathryn didn't care; she felt resigned. The guard screamed at her in Spanish. Cathryn gave her the haughtiest look she could summon. She would rather take a beating, and she sensed the guard knew it. The guard walked away, anger in every step. She spoke to another guard, one hand gesturing towards Cathryn. The second woman hit Cathryn's arm make her walk and prodded her to an area past the courtyard and into another area of the prison. They stopped near what passed for a kitchen. There Cathryn was directed to carry heavy garbage cans, and assigned to work with a Peruvian girl who spoke no English.

A sudden crashing sound that made her jump. A rusted metal can full of garbage fell over onto the already littered ground. Unidentifiable trash spilled out, and an animal darted away.

Was that a rat? A rat as big as a cat?

The Peruvian girl laughed. "*Gato*," she said. Cat.

Cathryn had heard there were no rats in the prison because it was populated with feral cats. These were not sweet tabbies like her beloved SusieQ and George, and this was the closest she'd ever come to one of them.

The third day as she moved the garbage cans around the inside part of the prison near the cell blocks she heard a woman call from an upstairs window.

"Hey down there! Are you American?"

Cathryn felt a rush of delight to hear English, even if it had a Scandinavian accent.

"I'm coming down," she called. "Stay there."

The white girl who approached Cathryn was Swedish, a little shorter in height, with a splotchy, square face. She asked Cathryn where she was from, and Cathryn told her about how she had been arrested by mistake. The Swedish woman smiled, giving the impression that it was neither here nor there to her if Cathryn was guilty or not.

"I'm Kadlin." She didn't extend a hand to shake but instead scratched at her shoulder where raggedy brown hair brushed her skin. Cathryn noticed that Kadlin's shirt looked pretty clean for the circumstances, but her jeans were just as filthy as her own. The prison couldn't afford uniforms so inmates wore whatever clothes they'd worn when arrested or had been given them by family and not yet stolen.

Cathryn's jaw fell in shock when Kadlin pointed to the upstairs window from where she'd called and said, "I'm up there, cell block A. Been here five years, now."

She asked if Cathryn had a boyfriend. Cathryn shook her head.

"My boyfriend's Peruvian," Kadlin said. "Pepe. He's a well-established drug trafficker." Her smile softened. "I have a nine year-old daughter, too."

Though Cathryn was afraid of the answer, she had to ask, "Where's your daughter now?"

Kadlin's mouth straightened. "In Sweden, with my mother. By the time I ever get out of here, I'll be lucky if she remembers me."

"You must miss her terribly."

"Sometimes I dream about her, and sometimes I hardly think of her at all. I get pictures once in awhile, but she no longer looks like anyone I know."

In her thirties, Kadlin looked older and spoke perfect Spanish as well as English. She admitted to a long-time drug abuse problem. "It's hard, you know?" was her explanation.

Cathryn told her about Dom, and how devastated she was by his betrayal.

"Was he your boyfriend?" Kadlin asked.

"No, it wasn't like that. He's younger than me—he was like a little brother to me," she wailed. "He used to ask me advice about his girl friends. I was touched when he offered me the ticket to Peru after his buddy couldn't go at the last minute."

Kadlin pursed her lips. "*Bastardo.*"

Cathryn felt new tears pooling in her eyes. She didn't want to cry like a baby, but it wasn't easy to hold them back. "How could I have been so stupid? I worked with him for four years. He was so nice. Everyone liked him. I should have seen a sign, but what sign? How would I know? I don't know anything about drugs."

"You'll learn here."

"Yeah, I'm learning, all right," she moaned. "And then I'll die. I just know I'm going to die here."

"I know how you feel," Kadlin said. "It's tough at first. You'll be sent to the B cell block. I'll talk to the *directora* and see when you'll be transferred and if I can speed it up for you. When you get there

I'll show you the ropes, who to stay away from, how to get drugs if you want, all that." She scratched her shoulder again.

Chapter 14

Another day on the garbage can detail Cathryn met an extraordinary American, Susan, a lawyer in her fifties. She was housed on the third floor of cell block B, the one for inmates awaiting sentencing. She had been there for two and a half years without a trial.

"If they don't bring me to trial they have to release me when I hit the three-year mark," Susan said. By now Cathryn had learned not to ask "why" questions. Susan said she was in for "corruption charges" stemming from the Montesinos witch hunt.

"I came to Peru thirty-five years ago as an exchange student," Susan said. She'd fallen in love with and married a cousin to Vladimiro Montesinos, Fujimori's right-hand man. Susan had lived in Peru for so long that now she had dual citizenship. "We had a daughter together, but the relationship lost its steam, you know? When I found out he was seeing another woman, I asked him for a divorce, but he wouldn't give it to me."

Divorce was difficult in Peru; it must be consensual, and still it could take years to finalize. Susan said that while she was still living with her husband, his cousin would come by often to visit. She had long conversations with Vladimiro Montesinos, a successful attorney who at that time wasn't in politics. She described him as "a fascinating man." They were friends for years before they became romantically involved. It was Vladimiro who encouraged Susan to go back to school and get her law degree.

"When my husband found out about us, he consented to the divorce."

With Vladimiro she had another daughter. He went into politics, and when their relationship ended, it was amicable.

"Vladimiro was good about sending the child support, every month without fail." Her smile was ironic. When the Fujimori presidency fell, Susan got embroiled in the never-ending Montesinos corruption trial because the money she had received from Vladimiro every month was seen as political payoff.

Cathryn said, "I'm sure you're the only woman in the world jailed for accepting child support. Too bad Vladimiro Montesinos wasn't a deadbeat dad."

Through the proper channels Susan had tried to explain the child support—she was a lawyer after all—but due process isn't part of Peruvian law. At least she'd been able to care for her youngest daughter while she was in prison, on the first floor of cell block A where women with children under three were quartered.

Cathryn felt like she was histrionic compared to Susan. Susan's stoic personality amazed her. Susan spoke as if this happened to everybody sometime in her life.

After days of hauling garbage cans Cathryn began to feel stabbing pains in her back. When she could no longer stand the pain she refused to haul any more garbage cans. Kate stepped in, speaking to the guard in Spanish. The guard backed down from Kate's imposing height and weight and menacing look.

Cathryn discovered that the guards were talking to other prisoners about her. She and Kate sat cross-legged on the ground one day when Rosemary, a sweet British girl, joined them. Cathryn liked Rosemary, who did a dumb thing one time and was now paying the price. In a sympathetic tone, Rosemary nodded towards the ever-present guards and said to Cathryn, "They like to see you do dirty jobs."

"Why me?" she asked. Cathryn tried to avoid attention as much as was possible for a tall, blond, white woman.

Rosemary's smile expanded her young face. "They believe that everyone in the United States is filthy rich, and you have legions of maids to do this kind of work for you."

Cathryn laughed. "I've never been able to afford the luxury of a maid in my entire life."

"Me, neither," Kate said. "But we could sure use one here. A maid could help me dress for 'dinnah' in the evening."

Her jest made the others smile. Kate didn't like that Cathryn was being singled out to do shit work, so she became her protection. With her size, passing Spanish, and blatant don't-fuck-with-me attitude, she made a formidable barrier between the guards and Cathryn. They knew they could only push her so far, and Cathryn felt no shame in hiding behind her.

Whatever words Kadlin had with the *directora* didn't help—Cathryn had to stay in Prevención. Even David Ryan had no influence. One day he came to check on her because her family and friends at home couldn't get in contact with her nor she with them.

"I'm the only consul they search," David told her. His tone was matter-of-fact, as if he'd grown used to being treated differently from all the other consuls who visited Santa Monica Women's Prison. He spoke to the *directora* about getting Cathryn transferred to a permanent cellblock, but she ignored him. It became clear to both David and Cathryn that she hated Americans.

As the rich American *gringa* in the prison Cathryn continued to face constant discrimination. The injustice and untruth of this made her heartsick. She would have liked to be able to say that it made her have noble thoughts about discrimination in America, accompanied by profound cultural revelation, but it did not. With day-to-day survival at stake, an animal instinct for self-preservation had taken over.

Her cultural revelation was a shocking dichotomy: One moment she worked in San Francisco, waiting on the wealthiest people in the world and their interior designers, and the next moment she was dropped into the dregs of the Third World to survive in the worst conditions imaginable. She couldn't integrate this contrast.

Cathryn cried—terrible crying jags that would last for days and leave her face bloated, her eyes scratchy. No one tried to console her. What could they say that would make a difference?

The money Cathryn's family sent to the U.S. embassy in Peru remained at the embassy. Unlike at Kate's Canadian embassy, at the American embassy their official position was that it was not their job to provide US prisoners with anything or with any services. David Ryan could bring her money—by prison rules one twenty-dollar bill per visit—and he was scheduled to visit his Americans only every three months.

Other prisoners had their embassies bring them money when they needed it, but Cathryn didn't have that luxury. Since she had no family in Peru to get things for her, she had to live without them. Cathryn remained in Prevención for one month, during which she had to survive with nothing. She felt humiliated and ashamed to be an American when the German, Dutch and Canadian embassies brought food, fruit, vegetables, canned milk, bottled water, and newspapers to their prisoners. Cathryn suspected that the U.S. government's every-three-month visit was just to see how many Americans were still alive. If so, they dispensed vitamins and protein powder.

"I've worked two jobs most of my adult life," she complained to her consul, "and paid the highest taxes because I am single, with no dependents and no property. And when I need my government to save me from living like an animal, where are they?"

In David Ryan's defense, Cathryn knew he understood her frustration and would have liked to do more. His explanation left her cold: "It's not our policy, and if I or my staff do these things for you on our own, there would be a reprimand. Any change toward our citizens in foreign prisons would have to be mandated by the President and/or Congress."

She was so grateful to Kate for sharing her bedding. How lucky she was that Kate was arrested the day after her. She didn't want to think about how much worse it would have been without her.

Cathryn vowed that if she survived this, those people in Congress were going to hear from her. Later, when she put what David Ryan said in a letter to Congress, he asked her to take it out.

The first thing Cathryn wanted to do upon awakening was go to work. She would be off to the interior design showrooms, or showing a client samples of Italian brocade chair fabric. Cathryn knew all about classic Asian furniture, and now she was getting a crash course in the illegal drug trade. There was no one in Prevención to commiserate with about this work-loss feeling—the mules couldn't relate to it.

Cathryn quickly learned that putting drug people together in one place disseminates information. The result: easier to move more drugs.

Kadlin explained it: "If you're a mule working out of Amsterdam and you get arrested in Peru, you arrange to have a Peruvian trafficker send a mule to your contact in Amsterdam. A portion of that drug sale, and all future sales made via this new connection, will be wired to you in prison."

"But how would you make that arrangement in the first place when you're already in prison?" Cathryn asked.

Kadlin smiled at her naiveté. "Most likely through one of the church organizations that's always trying to convert wayward prisoners."

She went on to explain the advantage to this. "The drug trade has not just replaced the mule arrested in the first place, but formed a new alliance to move drugs that was never there before. Plus, the arrested mule has secured a steady income while they remain imprisoned. Traffickers have lots of contacts within any prison. Their envoys come every visiting day."

And the most important thing was that you did not snitch, no matter what. You didn't talk, and if you do, you lied.

Cesar came to see Cathryn almost every day. She had gotten over her embarrassment about meeting him in such a filthy, slovenly condition. Each time she hoped he'd have positive news, though she'd become resigned to more of the same. Some days, all Cesar did was hold her hand while she cried. Some days he tried to make her laugh. Some days he came just to tell her that she needed to be strong and to eat.

"The courts are still on strike," he announced one morning.

"So this will all take longer." She felt a cloud of doom descend.

"Unfortunately, yes. But you are not alone, your case is not forgotten. Meanwhile I'm receiving more of your documents from the United States and processing them."

One day she was called out of Prevención, but it wasn't to meet Cesar.

The first thing Cathryn noticed about the woman standing before her was that she was taller, with large brown eyes and full lips, a classical beauty. It had been a long time since Cathryn had seen a woman dressed in a suit, and to her the woman looked almost angelic. When she heard her speak her name, she began to cry uncontrollably. The woman in the suit spoke English and said her name was Olivia and that she was an attorney.

Cathryn felt confused. "I already have an attorney."

Her smile dazzled. "Oh, I'm not here to represent you. Your sister asked me to check on you and see if you need anything."

Dierdre? Her sister's image came to her mind, sitting in the clever living room she decorated in burlap and plaster, holding a cigarette in one hand and a glass of wine in the other. Older than Cathryn, Dierdre spent a lot of time reading and Cathryn respected her sharp personality.

"She wanted me to give you this." From her handbag Olivia withdrew a laminated photo of the Mother Mary and a big, white fluffy feather.

Olivia had learned about her situation from an Argentine friend who worked for a friend of Cathryn's family. *How miraculously word travels in the universe,* Cathryn thought. *To cause this woman with her tidy suit and kind face to bring me gifts.*

Her shoulders began to shake. Knowing she was going to die, she couldn't hold back her tears. She felt lost and broken. She was going to die without saying goodbye to her family, without seeing any of them again, without any power to change her fate.

Chapter 15

Olivia returned several days later with incredible news.

"Your mother and sister are coming to visit."

"Coming to Peru?" Cathryn asked dumbly. "Here? To the prison?" The idea both thrilled and horrified her.

"They asked if you would give me a list of all the things you need so they can bring them to you." Olivia opened her bag, took out a twenty-dollar bill, and handed it to her. "Here, this will help buy things you need until I can come back."

Cathryn folded the precious twenty into a tiny square and tucked it in a little pocket near the waistband of her jeans. In a choked voice she managed to squeeze out, "Thank you so much."

"I have this for you—" Olivia withdrew a piece of white paper from her handbag. "A copy of a letter written on your behalf from your congressman."

The California Congressman in Cathryn's district had written the letter to the U.S. Secretary of State, the Honorable Colin L. Powell.

"Dear Secretary Powell:

"I am writing on behalf of my constituent, Ms. Cathryn Prentis, who is currently in custody at Chorrillos Women's Prison in Lima, Peru. After looking into the circumstances of Ms. Prentis' case, I am writing to express my concern and interest. I would appreciate it if you would independently assess her case and determine if an expedited disposition can be reached immediately.

"It is my understanding that Ms. Prentis was returning from a brief vacation in Peru when she was detained at the International Airport of Lima on the evening of October 21, 2003. She had apparently been asked to carry back a scuba carrying case for oxygen by a friend who was also on the trip with her. When she went through the x-ray clearance, an object was discovered that later tested positive for cocaine.

"Ms. Prentis maintains that she had no knowledge of the presence of cocaine and did not participate in any way in transporting it. I further understand that she has been extremely cooperative with DEA agents and local law enforcement in Peru.

"I have had the opportunity to discuss this matter with a number of individuals and have learned that Ms. Prentis is a longtime and valued employee at Petrocelli Antiques, an upscale antique store in San Francisco, California. Her employer at Petrocelli Antiques is equally impressed with her integrity and honesty.

"Moreover, I understand that the officials who are involved in the investigation of the case in Peru are impressed with Ms. Prentis' credibility and forthright nature. They have shared their observation with my office that she does not fit the profile of a drug trafficker, but instead leads a full and responsible life in the U.S. "

Cathryn's nose had begun to run from crying, and she had to stop reading. Olivia handed her a tissue.

When she read the words "does not fit the profile of a drug trafficker" Cathryn thought of Dom. She didn't think he fit the profile, either. Owning his own successful delivery business and having a beautiful wife seemed to her to indicate that he was also leading "a full and responsible life in the U.S."

Cathryn balled her tissue, sniffed and read the rest of the letter.

"I have had an opportunity to discuss this case in detail with Ms. Prentis' sister, her employes, staff at the U.S. embassy in Lima and the DEA special agents assigned to this case in Lima and in San Francisco. I want to add my concern to the growing list of concerned individuals in her case.

"It is my understanding that the DEA has proffered some suggestions to resolve this matter, which they are pursuing with Lima officials at this time. Those suggestions include serving Ms. Prentis with a federal arrest warrant so that she could testify against the perpetrator before a U.S. grand jury; having the U.S. take over her prosecution in exchange for Peru dismissing the charges; or

allowing Ms. Prentis to serve out her sentence in the U.S. should she be found guilty in Peru.

"I understand that criminal proceedings can often be protracted in Peru, but would appreciate any assistance your office could provide in moving the investigation and ultimate disposition of Ms. Prentis' case along. I will continue to monitor the case, since I am most interested in Ms. Prentis' well being and her ability to obtain a speedy resolution to this matter.

"Thank you for your personal attention to this matter and I look forward to hearing from you."

And there at the bottom was his signature: John Weatherman, Member of Congress.

Surely a U.S. congressman had influence in high places. Surely such a strong letter on her behalf would influence the powers that be to resolve this fast, and in her favor. Surely the Secretary of State would be impressed by this letter and intercede on her behalf with Peruvian authorities.

Cathryn knew that, even if this were true, all things governmental move slowly. The question was, would anything happen to affect her release before she wasted away to death?

Chapter 16

For three weeks Cathryn hadn't eaten anything significant. Her dirty jeans bagged at her hips. Her body had shut down—no appetite for food, no hunger pangs, no energy, no bowel movements. Her urine had further darkened, and she got dizzy if she stood too long.

But her mother and sister were coming to see her! That night she drank soup broth.

Late in the evening on Thursday, November 20th her mother and Dierdre flew into Lima. Visiting days for female visitors were Wednesdays and Sundays, but if visitors came from far away, and if the Consul of the Embassy requested it, the prison would allow special visits in Prevención. Cesar had had David Ryan write a letter to this effect so Cathryn could see her family on "non-visiting" days.

Friday morning they brought her from Prevención to sit in the waiting area. Through the bars she could see her mother and sister as they were processed to enter the prison. She thought she saw Olivia, too, but in her emotional state she couldn't be sure. When she heard her sister's voice she burst tears. A guard Cathryn had never seen before surprised her when she held her hand to hold through the bars and whispered, "*Tranquila*."

Cathryn was still sobbing when her mother and sister came through the last set of bars. Oh, for them to see her like this was so humiliating! Their hugs were awkward, and they sat down on the benches against the cement wall. They clasped her hands, wet from trying to wipe away her tears. Cathryn saw them steal glances around the open yard, taking in the equally shabby conditions of other prisoners and the disgusting filth of the place.

The only positive thing she could think of to say was, "I've gained a little weight in the last week." She had just started eating when she knew they were coming.

For a lurid moment Cathryn felt like she was in a VISA credit card commercial: *Round-trip ticket to Peru, $600. Tour to Machu*

Picchu, $200. Lawyer to represent me in drug bust, $10,000. Look of horror on mother's face when she sees my condition, Priceless.

As appalled as they were by her prison surroundings, they tried to be encouraging. They brought letters from people at home and showed her print outs of a website that had been created to disseminate information about her. There was even a place on www.BringCathryn Home.com where people could donate money to help. Cathryn's throat choked with emotion and she couldn't speak.

"But wait, there's more," Dierdre joked. She placed a purple duffelbag on the bench between them and unzipped it. "It's all yours, including the bag."

Inside were toothpaste, a toothbrush, soap, babywipes, toilet paper, Kleenex, Noxema, lotion, shampoo, conditioner, a bar of laundry soap, a Spanish dictionary and other incredible items.

Her mother explained that the micro-fiber zippered blanket had not been allowed in. "Zippers are not allowed," they'd been told. So she would cut out the zipper and bring the blanket back later. They wondered why the zippered duffelbag had been allowed. All Cathryn could say was, "Whatever the guard says goes, even if it makes no sense. You have to do what they say."

Besides the smudged and wrinkled skirt she wore, Cathryn had her dirty jeans, another shirt and a second pair of panties—other clothes had already been stolen. In the duffelbag were long-sleeved turtlenecks and flipflops. The high-heeled sandals she'd been wearing since she was arrested were no longer black, but a scuffed concrete color. The new flip-flops looked so clean they seemed to shout, "First World creature comfort."

And there was food: canned milk, tuna fish, instant coffee, crackers.

Her mother's smile was weak but brave. "I brought you canned Alaskan salmon, but they wouldn't let me bring it in because it was in glass."

No doubt tonight one of the prison guards would enjoy Alaskan salmon, sharing with no one.

There was a quilt made by Cathryn's Aunt May. For the rest of the visit she couldn't stop touching it; just the feel of new clean fabric was uplifting, comforting.

Cathryn felt like she was being ungrateful when she told her mother, "I need sheets and a pillow." She feared it would sound as if she weren't happy to have the quilt and soon-to-be-zipperless blanket, but her mother gave no indication of taking it that way.

"I'm not going to get you any of that because you're not going to be here that long."

"What makes you think that?"

"We'll get you out of here."

"How?"

"I don't know."

The woman is in denial, Cathryn thought. *Dierdre, too.*

Her mother handed her several small bills. Cathryn gave her a list of other things she needed: a plastic bucket to wash her clothes in, plastic eating utensils—metal utensils were not allowed—and a lock for the duffel so no one could steal her new treasures. These they were willing to bring…but no sheets and pillow.

At two o'clock in the afternoon official visiting ended. With her duffel full of new gifts, Cathryn felt like she was the wealthy American Peruvians thought she was. She returned to the cubicle, clutched her cache—already worried about thievery—and prayed nothing would happen between now and Sunday to prevent her family's next visit.

The next morning Cathryn jolted awake to hear a bitch of a guard outside the cell screaming in Spanish. She stumbled over bodies to get to the bathroom. A line had already formed and she almost wet her pants waiting for a toilet.

Oh, God, she prayed, *get me out of here. Please, God.*

For 160 women there were four toilets and four showers. Only three of the toilets worked and only one flushed. You had to force flush the others by pouring water from the bucket kept next to it until the water in the toilet appeared more clear and/or everything in the toilet had disappeared. There were no hand washing sinks, and no one washed their hands after using the toilet. If the laundry sinks happened to be empty of soaking clothes Cathryn could wash her hands there. She remembered the antibacterial hand gel, one of the little treasures in her new duffel bag.

Cathryn wandered out to the courtyard. Saturday was visiting day for men, but Cesar would not be coming today. He was to meet with her mother and Dierdre to discuss her case and its possible outcomes. She wouldn't know anything of their meeting until at least the following day, because on visiting days the phones were closed. Incidents had happened where women being released had been set up by other women in the prison. A phone call had been made to accomplices waiting outside announcing the woman's description and what she was wearing. As soon as she stepped outside the gates she'd been kidnapped or murdered.

In the courtyard, a little Peruvian guy approached Cathryn—dark hair slicked down, jeans, red tee shirt. Grinning like a school kid, he handed her a piece of paper. She looked at it and read, "gorgous, swethart" and other misspelled words. She removed a pencil from the pocket of her jeans, corrected his spelling, and handed the paper back to him. He gave her an intense look, shrugged, and walked away.

"You have an admirer," said Lourdes, a Spanish woman who might have been in her thirties, but it was difficult to tell because her face was so lined. Rosemary had told Cathryn to avoid Lourdes because she was a dyke.

"An admirer? I hardly think so."

"Oh yes, he definitely wants you."

Cathryn had no idea the guy was hitting on her. *There's no Prison 101 to learn this kind of stuff,* she thought. As much as she missed being around men, to even think of having a Peruvian "admirer" was too disgusting.

Chapter 17

Both inmates and guards were surprised that Cathryn's family came so fast from so far away to see her. She realized that a lot of the women in Santa Monica had brothers and sisters and mothers and fathers right there in Peru, but they weren't real "family" as in "someone who is there for you no matter what." She realized that just because you have family doesn't mean you have people who care about you. For some people, "family" is their friends because their blood relatives have disowned them.

Cathryn hadn't realized how much interest her mother and sister generated until they returned on Sunday. Everyone approached to cheek-kiss them, and while the appearance of several of the women repelled them they endured the traditional Peruvian custom with stoic grace.

It was Sunday, Women's Visiting Day, and the courtyard bustled with chattering women and frolicking children. If you closed your eyes, you might think you were at a big family picnic in a park. For the occasion Cathryn had rented a table and chairs. Before they sat down, she placed five *soles* in the hand of the girl who stood waiting next to the wobbly, broken down table.

"Everything here costs money," Cathryn said in response to her family's shocked expressions. "Everything."

They sat down cautiously on the rickety chairs. Cathryn had given Olivia a list of things she wanted her mother to bring. Her mother and sister had been frisked on their way in and been told they couldn't enter wearing any kind of hat or baseball cap. Cathryn had the impression that they'd been traumatized before they even entered the prison. As soon as Dierdre lit a cigarette, here came one inmate after another to ask for one, too. Dierdre handled being bum-rushed well, generous until her pack was empty.

In the middle of a conversation they were approached by Alice, an Australian inmate in her forties. She'd told Cathryn that both her father and brother, staunch Christians, had sexually abused her and she had been running drugs for a Nigerian out of Amsterdam since she was eighteen. Alice wore a ragged dress and a wicked smile. She leered at Dierdre, pointed at Cathryn's chest and asked, "Are her tits real or did she have them done in California?"

Dierdre was stunned that anyone would ask such a question. She had to take a minute to collect herself. "You shouldn't spend time thinking about these things." Dierdre withdrew a cigarette from her dwindling pack and thrust it at Alice. "Here. Go smoke it somewhere. We have things to talk about."

Alice continued to leer as she accepted the cigarette and walked away, hips swaying in exaggeration.

Her mother whispered, "Oh, Cathryn. You're among Philistines."

It was a far cry indeed from the elegant, exclusive San Francisco showroom where she had been surrounded by expensive antiques and waiting on the affluent and their personal designers. Now she slept on a cement floor with an uncouth group of women who would laugh at the concept of social manners, if they heard about them at all.

Susan witnessed this exchange and shook her head. She was the one person her family met and liked. She was the one person there who had any sense of manners, and her mother and sister warmed to her right away.

Dierdre and her mother made sincere efforts to be polite, but Cathryn could read repugnance on their faces. Her mother might have vomited right there if Cathryn had mentioned Alice was bisexual and had already propositioned her.

Cathryn couldn't take her family into Prevención or the cellblocks, but Dierdre wanted to see where she bought hard-boiled eggs and other food. Cathryn took her through the barred gate that led from the courtyard down an open area past the cellblocks into the area where the women used trash and twisted metal for clotheslines.

"In order to make money, women launder, dry and fold clothes for other people," Cathryn explained, as if she were Cathryn, the prison tour guide.

Cathryn showed her the outdoor kitchen and food vending stalls, where each cook had her own portable gas stovetop. Dierdre was horrified to see that eggs and yogurt weren't refrigerated. She was horrified to see the limp vegetables on greasy board counters, stained dresses of the kitchen workers, plastic bowls of grey, dirty water and flies scoping everything.

"This is horrible. Let's get out of here," she muttered, her voice sounding as if she were holding her breath. "Olivia told us to wash our hands a lot, but I had no idea..."

Cathryn had paid in advance for two chicken lunches, but neither her mother nor sister would touch them, so Cathryn ate them both while they pretended not to watch in disgust. She began to sense the limitations of both her time with her family and their separate realities. She caught Dierdre glancing at her watch, as if she couldn't wait to escape, and who was she to blame her?

"What time is it?" Cathryn asked.

Dierdre looked at her watch and frowned. "It's stopped. It says eleven-ten."

Her mother looked at her watch. "I don't understand. Mine's stopped, too. At eleven-ten."

The two p.m. visiting cut-off hour came fast. It seemed like her family had just arrived and now they were leaving. In her heart Cathryn knew it was possible she'd never see them again. Her stomach roiled with dreadful nausea. She wished they had never come, never seen her like this. Wouldn't it have been better to avoid this pain? She felt anger at herself—she felt truly grateful to have seen them.

They walked to the first set of barred doors, where they would say their good-byes. Deep hugs, more tears. Dierdre passed through the bars and turned back to face Cathryn. "We're getting you out of here somehow, some way. We aren't going to let you die here. So you hold on. We need you to be strong."

Cathryn watched her mother and sister move in the queue that led to the front gate. Before she lost sight of them she called, "I love you." Dierdre yelled back, "I love you." And they were gone, leaving a serrated knife twisting in her heart.

When the guards took her back to Prevención, several Peruvian girls laughed and mocked her. "I love you. I love you. I love you," they trilled. They pointed, giggled, and began their silly chant again.

"You wish you had someone who loved you," she hissed in English, not caring if they understood. But they understood her angry expression and backed off, still giggling. *Have to learn to say, "fuck you" in Spanish*, she thought.

That night, lying on her crumbling piece of foam, she pulled her aunt May's quilt tighter around her, as if there was a fragrance of civilization she could absorb, a fragrance that would magically transfer from the blanket into her skin.

We don't just wake up one morning and find we've lost our humanity, she thought. *We lose it by degrees.*

Chapter 18

Monday was the last day her mother and sister would be in Peru. Cathryn's tension subsided when she saw that they were admitted to visit. She felt so happy to see them again, even for a short visit. Before their flight they still had an appointment at the U.S. Embassy to meet again with David Ryan.

"There are lots of people back home who want to come visit you," Dierdre said.

"No!" Cathryn began to rub her fingers in a nervous gesture. "Never! I couldn't stand for anyone else to see me in this place. Tell them not to come. They can pray for me, but don't let them come here!"

Her mother cupped Cathryn's fingers. "We're going to do whatever's necessary to get through this."

Cathryn knew her mother meant to be reassuring, but she felt bleak about her future. She struggled to hold back tears so they could leave this shitty place remembering a brave face. It killed her to see them go, like a skewer running right through her entire body. The three women sobbed with their unspoken fear that they would never see each other again.

As they disappeared from sight, Cesar arrived, saying that he seemed more certain than ever that they could fight the charges against her.

"I would rather die here than plead guilty," Cathryn told him. She clung to the one truth she knew in life: that she was not guilty of conspiring to transport cocaine. Something inside her—not pride, she didn't think, but something—wouldn't let her tell the lie. It was her against them, and if she plead guilty, they would all win.

Dom would win.

After her family and Cesar had left Cathryn huddled on her floor-bed, hugging her knees. She felt isolated and defiant. She didn't give a damn about anything, including the cleaning work the guards came to get her for. When she refused to do it, they must have sensed her foul mood because they left her alone.

She felt even darker when later Dierdre told her on the telephone about their meeting at the US Embassy with David Ryan and the Peruvian Consulate General.

"What a jerk," Dierdre said of the Peruvian CG. He told them Cathryn would never be found innocent because he was Peruvian and knew all about how these things worked.

Dierdre said David Ryan "was gracious and kept his mouth shut."

The day after Cathryn's mother and sister left, she tried as much as possible to be by herself. Never alone, she had discovered that if she were grouchy enough the women would avoid her. Also, once you left Prevención in the morning for the courtyard, you had to stay out there all day until about 6 p.m.

Funny that when she'd first arrived at Prevención and the guards wouldn't let her into the courtyard she longed to go; now she didn't want to go there and see Kate's pitying look or hear the Peruvians taunt her with, "I love you."

Even the knowledge that Olivia had called Cesar and they planned to meet to discuss her case didn't raise her spirits. Olivia had great connections—at one time her father had been Lima's Chief of Police. Cathryn never could have predicted a friendship with someone like Olivia, but she never could have predicted that she would spend time in such a hellhole as Santa Monica Women's Prison, either.

In Prevención the women were packed in, like the proverbial sardines. Most of the time Cathryn slept on the floor, but Kate managed to get a lower bunk and Cathryn could sleep with her. Kate, a big overweight girl and skinny, tall Cathryn in one little bunk, but it felt like a hotel suite compared to the floor. Kate's embassy had purchased for her a clean foam roll.

Olivia exhibited a sophisticated philosophy and a highly-developed sense of perception. When Cathryn told her about how both her mother's and her sister's watches had stopped at the same time when they'd visited, Olivia said, "There is fragmented, draining energy here."

Olivia's manner made Cathryn feel she could be open and honest in a way that she couldn't be with anyone in the prison. "This experience is going to be your Ph.D. in life, Cathryn. What you're learning about yourself in this situation will help you for the rest of your life. Something will pass and you will leave this place."

But would she leave alive? Or dead?

Late the following night the guards came for her.

Chapter 19

On came the cold, fluorescent lights, startling everyone. Kate and Cathryn were dragged from their bunk, directed to gather their things and follow the guards. Cathryn did not think beyond the moment. To hope for anything was to feel profound disappointment.

They were taken from Prevención, down the dark hallways, through more bars, past the *directora's* office into the courtyard, past the administration building towards the main prison.

There they passed through a set of huge metal doors and were led past cell block A to cell block B. Through another barred door and up a circular staircase to the third floor and through another barred entrance. A long hall in each cell block, lined with rooms, led to a large room—the *salon*—where makeshift walls of bunks formed six cubicles.

Clutching her duffel, quilt and blanket, Cathryn was ushered into the *salon*. Lights flashed on, startling a floor full of sleeping women, and she was directed to put her things down. Room on the floor for one more—her. Making a total of nine women assigned to this cubicle. Kate was assigned to a neighboring cubicle.

After a month in Prevención where they were barred from visiting any of the cell blocks, Cathryn had been transferred to the prison proper. Cellblock B, third floor.

The only bright part of this was that now she would be able to buy toilet paper and toothpaste and soap—at hefty prices—from an in-prison store.

The following day Cathryn reported for roll call with the rest of cellblock B in the courtyard between the building and cell block A. Whereas in Prevención she gave her name for roll call, here she was to respond with the number of her bunk. Since she had to sleep on the floor the number she had to give them was followed by the word *suelo*. Cathryn was *diecisiese suelo.* Twenty-six ground.

After the roll call, Dolores, a Peruvian woman in her fifties and an old-timer who had seniority on the cellblock, gave Cathryn a gift—her own dirty, lice-ridden piece of foam that she didn't have to share with anybody else. Dolores' gesture both surprised and touched Cathryn and she vowed she would not take Dolores' kindness for granted.

Dolores asked about her mother and sister. "You are so lucky to have them helping you," she said.

Cathryn mentioned that their watches had both stopped when they were visiting on Sunday.

Dolores' eyes widened. Her voice softened. "It's this place. The people down there." She gestured towards the floor.

"What people down there?"

"All the people who were buried there long ago. This place was an old cemetery for a hundred years before they built the prison."

"Are you saying this place is haunted?"

The idea seemed to startle Delores. "Well, I suppose so. All I know is a lot of strange things happen around here. You be careful."

Great, Cathryn thought. *Now I'm living in Steven Spielberg's Poltergeist house. It's not the bitches out to steal my things, it's the ghosts.*

An old lady with a walking stick ambled by, talking to herself.

"Don't pay any attention to her," Dolores said. "She's crazy. She self-mutilated herself by banging things into her face and bled all over. She never has to do roll call or anything. They say she was jailed for chopping her children up into pieces and making soup out of them. Then I heard it was her husband she chopped up." With a bored expression Dolores made a shooing gesture towards the old lady.

"Which do you think is true?"

"Who knows? Anyway, she spent so much time here that when they set her free, she had nowhere else to go. So she just stays on, walking around, haunting the place like a living ghost."

Dolores also warned Cathryn about the stealing.

"Worse than at Prevención?"

"Oh, *si*. Watch everything or you will lose it."

Cathryn felt grateful for the lock her mother had brought her for the duffel. Anything not locked could be stolen at any time—despite shrines to Jesus and Mary tucked in corners on every floor of the cellblock. Cathryn learned that if you fell asleep without securing your belongings, the same women who stopped to cross themselves at the shrines would rifle through your things. Stolen items got passed to different women, kind of like the hundred dollar bill scam the Cuzco tour saleswoman had pulled. Even if you got the guards to search for your missing item, by that time it would have been passed off through a network of thieves and moved out of the prison on visiting day to be sold for income.

Such hypocrites, Cathryn thought. *They pray with the right hand and steal with the left.*

Amen, baby.

Chapter 20

Cell block B turned out to be not much different from Prevención. Cathryn still slept on the floor, living was squalid, the atmosphere dismal. In these new surroundings the cast of characters grew larger. Now there were hundreds vying for toilets and shower stalls. The food was no better or worse.

One improvement surprised Cathryn—she could pay someone to do her cleaning chores. Dolores arranged this for her, and she felt happy to pay. She thought of it as her own personal maid service. Now if they wanted her to clean a toilet—no big deal. Of course, as soon as she began paying, she was assigned easier jobs. Nevertheless, Cathryn paid 12 *soles* a month for the privilege. No more humiliation from the guards to clean toilets or empty trash cans.

There were many foreigners in Santa Monica Women's Prison, all there on various drug charges. Cathryn became fond of a pretty twenty-year-old Dutch girl named Serafia. Her father was a black man from Holland's former South American sugar colony, Suriname. He came to visit her once, but she was estranged from her mother and older sister. Cathryn had the impression that Serafia was a trusting, giving person who just got caught in bad business. A black Dutchman in the Callao men's prison regularly sent her fruit, which she shared.

There were other Dutch girls, plus South Africans, Brits, Thais, a few Belgians and an Israeli, and Germans, who outnumbered all of them. There were five Americans, but Cathryn only considered Susan and herself to be real Americans. The others didn't speak English nor understand anything about American culture. They were born and raised in Mexico or Columbia and had gotten American citizenship illegally or through relatives. They had not taken citizenship classes, or bothered to learn the language. Did that sound bigoted? Cathryn didn't care.

A large prison population from Spain mixed with prisoners from other Latin countries like Venezuela and Columbia. These women didn't hang out with the "foreigners"—they stayed with the Peruvians and other Spanish speakers.

Cathryn found that the foreign drug people weren't all bad. If they could dedicate one floor in any cellblock to just foreign drug people, it would have made living easier. People less likely to steal or do offensive things were the drug traffickers or *burriers*. Most of them spoke English as a second or third language. Moving drugs was all they knew, and when that job slowed, they often worked as prostitutes. They weren't aggressive people.

Cathryn hadn't been in cell block B long when one morning she awoke to the sounds of a huge commotion in the next cubicle where Kate slept. The words were all Spanish so she had no clue what it was about, but it sounded like a real bitch fight.

Kate and one of the German girls, Felda were fighting over *Mad* magazines. Cathryn didn't know or care who "won." She couldn't allow herself to get involved in dumb shit like that.

In her twenties, Felda, whose father was a black American GI, had dual citizenship and had been a longtime drug trafficker. She was always asking to see Cathryn's breasts. Cathryn's mother would call Felda, "hard." Felda bragged about her problems with Interpol, would tell you right up front that she'll get the best of you if you let her, and kept a Peruvian jail bitch to buy her clothes and other necessities. Because she'd lied, she was being prosecuted as a *burrier* rather than the trafficker she was. She vowed to kill the woman she thought had set her up, and Cathryn never doubted that she could do it.

That day Cathryn's highlight moment was getting to use the outside showers. Freezing cold water, but she was desperate to dilute the stink on her body. She could wash her hair in the bathroom sinks upstairs—also freezing cold water—and she found it easier to bear if she isolated washing to different parts of her body.

Cathryn still saw Kate daily, but they had grown apart. Cathryn felt wary of the women Kate was beginning to spend time with, women who openly did drugs. Cathryn suspected they were using Kate for her stipend.

Chapter 21

On Thanksgiving Day Cesar visited, bringing Cathryn two phone cards so she could call home.

Depressed to awaken and realize it was Thanksgiving in America, her experience of the actual call was devastating. Because this was an American holiday, the queue for the phones wasn't too long—small miracle—and soon she was talking to her mom and her dad and her sister.

She broke down in tears when Dierdre said, "We're setting a place for you at the table."

Oh, what she wouldn't do for her mother's turkey and mashed potatoes. *What wonderful holiday celebration food that so many take for granted,* she thought.

For the rest of the day Cathryn's thoughts never strayed from people back home. She knew they were doing their best for her, they cared what happened to her, they prayed for her—but their lives went on while hers sunk further into an abyss.

Peruvian courts were still on strike, but it had to end, and she would have to make an appearance. She used the last of her phone cards to call her friend Jim and ask him to send her—via the US Embassy so they wouldn't get stolen—something to wear to court. Her navy three-quarter length skirt and two jackets, she decided.

"Use your own good taste on choosing the jackets," she told Jim.

She returned to the cubicle and thought about what Cesar had *not* told her. She had sensed he wasn't feeling too positive about her case, so she hadn't asked any questions. When he referred to her case in vague sentences, she suspected the worst.

Cathryn began to think about how to escape from Santa Monica Women's prison.

"Two Americans escaped back in 1998," Kadlin told her.

"How?"

"That was before I got here, so I'm not sure, but only one got away."

"What happened?"

"The one who didn't get away broke her ankle in the escape, and almost had her foot amputated. But at the last minute the Red Cross came forward and paid for a doctor to treat her."

It was clear that any idea of escaping would require critical thinking and careful planning.

Whatever she did, Cathryn figured she would leave the place deaf. She was in the last cubicle by the TV, which blared incessant Spanish and the same horrible soap operas day and night.

Her assigned place on the floor also sat right under a glaring fluorescent tube light. Her light blue eyes couldn't tolerate bright sunlight or any fluorescent light. Her eyes ached and the guards wouldn't allow her to have sunglasses. Kadlin said she would go with Cathryn to the clinic to talk to the doctor about a special waver so she could have sunglasses.

Cathryn was beginning to get the pulse of things in this Third World women's prison. Many things were just like on the outside. The guards—known as "Inpees" for *Instituto Nacional Penitenciario*—were a lot like all the bosses and supervisors she had ever worked for. Some were authoritarian, some were sadistic, some were tolerant, some loved to dole out discipline, some were exploiters, and some just didn't give a damn either way.

There was also unwanted sexual attention. The same as anywhere, except here you recited the let's-just-be-friends line to a girl instead of a guy—and the girls did seem to take it better.

Cathryn's first move in the morning was to try to get to the outside showers where there'd be less of a line than for the ones inside the cellblock. If it happened that a lot of women were waiting for the outside showers then it would be useless to wait because after an hour the guards would close them.

After 8 a.m. roll call inmates would come by to hand out a piece of bread and something hot to drink. Most of the time Cathryn couldn't tolerate the drink but one morning it was real milk! She could put sugar and instant coffee in it. She began to notice a pattern—real milk appeared once every nine to twelve days.

In the courtyard she would sit with Susan at her table—for which Susan paid. Susan had been authorized to have a thermos of hot water—for which she also paid—and they would use the hot water to make coffee. They would eat their bread together.

The German Embassy had donated a table for their women, and Felda and the other Germans ate together. Cathryn noticed they were all chubby and healthy, those Germans. Susan explained: "Their embassy gives them a stipend and sends someone from their embassy every week to buy them food from an outside grocery store. They don't have to eat the slop we do."

Could this be why Felda had renounced her American citizenship?

After "breakfast" it would be time to start the workshop projects, like crocheting. The guards would reopen the cellblocks and the women could hang out there or in the yard. It was all about killing time. The laundry and shower areas would reopen too, and there would be a rush for the clotheslines and laundry sinks.

At six in the evening, the yard would be closed and everyone would return to their assigned cellblocks. After the evening roll call the women would be locked in for the night on their respective floors.

Conversations often centered on being out of prison: How great they had it when they were on the outside, all the splendor they lost, what they would be doing if they were out of prison—blah, blah, blah.

It reminded Cathryn of jobs she'd had where people talked about what they would do if they didn't have to work or if they won the lottery. Prison talk was just like a working stiff job—except they weren't killing time around the water cooler. Cathryn wondered if it was basic human nature to think that no matter how great or bad you have it something is always better somewhere else.

In long conversations with these foreign women who were now her contemporaries Cathryn continued to learn about the drug trade. Phan, a Thai woman in her thirties, had run drugs for years and spent time in prison in Thailand, but she was always in a bright mood.

"When I was arrested, I was interviewed by the DEA and I lied about everything." Phan spoke in a matter-of-fact manner.

They were sitting with Kate and Rosemary. By now Cathryn understood what Phan meant. If she had told them the truth, she would have risked being killed, even in prison. In the drug trade informers were not tolerated.

Cathryn began to think about what a dysfunctional, almost schizophrenic attitude existed towards drugs in America.

"When you think about it, legality has nothing to do with drug abuse," Kate said.

"Maybe the beginning of addiction is realizing that we are conditioned to look for the answer to our problems outside of ourselves," Cathryn suggested. "Can't sleep? Here's a prescription. Anxious? Take that drug. Depressed? Take this pill."

Kate laughed. "All you have to do is watch the commercials on TV, and you can see that legalized drugs is a huge business."

Cathryn frowned. "Makes pharmaceutical companies look like legal cartels, doesn't it?"

Rosemary lifted the hair from the back of her head and began to scratch the top of her neck. "If drugs are so bad, why are drugstores everywhere?"

"Because we think that if our doctor writes the prescription the drug must be good for us," Cathryn said. "And if it's produced by a pharmaceutical company it's safe to take."

Rosemary fluffed out her hair and shook her head vigorously. Cathryn thought how pretty she might be if she weren't so skinny.

Poor thing was due to have been out last month, but she couldn't get out because of the court strike.

"Do you think that helps the itching?" Kate asked her.

"No, but it makes my scalp feel better. Like it's getting extra air maybe."

"I don't think we learned anything from Prohibition," Cathryn said.

"What is that?" Phan asked.

Cathryn explained that part of American history from the 1920s. "When it was illegal, alcohol consumption not only increased, it provided a foothold for the establishment of organized crime. You've heard of the mafia?"

Phan's expression was unreadable so Cathryn couldn't tell if she understood or not, but she was on a drug-philosophy roll.

"We think making certain drugs illegal will keep them out of our country, but it doesn't. If the authorities admit to stopping five to ten percent of drugs moving across borders, think of what does get by and you begin to see the stupidity and ineffectiveness of the American War on Drugs. I grew up in a state where you can't buy hard alcohol at the local grocery store, only at the local state-operated liquor store. Liquor's taxed and regulated. What would happen if drugs were legalized and taxed? Wouldn't it be preferable to what we have now? It would mean people would have to take responsibility for who they are and what they do. Our society now seems to be based on victimization and blame.

"Keeping drugs illegal feeds corruption within government organizations and fuels drug syndicates. The cartels are getting richer and more powerful. Organizations like the DEA need the drug cartels. It's a weird, hostile symbiosis. Neither can survive without the other, because legalizing drugs would put them both out of business." Cathryn paused and took a breath and began to scratch her own head.

Kate and Phan and Rosemary stared at her.

"God, I hate the bugs," Kate mumbled.

"If the US was serious about getting rid of terrorism, legalizing drugs would be the first step in stopping the funding of terrorism," Cathryn continued. "I mean, if cocaine funds FARQ in Columbia and opium funds Al Qaida in Afghanistan, well… connect the dots. This one's a no brainer."

"Amen," Kate said.

Chapter 22

Cathryn was told it was possible for a woman to reduce her prison time by crocheting. She had noticed Susan spent a lot of time with other women with needles making things, which she said were "sold to the tourists."

For a monthly fee—of course—you could join a *taller*, or workshop, and get credit towards your prison time. How this worked was that if each month you made $150 US worth of items you would receive a certain number of coupons. Your lawyer could present them to the judge.

For lack of anything better to occupy her time, Cathryn let Susan teach her how to crochet. *I type 120 words per minute, and now I'll be using my hands to crochet tourist knickknacks,* Cathryn thought. She paid the crochet *taller* $25 US for the cost of the needles and yarn, and another $20 US for the first month. Later, when she asked for her coupons she was met with *no-hablas-ingles* stares.

Susan tried to find out where her coupons were. She said, "It seems they can't verify that you've been accepted."

They sat at Susan's yard table munching on Thanksgiving leftovers, compliments of Felda. Her Lutheran church group had brought the food for her, and she chose to share it with only Susan and Cathryn. This was a welcome reprieve from the give-us-this-day-our-daily-slop.

"What a joke the crochet *taller* is," Cathryn muttered. She suspected the *taller* system was a legal scam to get money out of the inmates.

"There's also a baking *taller*," Felda said. This turned out to be an elite thing based on equipment that had been donated to the prison, and ended quickly.

Rosemary said, "There's a gardening *taller*." This turned out to be so elite it was impossible to get into, for any amount of money.

Cathryn had joined the crochet *taller* because Susan was part of it and in boredom she was desperate for something to do. Something to make her feel like a productive person again. Something to take her mind off Dom's betrayal and her failing health and suicide.

It was nice to have coffee in the morning with Susan, Rosemary, Felda and Phan. Cathryn felt lucky that these women had accepted her into their clique, lucky to have found this little bit of civility in the women's prison.

Susan's face beamed. "I heard the court strike is over."

Felda scratched her head, peered into her empty coffee cup. "We heard that last week."

"No, really. This time it's really over."

Why couldn't Cathryn feel excited by this news? She would ask Cesar. Then maybe she would get excited.

A change came over Rosemary's face. "If it's over, and my paperwork's done, that means…" Her words trailed, as if she didn't want to say out loud that now she might be able to get out. As if to say it out loud might bring bad luck.

"We'll celebrate the rumor, anyway," Phan said. "Jorge is coming this afternoon."

Jorge was Phan's boyfriend. When he came on Saturdays to visit, he often brought her fruits and vegetables. Phan and Rosemary also had someone else they paid to buy groceries for them.

"Come to my table later," Phan said. She had been at Santa Monica so long she had her own table and bench.

That day Cathryn had her first decent meal—stir-fried veggies. Phan and Rosemary had worked out a deal with one of the outdoor vendors to use his stove to cook. *If Rosemary is let out,* Cathryn wondered, *how will that affect these deals?* Would Phan have to pay more to keep them going? Would she find someone else to split the cost? Phan was cute and resourceful. Plus she made bitchin' Thai food. Cathryn felt confident that Phan would work it out.

When Cesar arrived he was upbeat about her case. She felt better, too, with a tummy aching-full of Thai food.

"The court strike is over," he announced.

"So, it wasn't just a rumor."

"Now we can move forward."

Chapter 23

In order to keep your sanity, from time to time you have to lose it, Cathryn thought. Between her famous crying jags, life sometimes took on an absurd quality.

One day she got the mad idea to write a destination review of the Santa Monica Women's Prison. She dictated it out loud to Susan:

"Dear Michelin guide—We would like to bring to your attention the omission of an incomparable destination in Lima, Peru, the Penal de Mujeres Santa Monica. We love to stay here and spend as much time as possible enjoying the many outstanding amenities. Once you check in you'll never want to leave. You'll find the ambiance luxurious, the entertainment top notch, the cuisine exceptional, and the service beyond attentive. Please add this to your list of not-to-miss places in South America."

As they contemplated each word of description they choked with laughter. Susan's laugh was contagious—the more hysterical Cathryn became the more she laughed, and the more she laughed the more hysterical she became until her ribs felt as if she'd been in a bruising bitch-fight. No one else got the joke, and Cathryn was sure the other women thought they were crazy.

That night Cathryn laid awake contemplating her situation. Here she was in jail in a Third World country. What did she expect? Five-star dining? Conjugal visits with George Clooney? She imagined a genie had appeared, saying, *"There's been this huge mix-up...you said you wanted to live in Santa Monica, but I didn't know you meant the one by the ocean in Southern California, not the one by the ocean in Peru."*

She rolled over and clutched her quilt tighter around her shoulders, pulling the edge over her nose, as if that would block out the pervasive odors of the prison world. At least for awhile it would keep the cockroaches away from her neck and face. Her eyes teared, and she began to giggle. She thought of the looks on the Peruvian girls' faces that afternoon at her absurd remark when she'd left to go to the bathroom.

She had developed a crazy habit: she'd rise to leave the cubicle or table. One of the girls would ask, "Where are you going?"

"Today is Tuesday. I have a standing appointment with my masseuse."

Or, "I'm taking a dip in the pool and having cocktails with friends. What to join me?"

Or, "It's time for my Turkish bath."

Or, "George Clooney's waiting—hates it when I'm late."

Cathryn had often thought her humor far too dry for regular folks—not that she was now surrounded by "regular folks"—but Susan and Kate appreciated it.

She rolled her body, unable to find comfort. Her emaciated body had no cushioning for her bones, making every position painful. Turning her body on the foam, she tangled herself in the quilt. Every way she arranged herself, there was one torturous lump guaranteed to keep sleep away.

How can you see anything funny in this place? She chided herself. *This is serious shit, Cathryn, and comedy ain't gonna change the fact that you're dying, hour by hour, cell by cell.*

She stopped giggling and began to think about suicide—no humor there.

Cathryn was examining her hair for lice when they came to get her.

Inch by inch she took a long strand of her blond hair and meticulously ran the comb through it. She held the comb in to the light. In the space of a broken comb tooth she saw movement. Two little crabs moving as if they hadn't a care in the world. With her fingers she pulled them off and squished them on her jeans.

"You go to Callao for trial," the guard said. Not yet eight in the morning. Cathryn hurried to change into her one skirt. The guard waited with an air of bored impatience, The more professional skirt and jackets she had asked Jim to send had not arrived. Her shoe choices were the dirty, high-heeled sandals from the night of her arrest and the flip-flops her mother had brought. Cathryn wore the flip-flops—already taller than most Peruvians, she didn't want to intimidate some short judge.

Callao's Palacio de Justicia building also housed the Callao Men's Prison. The place smelled worse than the women's prison, something Cathryn wouldn't have thought possible.

"Because of the fish processing plants nearby," said the translator who accompanied her.

After she was let out of the transport van she had to walk by a bunch of ragged male inmates. One guy had his shirt off, his whole body scarred in what appeared to be a weird ritualistic cutting. Their stares made Cathryn feel like a pig in the market, albeit not a fat one.

Where was Cesar Xavier? How could she be going to court without her attorney? Had he been notified that she would be taken to court today?

Cathryn was led into a room to be searched. The door was left open, but this didn't prevent the female guard from grabbing her breasts. What was it with these women? Guards will be guards, she supposed, but at least male guards were a little more respectful. The female guard never looked at her face. It was as if Cathryn wasn't a real person, just a body with breasts—big, rich, American breasts. When she could no longer stand the hands on her Cathryn screamed.

Cesar appeared in the doorway.

"What's this? Why did you scream?"

"This guard keeps squeezing my breasts." Cathryn clenched her teeth to keep them from shaking.

He said something to the guard in Spanish. She gave Cathryn an indignant look when she answered. He translated her words as, "She can't enter the court because she isn't wearing a bra."

More back-and-forth Spanish between them. Finally Cesar said, "It's okay. It's all bullshit."

Cathryn had not yet entered the courtroom and already she trembled and choked back tears. They took her into a large room where she had to sit on a bench behind chain link fencing. The judge, translator, prosecutor, Cesar and the transcriber sat on the other side. They began to ask her questions. She stared at the spot on the wall above the judge's head where they'd hung a crucifix—no separation of church and state here.

Between great wracking sobs, Cathryn found it difficult to answer their questions. She never knew the human body could generate so many tears. Her nerves were so edgy that her feet itched and she repeatedly pulled at the edge her skirt.

Cesar had her tax returns, reference letters from her employer and publicity articles related to her career all translated and properly authenticated. He submitted them all as evidence of her law-abiding character. He thought the articles would be impressive because they documented the kind of work she did, and drug people did not have things like that written about them. Her impression was that even with her tearful hysterics and nervous skirt-tugging the court appearance went well. Cesar seemed pleased.

Outside the court they waited for the transport van to take her back to Santa Monica Women's Prison. Cathryn spotted a payphone—a payphone without a queue! With her last phone card she called her sister, though she had nothing to report other than that she had gone to court and Cesar had presented all her documents to the judge.

Dierdre bubbled cheer, seeing this as progress. But Cathryn still couldn't answer the unspoken question: when would she be coming home?

Cesar left her when she boarded the van. Chained in the back, she bounced through the streets of Lima with the other prisoners. Exhaust fumes blew inside, and her stomach lurched with nausea. In her throat she could feel the warmth of vomit threatening to erupt. How could Peruvians stand these poisonous, noxious fumes? As it became more difficult to sit upright.. Cathryn leaned her head forward but it didn't help—no position she could find would ease her queasy belly.

Why couldn't she die right now?

Back in her cubicle Cathryn crawled onto her raggedy piece of foam and curled her knees into a fetal position. The room circled around her, wouldn't settle in one place.

That night she was surprised to start her period. She remembered Rosemary saying that her periods had stopped for six months and another girl said hers had stopped even longer. Stress and bad nutrition, they said. Cathryn's face broke out so badly it reminded her of a pizza.

What a mess I am.

Chapter 24

They took Susan's table away for ten days and the women had nowhere to sit. Susan tried to explain, but Cathryn didn't care or understand.

Apathy had become her new best friend. Apathy would lessen the pain. Apathy would see her through the remaining hours and days until she died. Catatonic and lost, she floated through each day on a sea of indifference.

Friends and family at home in America seemed so far away as to no longer exist. They were no longer a part of her life as she was no longer a part of theirs. Cathryn looked forward to death.

Hunkered on the ground for hours, her mind obsessed on Dom. How right now he must be enjoying life somewhere, breaking in a new identity, living by a beach, enjoying good food, sex, companionship, while she did his time in hell.

Susan tried to interest her in a new crochet stitch, but with unanswered questions buzzing in her head Cathryn couldn't concentrate. How was it that they never saw a clue to indicate this dark side of Dom? How much cocaine did he move through the airport the night of her arrest? How many millions did he make out of duping her? Olivia agreed with the drug women—Dom must have set Cathryn up to be arrested as a diversion.

When Olivia and Cesar arrived on the same day to visit Cathryn broke down before she got into the same room with them. Cesar had no news, and Cathryn felt as if her court appearance at the Palacio de Justicia in Callao had been a meaningless sham rehearsal for something else, but what?

After they left Felda raised the subject of escaping. They were in the laundry room, looking for a place to hand wash some clothes.

"The best days to escape are Christmas Eve and New Year's Eve," Felda whispered. She didn't see escape as all that difficult.

"We can climb up the face of cellblock C, walk along the roof and use a crocheted rope to get over the fence from the roof."

Cathryn found a bucket and discarded it when she discovered a split in the plastic. "When you describe it like that it doesn't sound difficult."

"The problem is we need somebody to meet us on the outside to take us to Ecuador."

"Do you know somebody?"

"No. Do you?"

Cathryn almost laughed. She could never ask Cesar or Olivia to help her escape. They'd been so good to her, she could never endanger them. And unlike some of the girls, she was no good at being able to play Peruvian men on the outside to get them to do her outrageous favors.

"Don't look to me for the rope, either. I'm not that good at crocheting."

Felda wouldn't be put off. "This can work. I know it."

"Whatever."

Cathryn thought of the book she'd read during the eight and a half hour flight to Lima, *Adrift*, by Steven Callahan. It was the true story of how Callahan had stayed alive in a raft at sea for 76 days after his sailboat had sunk at night. She remembered how riveted she had been to his words, how as each day went by without food or water the odds increased against his survival, how big freighters passed right by and didn't see him. How she had wanted him to survive! Why of all books had she chosen that one?

Now Cathryn felt sorry she hadn't selected another kind of story—one about a prison escape.

"It took me five hours to track down your tourist photos so I could submit them to the judge as evidence," Cesar told Cathryn during his next visit.

He put out the cigarette he'd been smoking when he came in and lit another one.

"I finally had to pay the evidence clerk, almost a hundred dollars U.S." He sounded furious with the man.

"Bribe him, you mean."

"*Sí*, I had to bribe him." Cesar said he had the clerk's signature for the pictures, so he knew he had them, and the guy had had the nerve to ask, "How do you *know* I have them?" Cesar could have kept hammering the clerk, but how much was his time worth? It had been that common passive-aggressive thing where people drag their heels because they can, and it angered Cesar as much as it did Cathryn.

The whole custom of bribery in Peru made Cathryn feel vulnerable and defenseless. It was like playing a corruption game where no one has told you the rules. You learned them as you played, and then they changed.

"But your situation…" Cesar's voice broke with emotion. He began to review all the parts of her case that they had already discussed. Was he obsessing?

When he finished that cigarette and immediately lit a third one, Cathryn knew the stress of her case was getting to him. His next words made her feel doomed.

"The money that was wired to you six days ago hasn't posted at the embassy."

"Where is it?"

He took a deep breath, blew smoke out of both nostrils. "Who knows? These things often take longer than you would think."

Ten thousand dollars had been wire transferred from the American bank to the State Department, to be wired to the embassy in Lima. Ten thousand dollars designated to get Cathryn released floated out there somewhere while she rotted in a Peruvian prison. What if it was just—lost?

"Can't you do something?" she pressed, though she knew Cesar was doing the best he could on her behalf.

He sat on the bench, head lowered, not answering.

Two young, fresh-faced nuns, white habits flowing behind them, came rushing in to see her. They presented two little overripe apples dressed like Papa Noel, just for her!

One of them handed her a fax written in English. The apples and fax had been sent by her friend, Kara Stevens, whose aunt was a nun with the Sisters of Divine Providence. These young Lima nuns were part of that same order.

The prettiest one spoke something in Spanish. Cesar translated: "The whole order is praying for you. Do not give up."

Cesar spoke more with them in Spanish and they left.

"They'll come back on Sunday." Cesar added that they were also willing to teach her Spanish.

Before he left he handed her a phone card. "Call your family when you can."

Later in the day Cathryn managed to grab a phone. Her mother told her that a friend had written about her to the *LA Times*. If they did a story on her wrongful imprisonment, wouldn't that be a great thing? Wouldn't that influence the DEA and the State Department to do more to get her out? Cathryn remembered that she had signed a form saying the embassy couldn't give out to the press any information about her.

"Jim sent the clothes you asked for to the embassy," her mother said, "but they're stuck in customs."

"What does that mean?"

"Bianca at the embassy says customs won't release them unless they are paid two hundred dollars."

Two hundred dollars for a few old clothes! She hated this greed. She hated this corruption. She hated Peru.

After the call she retreated to the darkness of her quilt-tent, rocked back and forth and moaned a bitter lament. Felda found her there, coaxed her out, tried to cheer her with more of her escape plan.

"Don't worry." She was so confident. "I'll crochet the rope."

Chapter 25

To escape from Santa Monica Women's Prison they still needed someone on the outside to get them to Ecuador. Felda had bragged about being able to contact some guys to come visit them, but they never showed up. Cathryn figured they ran when they realized the address Felda gave them was a prison.

It continually amazed Cathryn how the women in Santa Monica pimped guys to get them things. But why should she have been so surprised? She had known lots of women in San Francisco who didn't marry for love. *Am I the stupid one?* she wondered.

On Saturdays the boyfriends came to visit. Kadlin's boyfriend, middle-aged Pepe, was a skinny Peruvian with bad teeth. With the energy of a used car salesman he told Cathryn, "You'll be here for years. Get used to it."

The way Pepe explained it made him sound like he knew everything. Though he came to visit Kadlin, he always found a way to talk to Kate. Cathryn suspected he was working Kate for her drug contacts.

Another man made Cathryn a "fucky-fucky" proposition. The polite Cathryn replied, "*No, gracias,*" and kept on walking.

Sometimes in the night, when the lights were out, Cathryn could hear girls going at it. Must be why they fought for the lower bunks— the ones with curtains. She covered her ears. She missed men. And it wasn't just the sex. She missed just being around a guy, hearing a man's voice, hearing a male perspective. She missed that essence of testosterone. There were no male guards, just female bitches, and men could visit only on Saturdays.

During the visitation, a woman came through the yard calling out in Spanish.

"What's she want?" Cathryn asked Susan.

"It's about getting your paperwork filled out so you can get a conjugal visit."

"A conjugal visit? Here? But hardly anybody here's married—"

"Oh, you don't have to be married," Susan said. "Kadlin gets a visit with Pepe each month."

Cathryn didn't want to imagine that. But she started thinking: what if she filled out the paperwork to have a conjugal visit and sent it to David Ryan at the U.S. Embassy? She would say, "Oh, David, here's my paperwork for a conjugal visit with George Clooney. Could you mail it for me? Oh, by the way, if Mr. Clooney isn't available, maybe you can send it to Brad Pitt? Thanks."

David would say, "Sure, Cathryn, just doing my job."

And she could hear George Clooney: "You want me to fly to Lima, Peru to have sex with a poor American girl who is down on her luck?"

David would say, "Mr. Clooney, I know this is a difficult assignment, but your government is asking you to put aside your personal feelings. If you complete this task, you will become eligible for a Congressional Medal of Honor."

Clooney: "But I don't *know* this girl."

David: "Mr. Clooney, just close your eyes and think of your country. Cathryn will do all the work."

Instead, what Cathryn got to look forward to the next day—Sunday—were the nuns.

That night Cathryn came out of the bathroom after brushing her teeth in the laundry sink and Lourdes attacked. Cathryn felt the breath rush from her lungs as Lourdes slammed into her, grabbed her arms. Like a crazed banshee, Cathryn fought back. She wouldn't have thought skinny Lourdes had the strength, but she wrestled Cathryn to the ground. She held Cathryn's arms and straddled her hips.

"Get off me you fuckin' bitch!"

Cathryn struggled while Lourdes humped on her and moaned and exaggerated her breathing. Several Peruvian girls stopped to watch, point and laugh. When Lourdes freed her Cathryn fled to her cell block.

The thing that pissed her off most was that in their scuffle she had dropped her toothbrush and it had touched the floor. Women walked, spit and blew their snot on those floors! In her Mike-Tyson-the-Hulk alter ego fantasy Cathryn busted Lourdes in the face, leaving her with no teeth to brush.

The next day Cathryn still seethed anger.

"Lourdes is a pig," Kate said when Cathryn told her and Susan what had happened.

"Just avoid her as much as you can," Susan said.

"I wish I were dead," Cathryn muttered.

Kate shifted her big body on the ground and scratched her crotch. "No, you don't. You know, one of the pregnant girls who came with us from Dinandro tried to kill herself by drinking Pinesol. Now she's in the hospital. I guess she'll make it but she lost her baby."

Cathryn remembered her first cellmate, the Peruvian girl who had just discovered she was pregnant. She squeaked, "Jenny?"

Kate sighed. "No, not Jenny, the other one. The one that was arrested with her husband."

Cathryn couldn't blame the woman, couldn't judge her. She was haunted by her own thoughts of suicide. She had already decided that she would OD. That was her back-up plan because she didn't have much faith in Felda's escape plans. Cathryn knew she could get sleeping pills. She would start to collect them. Nothing as painful as drinking Pinesol for the rich *gringa*.

While she mused over the quality of suicide, Susan and Kate had begun to talk about the quality of life.

"I'm a staunch Catholic," Susan declared. "but I have to admit I've had thoughts of death."

Kate gave her a disbelieving look. They thought of Susan as the strongest woman in Santa Monica.

"But I wouldn't call it suicide," Susan said. "Suicide is a crime. I'm alive, but this isn't living. This is survival in the worst circumstances."

Cathryn reached out her hand, but didn't touch Susan. "You're right. Without a certain quality, this is death in life. I feel like a person who has a terminal illness. So, how can killing yourself be a crime?"

"What God could blame a woman under these circumstances?" Kate asked.

There were no answers, and they sat for awhile without speaking, each lost in her own deathly thoughts. Cathryn could kill herself, but she did not want to see Susan die.

Her head swam in the direction of a personal plan. The businesswoman in her took charge—if she began collecting sleeping pills now, by January she would have enough to do herself in. Twenty pills seemed like a good goal number. So she would have to stay alive at least until sometime in January. Collecting the pills to kill herself gave her something to live for.

Chapter 26

A bitch in an upper bunk, without thinking to look, threw trash to the floor where Cathryn slept. They were so crowded on the floor the trash was bound to hit someone. *Must be my day*, she thought.

Now awake, she rose and headed to the bathroom. On the way back, Dolores approached her. Without any apology or explanation she announced, "Your cleaning duties are twenty *soles* a month now."

Cathryn had thought Dolores had understood that she was having a hard time getting money—she hadn't been shy about letting anyone know how destitute she was—but it was obvious Dolores still thought she was rich. Cathryn looked at her with no deep feeling about it one way or the other. *Whatever*.

She thought that it would be better for her if I she could have no thoughts whatsoever. What did cleaning duties and crochet credits and cockroaches matter? She'd be dead in January, anyway. Her Last Will and Testament was ready for David to take the next time he came with the who's-still-alive-checklist and vitamins. Cathryn planned to ask him to certify it and send it to her family. She wanted Jim to have her Turkman rug and her 1955 Packard. All the great stuff Dierdre had given her over the years would go back to her, and everything else, including her cats, to her parents. She hoped that if she died before David came around again that her signature on the will would be good enough.

True to their word, the nuns came on Wednesdays and Sundays to give Cathryn Spanish lessons. They sat in the visitor's courtyard and they stayed for several hours.

Hermana Amelia and *Hermana* Luz Maria were quite pristine in their all-white habits. Cathryn learned that *hermana* is Spanish for "sister." Only Sister Amelia spoke English, Cathryn didn't tell them she planned to kill herself. They were Catholics, after all.

The nuns were leaving about the time she expected Cesar, but this day he didn't come. She was still discouraged from his last visit, when she'd tried to talk to him about the possibility of being released on bail.

"That's not an option for foreigners," he'd said. "Flight risk is too real. Put it out of your mind."

So when he didn't come Cathryn went to the phones, waited in line, and tried to call the embassy. Ten thousand dollars had been wire transferred from her family's bank to the state department on December 2, 2003 to be wired to the embassy in Lima. Today was December 9, and she had heard nothing about its arrival.

Could this be why Cesar hadn't come? Because he hadn't been paid? He was Peruvian, after all. Did he suspect the rich American *gringa* was conning him? That she had no intention of paying him? He'd put a lot of time in on her behalf and had yet to see a *sole*. Had he reached his investment limit? Had he quit his efforts on her behalf?

The phone rang and rang. No answer at the U.S. Embassy.

These are bad signs, Cathryn thought. No release on bail, no visit from Cesar, no answer at the embassy, and $10,000 lost in never-never-government-land.

"Cath, Cath! You come," called Phan.

She lay on her foam mat under her dirt-smudged quilt, feeling rumblings in her stomach and dozing in a half-conscious state. Phan shook her arm. The rest of her body didn't move.

"In the clinic. Americans speaking English. You come."

The words "Americans speaking English" roused her from her dazed state. Cathryn crawled to her feet. "I'm coming," she muttered. She followed Phan to the clinic. The place gave her the creeps; she felt suspicious of everything there and everything that went on there. Even the head of the clinic had admitted there weren't enough cleaning supplies.

Today people with boxes and packets of supplies crowded the

room. An American Evangelical missionary group had come with doctors to prescribe medicine to the inmates of Santa Monica. Cathryn spoke to their leader, who confirmed everything she had heard about the clinic: the medications were all outdated and they reused needles.

They'd also brought with them drugs and donated used eyeglasses. The guards stood in line along with the inmates to get a free pair.

After the missionaries left, the head of the clinic said, "Today we're prescribing drugs that are current. Do you need anything?"

Cathryn remembered what the women had told her about drug trafficking through the non-profit organizations that visited the prison.

"Some Retin-A to help clear my skin?"

He scanned the shelves, and turned back to her. "Sorry, we don't have that, but I'll look into getting it for you." He selected a book from the table. "Here is a bible you can take, though."

So that was it. The hitch. She would be expected to "accept Jesus Christ as (her) personal savior."

"No thanks. If I have to do that, you don't have to bother finding the medicine. I'm a Pagan with a bent towards Mahayana Buddhism. You can keep your bible and give it to someone who will use it." It occurred to her that to get the Retin-A she could smile and take his bible and later dump it in the garbage. But she couldn't. It just would have been the wrong thing to do.

She turned to leave the room and he said, "If you know someone named Cathryn, have her come to see me."

Hearing him say her name stopped her. The skin on the back of her neck shivered.

"That's me."

His expression changed, as if something at Santa Monica had finally surprised him.

"Someone gave me a message for you. To tell you that May and Amy Nordgren want you to be brave and remember that people at home are praying for your release."

"My aunt and cousin…" she murmured. "Thank you."

Cathryn had to get out of there before the tears erupted from her eyes. She fled the clinic before she could break down into a blubbering idiot in front of this man who was doing the best he could to help the unfortunates of the world.

Chapter 27

Mid-December, Cathryn thought. In Santa Monica it was easy to loose track of dates. She had been arrested October 21, so to the best of her calculation, she'd been held in Peru 52 days now. Tick, tick, tick. The days went by and she remained in prison. How long could she hang on, living on so little? She needed more money for food.

Mailed packages were delivered to the inmates on Tuesdays and Thursdays, but she never received one. Week after week it was the same. *People have forgotten all about me*, she thought. She was old, helpless, hopeless news. No one cared, and she didn't blame them. Out of sight, out of mind.

There was no way she could know that many care packages had been sent to her at great cost by concerned people back home. During her entire stay in Peru's prisons, she never received a single care package through the prison system. The INPE's looted all of them.

December is summer in Peru. "January is one of the hottest months," Susan.. Several of them were sitting at her table—happy she'd gotten it back—crocheting and talking about nothing and everything.

"Olivia bought me sunscreen," Cathryn said. "I hope I'll be okay with that."

Susan said, "That'll help. You blue-eyed blonds need all the protection you can get. So have you decided if you want to run with me?" Each morning Susan ran around the yard for exercise.

"Yes. *Si.* "

Cathryn didn't tell her the real reason she wanted to begin to exercise. Eating all that rice and potatoes had done disgusting things to her gastrointestinal tract. Shitting had become painful, and she hoped exercise would help.

Later that morning Cesar came by. "The certified letter from Congressman Weatherman's office came today."

"That's good news."

Now she would have to pay to have the letter translated into Spanish for the court, about $40 US per page. And by increasing the margins and double spacing the typing, a good Peruvian translator could pimp that out to three pages. With translation, notary, and signature verification—a second party had to verify that the notary itself was genuine—the letter to be submitted as evidence into her case file would cost about $200. Everything took so much time, so much money.

Here was another reason she had to think twice about escape. Her congressman had stood up for her. Could she repay him for his interest and support by running? She had to weigh the horror of her likely death against everything she had been raised to believe about the value of friendships, about the value of honesty, about the value of giving your word.

After Cesar left Cathryn washed tee shirts and panties and hung them on the clothesline, her mind churning with thoughts of the *LA Times*, escape, suicide, and human values. She inverted a plastic bucket and sat down to watch her drying clothes. One had to be on guard all the time. Poor Kate had had so many things stolen from her. The thieving bitches would wait for her to fall asleep and rifle through her stuff. In comparison, stealing off the clothesline was petty.

After a couple of hours Cathryn had to pee. Still, she waited until the pain in her bladder was unbearable. She considered peeing where she sat, but didn't want to soil her panties and jeans. She'd have to wash them and sit watch while they dried on the clothesline.

Cathryn scurried to the toilet stall, forced pressure on her bladder to make the darkened urine expel as fast as possible, hurried back to her bucket seat. She looked at the clothesline and—two of her tee shirts were gone.

How long had she been gone? Two minutes? Four minutes? Someone must have been watching her watch her clothes. Waves of frustrated anger swept over her and exploded in sobs.

She took the remaining damp clothes from the line back to her cubicle and went to look for Felda. The big German would help her kick ass—in Spanish.

"Everyone I talked to who was standing nearby said they didn't see anything," Felda told her later, a helpless note in her voice.

"How convenient."

A bitter bile taste filled her mouth. Those Peruvian bitches. She hated them all.

Dierdre's words sent Cathryn's head in a wild spin. "Dom has hired an attorney."

She had managed to get to a phone and connect with her family.

"Are you kidding me?" Cathryn said, mind reeling.

The line crackled a little, and she distinctly heard her sister say, "This attorney called Angela and asked for a letter of recommendation for Dom."

In her shock Cathryn repeated her words, adding language that for her in prison had now become normal usage. "A letter of fucking recommendation?"

"Angela took his name and number and turned it over to the DEA. I guess that's all she could do."

So why would Dom hire an attorney? Because he knew if he told the DEA the truth they might come after him? But where was he? Did hiring an attorney mean he was back in the U.S.? Or still in Mexico where he'd gone the night she was arrested?

She posed these questions to Cesar when he came to see her that afternoon.

"The DEA has no jurisdiction over him," Cesar said. "He never committed a crime in the U.S. His crime is here in Peru." Cesar had other stunning news. "I met with the judge. He told me someone had offered a person in his department a lot of money for a copy of your file."

"Who?"

"Who knows? But they'll get it eventually. There's enough corrupt people working there. One of the court assistants will do it for the right amount of money."

"Unbelievable."

But this was Peru. It was believable.

Later, sitting and crocheting with her friends, Cathryn told them about this latest development.

"It was the best thing that Dom got away," Susan said. "As an attorney I handled enough drug cases to understand how drug people operate."

Kadlin said, "Most drug people frown on duping people to carry drugs. All this could backfire on him."

Without missing a click of her needles, Susan said, "You're naïve to think he would confess to the truth. He'll lie not just to implicate you, but to save his ass as much as he can."

Felda put down her crocheting and looked towards the east wall of the prison, as if she were imagining a frightening world outside. "There's one thing. Dom could have you knocked off so you could never testify against him."

"Killed?" The word came out of Cathryn's mouth as soft as passing gas.

"Or he could kill someone in your family to send you a message."

When Felda looked back Susan gave her a sharp look as if to say, *that's enough of that kind of talk.*

But it was too late. Cathryn thought of her sister or her mother or her father or her brother being harmed because of her and felt a sick nausea in her stomach that gripped her like a clammy fist. The rest of the evening she couldn't make Felda's words go away. They played themselves over and over in her head like a bad Fellini film.

That night as she lay on her foam mat she couldn't sleep. She felt as if her whole body was enveloped in an orange ball of fear. Fear for her life. Fear for her family. Fear for her future.

Cathryn had an epiphany: *My old life is over. If I survive this I'll never be able to go back to it.*

One of the Spanish girls, she'd heard, had a psychotic break and "went off the deep end." It occurred to Cathryn that she might have been better off if she'd lost her mind. What was she using it for, anyway? Felda's words crept back to her, like sly dingo dogs lurking at the edge of the firelight, reminding her of danger. What if Dom arranged to kill someone in her family? For several hours she cried before her body escaped into restless sleep.

Chapter 28

Santa Monica Women's Prison designated Wednesday, December 15th, 2003 "Christmas Visiting Day." Cathryn skipped her morning run—too much activity in the yard, with people arranging tables and milling around in expectation.

Instead she waited in the yard for the nuns to come for her Spanish lesson. To pass the time she began to count the feral cats she saw. So many of them lived in the prison. She wondered what had happened at home to her own SusieQ and George.

She could imagine them sitting at the window watching the cars come and go, wondering when the big blonde would return to feed and play with them. They must have been suffering—they were old and needed special attention. Cathryn didn't know their ages, since they had been abandoned, grown cats that had just appeared at her back porch, flea ridden and starving. Poor things, to have been abandoned twice in their lifetimes. Those cats had given her such unconditional love. They never cared how much money she made, how big her tits were, what kind of car she drove, what her political affiliations were, how old she was.

Cathryn stood for a long time in the Peruvian summer sun with her conjugated verbs. No nuns came on Christmas Visiting Day, and she lost count on the cats. Soledad, Olivia's assistant, found her and they moved to a shady spot to talk. Soledad handed her two 100-*sole* bills. In her broken Spanish Cathryn tried to tell her they were useless here.

"I need small bills and lots of coins."

Soledad smiled and nodded. Cathryn hoped she understood that she was grateful for the money. She raised her hand, palm outward. "Wait." She ran to find a pencil and a piece of paper, scribbled "fruit, vegetable, broccoli, jelly." Cathryn hungered for jelly on her bread at breakfast. She gave the paper to Soledad, closed her hand around it and the two bills. *"Por favor, compra para mi."*

"*Sì, sì.*" Soledad gave her a broad smile and left.

"Who was that?" Susan asked when she sat down at her table.

"Olivia's assistant. I think she understood what I wanted. I hope she'll come back on Monday with food."

"Maybe," Susan said. "What about your Christmas allotments?"

Each prisoner had been given three visitor passes, or "allotments" for the visiting days before Christmas and New Year's. Since the courtyard could only hold so many people, the allotment system reduced overcrowding during this time. Peruvians with family in Lima could barter with foreigners or prisoners without family for their allotments.

Sarcastic laced voice Cathryn's voice. "I gave my allotments to the Peruvian girls in my cubicle who steal my stuff and throw trash on me."

"You *gave* them away? When will you learn? Felda sold her allotments."

It had never occurred to Cathryn to sell her allotments. She shook her head, marveling at her stupidity.

Susan's daughter, Elena, arrived with gifts. She had a present for Cathryn: two pairs of running shorts she no longer wore.

"*Muchas Gracias.* Now I can run in the mornings with Susan in style."

Rosemary, Felda, and Alice came to the table. Rosemary bubbled with excitement.

"The paperwork is starting for me to be released. And my father is coming to visit me."

"Your father—that's great!" Susan said.

No one acknowledged her paperwork announcement. You could get excited about something like that and be painfully disappointed. No one wanted to encourage that.

Anyway it wasn't either of those things that had Rosemary enthused. She'd also received a letter from a foreign inmate who'd been released a year ago. After her release, the woman had escaped through Ecuador. Rosemary was impressed and thinking of doing the same.

Changing the subject, Felda said, "All the girls keep asking me why you have the legs of a teenager."

"Because I *am* a teenager." Cathryn smiled.

Felda had been watching Susan scratch and had begun to scratch her own head. "You should be in the beauty contest they have every year."

"What beauty contest?" Cathryn's laugh was acidic. "Is this a joke?"

Felda's face was solemn. "Every year here there's a beauty contest for Miss Santa Monica."

Cathryn gave Susan her where-does-this-shit-come-from? look, but Susan nodded. "It's true."

Cathryn shook her head, thinking of her blond hair full of lice. "I'd die of embarrassment. I don't want anyone to ever know I was in this hellhole."

The next day Cesar arrived, animated. Waving his perpetual cigarette he gave Cathryn the pep rally treatment—don't despair, don't give up, don't lose hope. He made her laugh, which made her feel so lucky to have him for her attorney. She believed he was doing everything possible to fight for her release, that he would be able to get her out.

But as she watched him walk out of the prison Cathryn had a cold premonition that blew over her like a winter-in-the-Northwest wind. She retreated upstairs to her cubicle, aching for solitude, and pulled the quilt over her head.

She felt castrated. She had lost her work, her meaning, her self-confidence, her *joie de vivre*, her every-fucking-thing. She felt like a guy who had a meaningful sex life and had to step aside and watch his wife or girlfriend look elsewhere for what they needed. She'd lost her metaphorical balls.

All of a sudden the solitude she'd sought felt claustrophobic. She needed to talk to someone. She threw off the quilt, got to her feet and went downstairs to the yard to look for Susan. No one else here except her and Susan had ever had a steady job. They couldn't understand what it was like to awaken in the morning to go to work, share a camaraderie with office mates and customers and suppliers, accomplish meaningful tasks, and to miss all that.

"It took me a year and a half to get over missing it," Susan said.

"How did you stand it?"

She shrugged, scratched. "I had other things to worry about. My savings are almost exhausted. All my property's been embargoed…" She brightened and smiled. "but my niece delivers lunch to me three times a week, and I get to see my kids. It could be worse, I suppose."

"How long can a sane person hold on without giving up hope?" Cathryn asked. "When do we throw in the towel?"

"You're asking how life can be so unfair."

"Yeah. Is our life going to make a shred of difference in the greater scheme of things? What does this fucking nightmare mean?"

"Heavy questions, Cathryn."

Not hearing the indulgent smile in her voice, Cathryn rattled on. "Why Us? Why are we in this hellhole suffering when there are plenty of guilty people out there who'll never see the inside of a prison?"

"You're afraid you'll die here."

"Damn straight," Cathryn wailed. "I don't want to die here! How can we fight the power when we're so fucking powerless?"

"Certainly we'll never get the time back. It's gone forever from our lives."

Cathryn groaned. "Thanks for the encouragement."

"You started this stuff. If you want encouragement, think about Nelson Mandela."

Nelson Mandela. The idea of his ordeal stopped Cathryn cold. Her voice became reverent. "How did he survive thirty-something years of this shit?"

"The point is, he did."

"So we can do what we have to do, I guess." Cathryn felt no feeling of power in the words.

Chapter 29

The lights had just come on.

"Good mooooooorrning Liiimaaaaah." Georgia did a good Robin Williams imitation.

A skeletal British woman in her fifties, Georgia was from South Africa. She had missing teeth and smoked like the proverbial chimney and farted all the time, but she could make a great joke. Georgia had the bunk above Susan in the next cubicle.

"You'll never get out of Santa Monica in less than two years" was Georgia's constant advice to Cathryn.

It was another Christmas visiting day, with the Germans all getting Christmas packages from their embassies, Peruvians getting presents from their families, other foreigners getting care packages from home. But no one came to see Cathryn—no care package from *her* embassy—so why bother going downstairs to the yard?

She spent the day upstairs in her cubicle. In the evening Felda came with her jail bitch's Walkman.

"You can borrow it for awhile," she said. "The Jazz Hour is on from seven to eight."

It was the best—the only—present Cathryn had all day. She heard Sinatra, Dinah Washington, Eartha Kitt... she almost felt human again. She found another station that played Radioheads and some old Pearl Jam. Who would have thought she could find that in Peru? She remembered her CD Player that had been confiscated. *Fuckers*, she thought.

One of the bitches in her cubical had stolen her soap while she slept, so she hadn't bathed this morning. If she stunk, she stunk. *No one would smell me through their own stink anyway.* And she should bathe for these people? *Fuck 'em.*

While on her internal tirade, she thought of the girls who whistled at her, how it unnerved her, and ought. *I hate this fucking place.*

Merry Christmas? Pulleeeeez.

The next morning Cathryn awoke to discover some bitch had stolen one of the pairs of running shorts Susan's daughter had given her. She exploded, screaming at everyone within hearing distance. In that moment she wanted to kill the thieving, fucking bitches. She ran to find Felda, brought her back to the cubicle to translate.

In Spanish Felda told them off. Told them they should be ashamed of themselves for treating her like that after she'd given them her Christmas visitor allotments so they could see their stupid, fucking families, and how dare they steal her shit in return.

"Tell Ava," Cathryn shouted, "she better keep her friends out of here or else."

Serafia, from her top bunk, cried, "She's right, Ava, you better keep your stupid friends away from here."

Ava screamed something back in Spanish and the shouting match was on. Peruvians versus Foreigners—Cathryn, Felda, Serafia. Ava stepped on a lower bunk to raise herself so she was right in Serafia's face. They yelled slurs back and forth. The Suriname woman grabbed Ava by the hair. The Peruvian woman's screams echoed on the ceiling and floor. The entire cubicle erupted into a throbbing, pulsing bitch fight complete with flying hair and thrashing arms and screaming obscenities.

Someone went to call a guard. The women realized they had to stop or they would all end up in *calaboso*, an isolation cell—no one but you and the dark and the rats.

Cathryn had heard about *calaboso*. "It's so horrible," Kadlin had said, "that you have to stuff a water bottle in the hole you shit and piss in to keep the rats from coming up." There were no feral cats in that part of the prison to keep the rat population in check.

Cathryn had yet to see the *calabosos*. She was sure there was more than one isolation cell because usually more than one person got in trouble at a time.

"They're on the other side of the kitchen," Kadlin said. "You have no contact with anyone except for the person who delivers your food."

The threat of being sent there quieted the women. That night the Peruvians on the lower bunks in the cubicle all shut their curtains and the ones in the top bunks regarded Cathryn and Felda and Serafia with cold, silent hostility. That was fine with Cathryn. No stupid cunts yapping and making noise and stepping on her bed.

But even Georgia's funny jabs couldn't quell the rising tension in all the cell blocks and the yard.

"They should assign all us drug people to one floor of a cellblock and let the Peruvians live with themselves," Cathryn said to Susan the next morning while they ran.

"You're right."

"But nooooo. That would be too logical."

"Too easy."

Cathryn had made her point about the stealing, but it had resulted in open war in the cubicle. Foreigners versus Peruvians.

Later that morning she had to go to the office of the head guard to defend Serafia. Big-mouthed Ava had thought she could get them in trouble by reporting the fight. Something about Ava—not just that she was Peruvian and short and fat—implied someone shifty, conniving, someone capable of anything.

When Ava saw that Cathryn had brought Susan along to translate, she lowered her voice, became less indignant. Because Susan spoke perfect Spanish and because she had been part of the Montesinos corruption thing, she was considered a VIP—a Very Important Prisoner. No one wanted to fuck with her in any way.

Ava shifted her body, nervous about talking to Susan. Because of a previous incident concerning a stolen bag, Susan already had it in for Ava, and Ava knew it. In the head guard's office she now found herself confronted by an angry VIP foreigner armed with perfect Spanish.

The guard decreed that Serafia would go to Prevención for a couple of hours, and Ava's gang of thieves would not be allowed to hang out near the cubicle. Ava agreed to everything so that Susan wouldn't tell the head guard about the incident with the stolen bag. To be caught stealing could mean an entire month in *calaboso*, and Ava feared that more than Susan's wrath.

Because of Cathryn's friendship with Susan Ava became afraid of her, and that was just the way Cathryn liked it.

Chapter 30

Olivia, as an attorney, could visit Cathryn any time.

"This place is destroying me," Cathryn confessed to her. "I used to be a peace/love kind of person. I used to believe in the goodness of people, world peace, non-violence—all the things Ghandi stood for. This place is turning me into a *kill-before-they-kill-you* kind of person."

"This is your Ph.D. in life," Olivia said.

"I hate the person I am now."

"What you learn here will pave the way for you. If you handle this right, you will be able to put this karma behind you."

"I don't know that I know how to handle this right."

"You will find your way. I, too, can feel how hideous the energy is in this place, but in spite of it, you will find your way."

Olivia was the best medicine—relaxing, calming her—and Cathryn always felt much better after talking to her.

"I bought you groceries. Cesar will bring them by tomorrow."

That meant Cathryn would be able to eat something green. *God bless Olivia and Cesar.*

"Are they painting the salon?" Olivia asked on her way out the door.

"Yeah." Cathryn felt bitter about it because she knew the inmates would be the ones paying for it. The paint they used on the inside walls of the salon had been watered down so much it covered little. The painting scheme was just a cover for the *directora* to extort more money from the prisoners. Just ten *soles* per person—that is, Cathryn assumed it was ten *soles* per person. It wouldn't have surprised her to learn the foreigners paid ten *soles* and the Peruvians paid less.

So what would happen if she refused to pay? Ten *soles* equaled just a couple of dollars, but she shuddered to think of the retribution for *La Americana*. She would have to be prepared to lose something, to be denied some small privilege—like when Susan had her table taken away for ten days—or to be assigned extra work details, or to be thrown into the *calaboso*. Never ask, how much worse can it get when you're already at your lowest.

Cathryn paid her share for the shabby paint job.

When Cesar brought the groceries Cathryn went into euphoria. Yogurt! Honey! Peanut butter! Butter and fruit and crackers and cookies and milk, beautiful, lovely milk! She could have *café con leche* in the morning.

"Please, please thank Olivia again for buying all this for me," Cathryn gushed.

"Dierdre called me." Cesar frowned. "She's worried and upset that you haven't called home in a long time."

Cathryn's heart lurched. "Please explain to her the phones now are closed on all the additional visiting days they've scheduled for the holiday season. When they are available the lines are longer than usual, and many of the phones are broken. I'd write, but I can't buy stamps here and there's no mail drop."

All this he knew but Cathryn raved on anyway.

"The U.S. Embassy only comes by once every three months, and they've made it clear that they can't—or won't—mail letters for us. I don't know what else I can do to make contact."

Cesar made sympathetic noises. "I will come see you on Christmas."

Cathryn didn't know how this would be possible because he had to have a special visitor's pass, and she had given hers to the thieving bitches in her cubicle.

After Cesar left, Felda found her. She let her listen to the Jazz Hour again, and gave her a white shirt for Christmas. A real Christmas present for Cathryn. The shirts had been in the plastic Christmas buckets the German embassy had given their inmates that day, along with food and clothes and shampoo.

And I got fuck-all, Cathryn thought. *I've paid so many taxes to the wealthiest nation in recorded history, and they can spend four-fucking-billion dollars a month in Iraq and can't mail a lousy, fucking letter to my family so they'd know I'm alive.* She vowed that if she got out of this mess alive she would write a letter to each goddamned senator and congressman telling them what hypocrites they were. *Human rights? Puleeeze.*

Cathryn felt ashamed to be an American.

Christmas Eve day. The idiot bitches had "decorated" their cubicle with some of the stupidest Christmas junk Cathryn had ever seen. It reminded her of decorations in her classroom during first and second grades.

When Serafia and Cathryn were asked for a contribution to pay for it, Cathryn asked Susan, "How do you say, 'go fuck yourself' in Spanish?"

"There's no real translation for that. Tell them, *Vaya a la mierda* instead."

Cathryn repeated it four times and the Peruvians backed down.

The phones were open for a little while, and Cathryn was able to call her father before the circuits overloaded and they were cut off. She was crying when it happened, and he had just repeated—for the umpteenth time—"Be strong. We're doing everything we can on this side to get you out."

Cathryn tried to call Dierdre and Jim, but the connections wouldn't go through.

For Christmas Eve the prisoners were allowed to establish tables between cellblocks A and B. Balmy, humid weather marked the Peruvian summer. Phan and Susan put their tables and benches together to make a bigger table that would include Rosemary, Felda, and others. Phan made a killer Thai hot sauce that made the chicken dish Rosemary had paid to be brought in quite palatable. Cathryn's stomach had shrunk so much that four bites made her full and afterwards she felt uncomfortably bloated.

Outside music blared, boring Latin sounds, no good salsa. *What a shame, when there's so much good Latin music,* she thought. *Only morons like prison guards would spin shitty disks.*

"Slimy Latin lounge—'Quando, Quando, Quando' and 'Guantanamero'—would be an improvement over this Mexican polka shit," she said to Susan. Cathryn found it impossible to conjure a joyous Christmas mood.

From a South African Cathryn scored five Mellaril, 200 mg, for ten *soles.* She told the woman she needed them for sleep, which of course was a lie. She needed them to kill herself. The pills were big and orange and strong and Cathryn suspected they were psychotic tranquillizers.

Kate saw her make the buy. "I took one of those and it knocked me out big time," she said. "Break them in two or three pieces." She too thought Cathryn was buying them for sleep.

Cathryn calculated that she would need five more to accomplish her suicide. *Ten of those monsters should do me in just fine. If I'm going to kill myself, I want to do it right the first time.* She wrapped the pills in plastic and hid them at the bottom of her Noxema jar.

Chapter 31

With no refrigeration, Cathryn found it a challenge to ration her food. Her yogurt was long gone. Once the can of evaporated milk had been opened, she had one day to drink it all. The image of leafy green vegetables teased its way through her head. Steamed broccoli with melted cheddar cheese, a leafy green salad with shrimp and vinaigrette, or celery with wild smoked Alaska salmon. These were her torturous Christmas fantasies.

Food continued to be a survival issue. To not have it was physical torture, to think about it was mental torture. Susan's family had arranged a tab at the little store across from the prison so she could buy things there and thus avoid contamination. When Cathryn had bought jelly in the prison, she had discovered it had been opened, and someone had already eaten out of it. She screamed and got her money back, but the lesson stuck. That was the last time she bought anything inside the prison.

Susan said she should buy the carbonated water. She thought they were refilling the regular water bottles from the tap. Cathryn suspected she was right, and she'd been paying top dollar for it —six *soles* for one litre. In Santa Monica you had to be vigilant every second. You could never relax.

"Open the carbonated water right after you buy it," Susan said. "If it doesn't fizz like crazy, it's been refilled, and you get your money right back."

Christmas morning meant there wouldn't be a hideous line for the laundry sinks. So there Cathryn was, scrubbing her clothes by hand like her four great-grandmothers in Minnesota and Idaho did a hundred years ago. She concentrated her thoughts on them so that she wouldn't think about her family back home and make herself sick and more depressed.

On Christmas day no visitors were allowed, so they opened the phones for three hours. Cathryn didn't try to call—everyone who tried to call the U.S. or Europe said the circuits were overloaded, and no calls got through.

She felt glad Cesar couldn't come. She liked the image of him happy at home with his family rather than miserable in prison with a client.

Most of Christmas day Cathryn spent in the cubicle, crying. Christmas night the *directora* held an inspection. She planned to hand out an award for the nicest decorated cubicle on the cell blocks. The Peruvians in her cubicle wanted Cathryn to put her floor-bed away for the inspection.

"Vaya a la mierda y dejame sola," she told them. Go fuck yourself and leave me alone.

A new surprise: that night for dinner they handed out an edible piece of chicken.

But Cathryn's personal Cold War continued.

Merry Christmas, fuckers. Peace on Earth can kiss my ass.

The days after Christmas the women crocheted because they were bored, and there was nothing else to do. Sometimes after roll call they would just go back to sleep. Cathryn would lie on her foam mattress, scratch and cry until she fell asleep from exhausted emotions. Sleep was her escape, but it was sporadic and temporary.

Some of the women found places to do drugs, mostly marijuana and cocaine. Cathryn suspected some of them did drugs just because they were bored, and others did drugs because they were addicted. How easy it would be to think drugs would take away your pains, dull your aching senses, make you feel better.

Cathryn tried not to think about her poor, sleep-deprived immune system, tried not to think how overloaded it must be.

When she mentioned to Susan she was thinking of paying the *delegada* for a bunk, Susan advised against it. The *delegada* was a kind of liaison person assigned to each floor of the cellblock. Her job was to make sure the cleaning duties were done. She also collected money and assigned new people to sleeping cubicles. The guards were there to maintain order and make sure no one escaped. If there was a problem on the cellblock, it was the *delegada* who went to the *directora* of the prison about it.

That night Susan gave Cathryn one of her tranquilizers, and it knocked her out from 6:30 p.m. to 5:30 a.m. After that much sleep she felt better; she felt subhuman instead of inhuman.

Susan spoke to the *delegada* and had Cathryn moved into her cubicle. She still slept on the floor, but she was farther away from the blasting TV and the insufferable fluorescent light. While she felt grateful to Susan for this move, she discovered that in Susan's cubicle there were way more cockroaches. Susan explained that the girls there had family bringing them food that they were careless in storing.

"Also, the bunks in this cubicle are hollow instead of solid wood, perfect living quarters for the roaches."

Cathryn was now in the same cubicle with skinny Georgia of the missing teeth and constant farts, who slept above Susan. While smoking was forbidden in the cellblock, Georgia lit up anyway. No one wanted to say anything to her because she could be so belligerent and obnoxious.

Cathryn's body weakened. From the gruel she contracted food poisoning, followed by foul diarrhea. Knives sliced her throat when she swallowed, and she developed a rattling cough.

Chapter 32

Noise and lights exploded in Cathryn's brain. It was after 11 p.m., and she had just fallen asleep. She shot up, clutching her quilt, as guards shoved around her to get to a lower bunk where one of the Peruvian girls slept.

The women watched in silence as they dragged the girl from her bunk. She stood shivering while they shook her down, going through all her stuff, piece by piece. Most of what she had didn't belong to her. Cathryn watched to see if she had any of her clothes, but she didn't. It had been discovered that the girl was part of a huge thief network. The guards hauled her off to the *calaboso* for a month. Thirty days in the hole. How could anyone survive that?

Afterwards Susan talked to the *delegada* about letting Cathryn have the now-vacant bunk. The *delegada* stalled, and they both knew why. She wanted to extort it out of the rich American *gringa*. However, she didn't dare say that to Susan.

"It's stupid for Cathryn to sleep on the floor when there's a bunk free," Susan told the *delegada*. Her tone indicated that if the bunk wasn't given to Cathryn, Susan would go straight to the *directora* for an explanation.

Cathryn was assigned the bunk. She spent a day cleaning her new space. The Peruvian girl had been filthy. Cathryn had seen her blow her snot on the floor, so she would have to wipe down the bunk with babywipes before she'd feel comfortable. Like all the lower bunks, Cathryn now had curtains, which meant some precious privacy. Susan gave her a little shelf that she hung from the overhead bunk.

Cathryn was meeting with Cesar the afternoon Georgia gathered all the foreigners in their cellblock for a meeting in Prevención with the *directora*. Because of the corruption and stealing, they wanted to lobby for a floor for just foreigners. Cathryn had not committed to going to the meeting because she didn't want reprisal from the *delegada*. In going to the *directora*, the women were going behind the *delegada's* back to complain about corruption and there was bound to be payback. Also, the *delegadas* were all Peruvian, and when it came down to any incident between Peruvian and foreigner, they always sided with the Peruvian. The exception to this was Susan, who had lived in Peru so long that she had dual citizenship.

Cesar said he wouldn't be able to come by for five days because the courts would be shut down through New Year's. He would be spending the time with his family. Then Olivia arrived, on her way to Cusco to stay in the Sacred Valley for five days. Between them they handed Cathryn twenty letters from people back home. She was touched—some of the letters were from total strangers who'd heard about what had happened to her.

Later Cathryn was happy to learn that Susan hadn't gone to the meeting, either, because it backfired and everyone would be punished. The *directora* planned to move all the foreigners who had received their sentences out of Cellblock B and into Cellblock A. They hadn't been moved before because there was no room. Felda, Serafia, Georgia—they would all be forced out the following week. Alice and Susan and Cathryn would stay because they hadn't received their sentences. Now the others would have to sleep on the floor in Cellblock A. The women were stunned and angry.

With no notice, Rosemary went free, leaving Santa Monica Women's Prison at 5 p.m. If an inmate served one-third of their sentence, they got paroled. That meant they had pleaded guilty, been sentenced and received time off for good behavior and work in the *talleres*. At that point foreigners would escape from Peru through Brazil or Ecuador. Cathryn wondered if Rosemary planned to do the same.

Since neither Susan nor Cathryn had pleaded guilty, they had no parole date to look forward to.

It would be lonelier without sweet Rosemary and her lilting British-accented voice. And it was nice of her to leave Cathryn clothes. Some of the shirts had belonged to Rosemary's father, who'd left them when he'd come to visit. Cathryn buried her face in one of them, eager for a whiff of testosterone. And it was there— faint, but recognizable. How much she missed the company of men.

Chapter 33

Cathryn's head itched incessantly. The only women who didn't seem to get lice were the ones who brought their own foam to sleep on. Head lice was so rampant in the prison that the Peruvians groomed each other's heads like monkeys in the zoo. No head lice shampoo was sold in the prison and the doctor didn't carry it—logic escaped Santa Monica.

Cathryn felt too weak to run in the yard with Susan. She had gone so long without food that her bowels had shut down. Her body felt like her life force was leaching out in a slow insidious drain. She scored another five Mellaril. The best time to take them would be at night right after roll call. That way her body wouldn't be discovered until morning. She thought again about the *Adrift* guy. Strange that as an outsider reading Steven Callahan's experience she coaxed him to struggle on, to not give up, yet she couldn't do the same for herself. So much easier to succumb to death.

Of course she might not need the Mellaril after all—she might die of natural causes.

In the yard on the day before New Year's Cathryn sat with Susan, discussed age-old questions, and for a while this distracted Cathryn from the ravages that weakened her body. Were they victims of an existential, random, chaotic world like Camus wrote about? Why do we suffer? Didn't suffering just make you bitter and mean and prematurely aged? Was suicide all that bad?

"How can anyone judge us if we have to make that kind of decision?" Cathryn wondered aloud. She was ready to embrace suicide.

Susan admitted to passive wishes to die. Though she was a vehement Catholic—for whom suicide is a sin—she admitted to losing hope in this hellhole.

Cathryn said that the parts of Christianity she liked were to treat other people the way you want to be treated, to not judge others so you yourself will not be judged, to love your enemies. Difficult things to apply in this world.

"I don't believe that I need to be motivated by guilt or fear to do the right thing," Cathryn said.

Susan wondered about Buddhism. "There is no God," Cathryn explained. "Just the Mystic Law, meaning the fundamental truth, which supports all universal phenomena and the Buddha who is enlightened to it." Through Buddhism Cathryn had seen people overcome addictions and resolve dysfunctional family relationships.

In the end they agreed that it's easy to call yourself a Christian, but another thing to practice Christianity. Likewise, it's easy to call yourself a Buddhist, but difficult—at least for Cathryn—to practice it.

It saddened Cathryn that Kate—maybe in her own kind of survival mode—had fallen in with a rough crowd. She did cocaine with them, loaned them money she never got back, lived what looked to Cathryn like a pretty precarious existence.

Cathryn hated the woman she had become—wretched, suicidal, bitching at the world with her last breath. In addition to weakness and aching bones and chronic cough her face broke out with painful eruptions. She could see the headlines: "American woman found dead in Peruvian prison, face covered with pimples."

The first three days of 2004 Cathryn, sick, laid in her bunk, dizzy and nauseous. Her ear felt like it was embedded with a knife. Her chest felt like someone sat on it, and each breath felt forced. When her lungs began to rumble she knew she had pneumonia.

It couldn't have happened at a worse time. Because of the holidays she had no contact with Cesar or Olivia and no way to get in touch with them. Susan was in Prevención visiting family and friends. Cathryn was afraid to go to the clinic, afraid they would give her an injection with a dirty needle. Pain and fullness in her left ear confirmed infection. She expected dizziness and vomiting would follow.

She began to obsess that if she died in Santa Monica Women's Prison, Dom could slander her. He could say she was a drug dealer and place all the blame on her. *When you're dead, no one can speak for you,* she thought, remembering what they did to Nicole Brown Simpson. She wanted to survive this so Dom wouldn't have that opportunity. In her delirium she called out to her mother.

She scored antibiotics from Serafia, who had gotten them from her embassy. She also took a Mellaril. Remembering Kate's advice, she broke the big, orange pill in two pieces. One half knocked her out for a long time.

On the 4th she took another antibiotic and her ear began to drain. She could feel it drip into her throat. All day she stayed in her bunk with the curtains closed. With no fat on her bones, she felt pain at all contact points, making sleep difficult.

She passed the time chanting from the Lotus Sutra, a teaching that difficult, negative or painful situations can be transformed into something positive or into a source of value. Overcoming painful circumstances in order to grow as a human being. Cathryn believed that chanting created a powerful vibration within the person and their environment that triggers a chain reaction, awakening the highest potential. You could chant for anything—a new car, money, a satisfying relationship, appreciation for one's life, other people's happiness or health, spiritual awareness, getting well, getting out of jail, proving your innocence.

When she awoke the next day Cathryn knew she was a different person. After roll call the night before she had fallen into a deep sleep, and though she still felt weak, in some ways she felt stronger. As she walked to Prevención to see Cesar she felt as if a great weight had evaporated.

"I'm going to ask for your release on bail," Cesar said. "Though the request will be turned down, I must do it."

Cathryn had an epiphany that she was privileged to go through this, and that if she survived it, it would be an opportunity to free herself forever.

Why had she felt such a compulsion to cling to her old life? So many things about it had made her miserable. Most of her relationships had been dysfunctional. She'd over-sympathized with people, becoming their "therapist" and thereby absorbing their sick energy. She'd allowed herself to be manipulated by other people's desires and needs, putting theirs before hers. Afraid to demand her real worth, for years she did the jobs of more than one person.

This prison experience had given her the chance to see who her real friends were and to let dead weight fall away. She didn't feel any jealousy for people back home, most of whom were in prisons, too— trapped by bad marriages, bad finances, addictions, fears. But their prisons were less obvious because they could carry their chains and bars around with them wherever they went.

Cathryn's Buddhist friends had never been negative or fearful about what had happened to her. They said this was an opportunity to change her karma, to challenge the dark side of her nature, to turn this horrible, hideous poison into a beautiful beneficial medicine. While Cathryn contemplated suicide, they believed she would prevail over this disaster.

Cathryn gained a fighting spirit she'd never thought she had. She saw the gift in this thing that had happened to her.

Chapter 34

Cesar arrived in great spirits. "All your documents are complete, translated, certified. I think you have a chance to be released on bail."

Cathryn couldn't allow herself to believe in anything that might or might not happen. She knew she should be happy, and managed a grateful smile for her attorney.

After he left Dolores informed them that the stove used to make the hot water for women with thermoses had broken, and they would have to pay to buy a new stove. Everyone would all be levied another ten *soles*.

Cathryn protested. "I don't use the water."

Dolores shrugged. "No matter. Everyone pays."

Cathryn was tired of being hit on for money. If they didn't want money outright, they wanted to borrow money. Each time Cathryn looked at the salon she thought of the painting scheme that had been used to extort money from the prisoners. Now there was a new levy for the bathrooms—a weekly cleaning fee, they called it. The *delegada* said Cathryn had to pay for the curtains on her bunk—the equivalent of twelve dollars.

"But they were there when I got there," Cathryn protested to Susan.

"Better if you just pay or they won't just take away the curtains—they'll use it as an excuse to kick you out of the bunk."

It wouldn't have been so bad if Cathryn had had a stipend. But she couldn't handle the thought of being back on the floor with the cockroaches. She paid. She paid another five dollars a month for Dolores to do her kitchen and serving duties, and she was still paying another girl for the regular cleaning duties.

These little amounts don't sound like a lot of money unless you don't have it and you don't have any source of income. Cathryn could squeeze it out of her money from the wire transfer, but she needed that money to get her documents translated, notarized, certified, etc., and for her attorney fees. Plus the corruption costs—like paying customs $200 to release her skirt and jacket. No matter how frugal she was, the money from the wire transfer evaporated fast.

A rumor erupted that Susan could be moved to a new prison being built in Ancion.

This new facility, about an hour away, would house the terrorists and corruption people. Cathryn wondered how she could keep on without Susan. She felt selfish to think about herself. A move like this would be devastating for Susan because her family couldn't often travel that far to see her. Cathryn thought one of the reasons Susan was able to maintain was that she could see her family and receive food from her niece.

Susan was terrified because the Montesinos had come down hard on the terrorists—who knew what could happen to her if she were housed with them?

"You should have your attorney go to the U.S. embassy," Cathryn said. "They pay the Peruvian government millions of dollars each year. They could at least put pressure on them to keep you safe."

But Susan had appealed to the U.S. government in the past and discovered they wouldn't help her. Was she afraid of again being shunned by her country? Cathryn felt guilty that the embassy did more for her than for the other four Americans.

The ten thousand dollars her family had wired had been kept at the embassy, and Cathryn wrote letters to David Ryan saying how much needed to be released to Cesar.

In order for the judge to consider her release on bail, Cathryn needed to provide an address in Lima where she would be able to stay. She hesitated to ask Olivia because she didn't want to be a problem to her if she had political aspirations. Olivia's opponents would say, "You let a known felon live in your home? What kind of judgment is that?"

So Cathryn asked Susan if she could use her address in Lima if the judge agreed to release her.

"Of course." Susan gave her the address and cell phone number for her son-in-law.

Chapter 35

Cathryn didn't know if the nuns knew about the homosexuality that existed in the women's prison. For example, Alice had taken up with an ugly, fat Peruvian girl, probably to make her previous partner, Charlene, jealous. So many of the girls hooked up with other girls that Cathryn no longer gave it much thought.

She rented a table in the visitors' courtyard for the nuns when they came to give her Spanish lessons. Sisters Amelia and Luz Maria always stayed as long as they could, sometimes for hours. Cathryn could never anticipate when they would show since she didn't have a phone, and there was no way they could leave a message.

While Cathryn adored Sister Amelia, she had no respect for the various Christian groups that visited the prison. Phan—the Buddhist—was a member of one such group that came in two times a week to convert the wayward. Most of the women pretended to be converts just to get goods and services.

Before she left, Sister Amelia and Cathryn said a powerful prayer together. A Russian woman, who came in with the evangelicals to convert the Catholics, had been standing near them, eavesdropping. She asked, "Were you arrested for drugs?"

"Yes, but I intend to be found innocent. I was carrying luggage for another person."

The woman rolled her eyes. "That's impossible. You'll never be found innocent." She told how she had come to Peru to transport drugs and was completing her probation by working with the evangelicals.

Cathryn said, "You have your faith, and we have ours. We'll see who accomplishes the impossible."

The days slipped away, and nothing seemed to be happening on her case. Cesar still reassured, but couldn't say when there might be a turning point. In mid-January David Ryan and his assistant came by on their three-month visiting tour to hand out vitamins. Cathryn gave him a copy of her last will and testament, which she asked him to certify and send to her family.

"I know I won't survive this in terms of years," She said. She had never had a formal will before, but she thought it was a wise thing to do. Otherwise, she was at peace with whatever happened.

"Did you bring my CD walkman and my sunglasses?" she asked.

David's face reflected a picture of resignation. "I'm afraid they confiscated them when they searched my things on the way in."

Cathryn knew things like sunglasses, belts, shoelaces and zippered items were not allowed, but women had them anyway because monthly they paid for the privilege to a guard or someone else in authority.

"The German and Spanish consuls sneak these things in all the time for their inmates. They never get searched. They're just searching you because you're American. And the *directora* despises Americans."

David agreed, and asked her, in a mild tone as if it were an afterthought, "Are you going to plead guilty?"

By now Cathryn thought he should know where she stood. In irritation she said, "Never will I plead guilty to a crime I didn't knowingly commit."

He smiled. "Good."

He left her with the impression that he hadn't let his government job strip him of his humanity.

The next day when Cesar arrived he chain-smoked, worried. Finally he asked, "Cathryn, are you planning to kill yourself?"

She waved a hand in the air. "This place will probably kill me before I get around to it." For the most part Cathryn told him the truth. She left out the part about the Melloril, because he would tell the guards, and they would shake her down. "The reason I've held on as long as I have is because of Susan, and you coming to visit me. But I know I can't hang on forever." The idea of Susan being transferred to Ancion haunted her.

She babbled on about the quality of life necessary to maintain one's humanity. "I'm here because I was conned and the person who should be here is probably on a beach enjoying life. I know life's unfair, but that doesn't mean I have to keep participating in that unfairness. Little by little I'm dying here. I've almost died once, and if it happens again, I may not have the strength to overcome it. It's just a matter of time. I can put up a valiant fight, but no one could keep it up forever."

Cesar listened, letting her vent all her pent-up frustrations. She paced the cement near where he sat, albeit without much energy.

"This ain't no Hollywood movie. There aren't jump cuts or montages or fast-forward sequencing. This is the long, grueling, ugly, realism of daily life as it passes from one horrible moment to the next. There's nothing glamorous or beautiful about it. And it's killing me…"

Her voice trailed off with the last of her energy and she sat down. Cesar lit another cigarette and took a deep drag. For a long time they didn't speak.

He stubbed out his cigarette. "I'm submitting papers on Wednesday for your release. If the judge accepts the submission, I will have an oral argument before him. I've asked David Ryan to be there."

"Thank you," she murmured.

"Cathryn, if you get this, it will be unprecedented."

Chapter 36

One evening Guards burst into the cubicle, blew whistles, waved arms and spewed out Spanish—some kind of instructions? Cathryn didn't understand a word. Evening roll call had been completed and the women were in for the night, but Susan said they were making everyone go outside and clean.

No one seemed alarmed by this sudden event. Felda and Alice were in good humor, and they began cutting up, making Cathryn think of a Fellini-movie version of summer camp.

The day had been a busy one for Susan—her 55th birthday—and she'd had lots of visitors, one of whom had brought her a chocolate cake. She'd saved a piece to eat together with Cathryn. In their cubicle they laughed that it was just the two of them and the cockroaches eating the cake. Susan said her best birthday present, from her kids, had been roach motels, which she wedged into the upper bunk.

That night Cathryn lay awake a long time, again haunted by visions of Susan being sent to Ancion. What would she do without her? How would she get through the days?

Cathryn would not tell Susan that Cesar had spoken to her oldest daughter and her son-in-law, who told him they didn't want Cathryn to live with them in Susan's house.

At midnight a guard came to the bars at the top of the stairs and sent someone to find Cathryn. The guard told her that in the morning she would go to court at the Palacio de Justicia.

This had to be some mistake. Cesar had not mentioned anything about this appearance. Did he know about this?

Cathryn gave thanks that the next day wasn't a visiting day with closed phones. She got Alice, a big girl who wasn't intimated, to fight her way to a phone as soon as they opened and call Cesar for her.

But before Alice could report back Cathryn was taken with several other women in a filthy transport van. From inside, she always knew when they arrived at the court in Callao because it stank so bad.

For a long time Cathryn sat in a room with several others. She was speaking her broken Spanish with a guard, Eduardo, when Cesar arrived, all professional in his meticulous suit and tie and perpetual cigarette.

"I have no idea what is going on, or why they've summoned you. I wasn't notified." Then he disappeared to find out what he could.

They called Cathryn into court—more of the same. She on one side of a wire mesh wall and the interpreter, court recorder, judge, and Cesar on the other side. This time all she had to do was sign papers to get back what was left of her souvenirs. Of course, she couldn't take them with her back to Santa Monica, so Cesar agreed to keep them for her.

Afterwards Cesar said he felt the judge had called Cathryn to the courthouse because he wanted to see her again. Cesar had told him about her situation and would he consider letting her out? Cesar said the judge told him that he felt the *gringa* to be a good person.

The lady translator was the same one who'd been in court with her before, and Cathryn was able to have a brief conversation with her.

That was it—her big day in court.

Back in the holding room Cathryn sat again with the guard, Eduardo. She told him what had happened to her. He said she was stupid to trust a Peruvian, she should never trust a Peruvian, blah, blah, blah.

So that meant him, too? And her attorney? Olivia? No one?

Eduardo took her outside to wait and let her call Dierdre from a payphone. Her sister had news. She'd spoken to a friend who knew a journalist who wanted to write about what happened to her, but not until after the primaries. God, her suffering was being pre-empted by the presidential primaries!

After she hung up, Eduardo asked her if there was anything she needed.

"Vegetables, green ones."

"On men's visiting day I bring you," he said.

Cathryn thought of Phan and her boyfriends and wondered if dark, stocky Eduardo, who came to the height of her shoulder, was hitting on her. Had she smiled enough to get vegetables? Could she learn to play this game?

On the way back the van stopped to add more prisoners and another guard, Jorge. Jorge took one look at Cathryn and rattled off some Spanish. A girl in handcuffs next to her began to laugh. In broken English she told Cathryn Jorge said when he saw her his heart did something. She tried her best to translate for him, but the gist was that the guy adored Cathryn. "Tell him to bring me vegetables on Saturday." Phan would be so proud of her.

It's not like I'm prostituting myself for vegetables, Cathryn told herself. She thought of girls all strung out on crack, willing to do any kind of sex act just to get another rock. Cathryn just felt desperate to eat anything green. She felt like she'd do anything for broccoli.

Her attempts to "work the guys a-la-Phan" backfired. Asking Jorge to bring vegetables pissed off Eduardo, and the two guards got into a fight over who had homesteading rights on Cathryn, who saw her first, blah, blah. She didn't care. She'd give a big kiss to the first guy who walked through the prison doors with a bouquet of broccoli. Forget flowers, forget candy, forget pronouncements of love…she wanted someone to express their attraction for her with fruits and vegetables.

❖

By the time Cathryn got back from court, the overcast day had become night. All the toilets on the cell blocks were shut down—no water. Lima was in the middle of a summer drought. One hundred eighty women on her cellblock and nowhere to shit or piss until 6 a.m.—and she had thought things couldn't get worse.

Next day they learned that because of the drought the water would be turned off in the prison from 5 p.m. until 6 a.m. each day. Soon the bathroom stink became so unbearable that Susan and Cathryn decided not to eat or drink anything after 2:30 p.m. When they had water, it was too cold for showering and hair washing. What did Cathryn care if her hair looked like shit? Washing her hair wasn't going to stop the lice, so why bother?

The days continued to drag. Cesar had no new news. He waited on one document to go before the judge, and remained hopeful.

When Cathryn's period came she saw just two little drops of blood. Her body had shrunk and on such a bad diet she suspected that before long her periods would stop altogether.

Raging headaches plagued Cathryn. There was so little to eat. In the morning she could get just two pieces of white bread. Male visiting day had come and gone with no guards bearing vegetable gifts. She became so weak she now spent most days lying in her bunk.

Everyone seemed to be in a bad mood. The water was still shut off at night, and all the women vied for what little resources there were. Alice, in a vile mood, shoved Cathryn to the floor in the morning to be first out of the cubicle. Susan had taken to eating her breakfast alone. Women who'd been couples were fighting. Everybody seemed pitted against someone. Cathryn had never felt so alone.

What would death be like? She wondered. Would it be more of life but in a different dimension? She already felt dead. How did she know she hadn't already died and this was Hell? Or maybe this was heaven, as good as it gets—a kind of cosmic joke.

Just as she thought that this was her darkest hour, Olivia arrived with groceries. Milk—yogurt—broccoli—cauliflower—a treasure of life-sustaining food! She would have a decent meal. Cathryn gave some of the vegetables to Phan to stir-fry. She would share them with Phan, Susan and Felda, but in her heart she felt like a selfish bitch because she wanted them all for herself.

Chapter 37

The water shortage continued with no end in sight. The bathroom stank beyond gagging. The women collected reserve water in bins during the day so they could force flush the toilets at night. But by 10 p.m. the reserve water was gone and the toilets were filled with piss and clogged with shit. One morning the water never came on in the bathrooms. At the outside showers, where there was water, fights broke out.

One day Cathryn was able to get through on the phones to just about everyone at home—her parents, Dierdre, Marge, Jim. Jim said he'd sent her a letter and Raisinettes, but she had never received them. Which bitch-guard had eaten her chocolate-covered raisins?

It was comforting to hear their voices, comforting to catch up on the news in their lives. What had happened to Cathryn had taken a toll on all the people she loved; she told them all she was feeling better, which she hoped made them feel better.

In the afternoon, Cesar came by, upbeat, repeating that Cathryn must be patient. He had written his oral argument for the judge, to be presented the following Monday at 8 a.m. Cesar took a deep drag on his perpetual cigarette. "After I give my oral argument, the judge will make his decision known within a few days."

The more Cathryn tried not to think about it, the more obsessed she became about Cesar's oral arguments to the judge. What if all Cesar's good intentions didn't get her out? What if she were here for a long, long time? What if she died here?

Under a statute that stated it was a greater crime if three or more people were involved or it was nine kilos or more, Cathryn could get twenty years without time off for good behavior or *taller* work. While the scuba tank had contained just 8.7 kilos, the system considered Dom's cousin Luis to be a third man. Cathryn knew

Cesar was fighting hard to get it down to two people involved, so she couldn't get the 20-year sentence.

Cathryn tried to reassure herself that the judge knew that if she had been dealing drugs she'd never have told the truth, because who would risk twenty years? Cathryn told the truth because she didn't know anything about the drug trade and—worse yet—she hadn't known she was transporting drugs. If Cesar could get them to see that two—not three—people were involved, or if Cathryn "confessed", she could get six years.

Was it better to lie like the rest of the women and just do a little time?

The first Monday in February 2004 Cesar gave his oral arguments to the judge. All day Cathryn wondered how it went. She wondered about the judge's reaction. She wondered what it meant that Cesar hadn't come by in the afternoon. She paced, she sat, she cried, she paced again, she lay in her bunk—nothing eased her torment of worry. She tried to crochet, but could not concentrate. She couldn't stand the water shortage and the smell of shit one more minute.

That night Cathryn took a third of a Mellaril and zonked out. The next morning she felt so weak she had trouble standing for roll call. At any moment she expected to faint and fall to the ground. In the afternoon Cesar came, dressed in a nice suit. He told her that David Ryan had appeared for the oral argument.

"It lasted forty minutes instead of the usual five." Cesar bobbed his cigarette to indicate that this was a good sign. "The judge should decide in the next few days. We must be patient and positive."

Patient and positive spiked with uncertainty was killing her.

As Cesar turned to leave Olivia arrived.

"I came by last Wednesday, but they wouldn't let me in," she said. Cathryn didn't bother to ask why. There was never any rational explanation for these things.

Olivia looked so fresh and beautiful, such classic beauty in her face, such a tailored suit.

Next to Olivia and Cesar Cathryn felt like foul slime.

The following day Cesar never came. So, that must mean no word about her case.

"I can't believe you've lasted three years in this place," Cathryn said to Susan. "You're a trooper."

There was still no word on Susan's possible transfer to Ancion and Cathryn knew the uncertainty weighed on her. The idea of another prison, maybe worse than this, further away from her kids…Cathryn couldn't imagine.

The shit, the stink, the filth, the crazy fucking bitches were bad, but the worst thing was the waiting. Waiting to get decent food, waiting for the phone, waiting for the toilet, waiting for the next explosive uproar, waiting to hear about your case, waiting, waiting, waiting. Cathryn felt that any second the waiting could make her go psycho.

The more time passed, the more hate Cathryn felt for everyone and everything, hateful and vengeful. She disgusted herself. Maybe she was better off dead.

One of the Dutch girls went to court and told her afterwards, "Eduardo and Jorge were asking about Cathryn, *la Americana*. They said to tell you, hello."

Fuckers—where were the vegetables they were supposed to bring?

On Thursday, four days after he'd given his oral arguments to the judge, Cesar arrived. Cathryn felt stunned when he presented her with packages from her mom and her friend Kara. Her first care packages—Tampons, toothpaste, peanut butter, packets of mustard, mayo, ketchup, honey mustard, instant coffee, lotion, soap, shampoo, hair conditioner.

Other packages had been sent to Cathryn at the prison, and when people realized she never received them, they began to send packages to Cesar. Cesar told her he stood in customs for eight hours before the packages were released to him. He told Cathryn that someone from the U.S. had called the U.S. embassy in Lima to get the address so they could send her packages and was told absolutely *not* to send anything there because they "did not have the staffing for it."

Regarding her case he said, "The judge went to Dinandro to talk to the detectives. He wanted to see how detailed their investigation was and if they thought you were innocent."

Cathryn said nothing.

"Don't worry. I know you're innocent." He told her that if they released her on bail, she would have to put up a lot of guarantee money—about seven thousand dollars—that she would lose if she fled Peru. If she were found guilty or returned to prison, she would get it back.

Cesar came again on Friday morning and announced, "The judge has issued his decision, but I haven't seen it yet."

Cathryn tried not to think about it for the rest of the day. But there was nothing else to think about, nothing else of interest, nothing else as significant. Was it possible she might get out of this hellhole?

At 12:45 p.m. on Saturday, February 7, 2004—visiting day for men—Cathryn sat crocheting with Susan when a Peruvian girl came running around the corner, rattling away in Spanish.

Susan grinned. "You're going free!"

Cathryn hesitated, and stood. She'd dreamed so long of this moment that the reality seemed like a weird, freaked-out dream. Would she wake to find herself lying in her bunk, emerging for roll call, fighting for a shower?

She ran, as if she were afraid they might change their minds, upstairs to get her things. All the women were stunned. Dolores screamed and hugged and kissed her. With her plastic carry box under one arm and her duffel bag—containing her jar of Noxema with the hidden Mellaril—Cathryn walked out into the courtyard, ready to face the real world.

Cesar greeted her, beaming indescribable energy. Everything felt wild, strange, unreal.

Women filled the courtyard, talking. Alice sat with Kadlin and her Peruvian drug-trafficking boyfriend, Pepe. Cathryn was delighted to be released in front of Pepe, who three months ago had said she'd never get out early.

"I put the shelf Susan gave me on your bed," she told Alice.

Several women hugged and congratulated her. Susan gave her the telephone number of the prison to call. With no new rumors about transferring Susan to Ancion, Cathryn carried away with her the image in her mind of Susan's safety.

In the courtyard in front of the bars, Cesar and Cathryn stood with her stuff and waited for the guard to open the door. Inside Prevención they had to wait again. An old man beckoned, and they followed him into a dingy office. He took her fingerprints and matched them to the ones she had given when she'd arrived. Once he verified that she was the same Cathryn, she and Cesar were let through another set of bars. In front of them now were the solid steel doors that led to freedom. The guards opened them, and they stepped into bright sunlight.

My god, a street full of cars!

Cesar flagged a taxi. They loaded her things inside. He observed that her clothes were all raggedy; he'd take her to buy new things. At the market she saw clothes, shoes, socks, caps, purses—all new. She bought a skirt, shirts, a pair of sandals.

So many things that other people take for granted, she thought. A city boulevard with cars, being able to buy something from a market, not having someone breathing down your neck every second, using a toilet that flushed. She felt dazed, overwhelmed by all the colors, in sensory overload. She thought of the *Adrift* guy, whose eyes hurt from the sight of bright reds and yellows after months of seeing only ocean blue and gray.

Cesar took her to his country club on the beach where they sat outside. In Spanish Cathryn ordered a beer. So much going through her mind—she couldn't concentrate on any one thing. Just people-watching was a trip, not the same women, always in the same clothes. And men—everywhere she looked! Men walking, men in conversation, men doing everyday things.

Cesar couldn't stop grinning, he was so happy for her. They walked to a payphone to call David Ryan and Olivia and her parents. Later she couldn't remember any of their conversations, but oh, the thrill of using a payphone—that worked—without waiting in line, without having to battle someone to use it!

Afterwards Cesar took her to the club's restaurant. "Let me buy you dinner."

Cathryn ordered steamed broccoli and seafood—flounder, squid, crab, lobster. Looking out on the vast ocean, in a restaurant, eating that gorgeous food, she had an epiphany. She missed Susan. Leaving Susan behind tugged at her soul. How she wished Susan could have been there with them, free, sharing the moment.

When Cathryn left the table to use the bathroom she saw herself in a full mirror for the first time in four months. She didn't recognize this woman.

Chapter 38

Cathryn hadn't been prepared for what she'd become. That haggard, hollow, holocaust look. Her belly tightened. She feared she might faint. She knew it wasn't the beer that made her dizzy. She hurried out of the bathroom—back to Cesar, the view, the table with its dirty dishes—in a futile attempt to erase from her mind that frightening woman in the mirror.

After the meal they walked along the pier, not talking much. Cathryn stared at the vast expanse of ocean and felt the sea breeze on her skin. The smell of ocean was like something she recognized, but couldn't remember.

Cesar took her to Olivia's house, where it had been agreed that she could sleep in the guest room. Her last real shower had been before her arrest. To shower in prison meant to put a washcloth under ice cold water, suds it with soap and wash her face, pits, crotch and feet. That night she stepped under hot water and let it spray all over her body until she thought others in the house would think she was drowning herself. Her last thought before she fell asleep was that it'd been selfish to use so much hot water. Everything seemed dream-like, surreal, temporary.

In the morning when she awakened she found the bed, the room—everything—startling. She told herself she no longer had to fight for a shower, scramble outside for roll call, fear for her survival. Being thrust out of immediate survival mode jarred her senses. She felt ready for battle, but outside the window—a real window with real curtains—birds cooed. Olivia's house seemed so tranquil.

A concrete, flat-roofed home in the San Isidro district of Lima, Olivia's house was average by neighborhood standards. On the ground floor a little courtyard, the garage, living room, dining room and kitchen. Upstairs a bedroom each for Olivia, her mother and her two sons. Plus the guest room. Lots of hardwood floors and area rugs. Off the kitchen was a stairwell for the maids who lived in a little room on the third floor. There was a laundry room and a place outdoors to dry clothes.

The guest bedroom contained a double bed, dresser, night stands, built-in closets. And quiet! In prison Cathryn had become accustomed to such incredible, constant noise. The tiled bathroom—toilet, washbasin, stand-up shower—reminded her of an American seventies-style bathroom.

Olivia's maids liked Cathryn because she made her own bed and washed her own clothes. If she left her coffee cup in the sink in the morning she felt guilty, because they would insist on washing it for her.

Olivia and Cathryn walked to the beach where they did a variation of Tai Chi, and meditated. Cathryn marveled to see people parasailing.

"This happened to you so you could change," Olivia said. "You should not try to pick up the pieces of your old life."

Cathryn knew she wasn't the same person who left the U.S. four months earlier to see Machu Picchu. As enjoyable as it was to walk the short blocks from Olivia's house to the beach, Cathryn felt vulnerable, frightened, nervous. She startled easily.

The terms of her release weren't yet clear to her. She knew she had to live at the address she had given the court, she couldn't engage in criminal activities, she couldn't leave the city of Lima and, of course, she couldn't do drugs.

Cathryn wanted to learn the layout of Lima, but felt too overwhelmed to try to deal with it on her own. So one day she asked Cesar if she could accompany him as he dealt with his cases. While he drove all over Lima, Cathryn waited for him in his car, and began to recognize main streets.

They went to the American Embassy and talked to David Ryan, who was thrilled to see her. They chatted about his forthcoming month-long family leave while his wife would have her baby.

Cathryn liked David and felt that though his hands were tied in many areas, he'd always been on her side.

She wondered how many days/weeks/months it would take to get used to having her freedom, to not have to defend the smallest thing she owned. She couldn't shake the fear that someone would steal her things. The smallest changes frightened her. What simple things she had taken for granted. A walk to the neighborhood grocery store, to the local pharmacy—so nice to walk to places. She bought soap, lice shampoo, skin lotion, and toothpaste. She longed to buy the make-up she saw, but it was too expensive.

Cathryn found a nearby *cabina de internet* where she could access her email. How strange it felt to log onto her email account, send emails and read them. She felt a strong urge to hurry, as if at any moment the privilege would be denied her.

Online, Cathryn was stunned to discover that, in a well-meaning gesture, her aunt and uncle who had built the *BringCathrynHome* website had posted Olivia's street address.

She felt sure Dom had drug connections in Lima. You heard all the time about Peruvian officials getting assassinated or their dumped bodies being found.

In panic she telephoned her sister. "You need to take it off! Right Away! *Now!*" she babbled. "I'm a sitting duck here if someone wants to kill me!"

Chapter 39

What was wrong with the print in the Lima morning newspaper? Sunlight splashed across the table in Olivia's kitchen where Cathryn sat drinking coffee. As part of studying the language she wanted to read Spanish, but found she couldn't focus on the words. She realized it was hard to see far away as well.

After perfect vision all her life, her eyesight was failing. She knew it was the result of the diet and stress she'd endured during the previous four months. She didn't have any money to see a doctor. Once she began eating decent food, her long-distance eyesight and her close-up vision improved a little, but she continued to need cheaters to read.

Her ordeal had affected her skin as well. Pimples, red and tender, dotted her face. No cream from Pharmax would cure them—she would just have to wait until her life leveled out.

Cesar took Cathryn to visit museums. In the Museum of the Spanish Inquisition, she saw a diorama of a court where people pleaded guilty to heresies they never committed. They had been told that if they said they were guilty—though they weren't—they would go free. Instead they were killed. Cathryn felt like ants crawled on her body. The place reminded her too much of what had happened to her, with the DEA telling her to plead guilty.

Cesar told her she would have to present a monthly summary to the judge of what she was doing, and going to cultural places like museums would look good. She made herself a mental note to remember to keep her ticket stubs and brochures to document these activities.

Diedre and her parents were happy and relieved that she was no long in prison. Her mother cried while they talked. Dierdre, always good at keeping her emotions controlled, had a clean note of relief in her voice. To be able to tell them she was out of prison, that she had accomplished—with Cesar's help—the impossible, made Cathryn's voice choke as well. The conversations seemed like part of just another dream she'd had so often in Santa Monica Women's Prison. Each time after she hung up, she again gave way to tears.

Five days after being released from Santa Monica, on Thursday, February 12, Cathryn had to go to the Palacio de Justicia to report to the judge. The appearance was informal. She signed papers and Cesar gave her a copy of the decision allowing her freedom. "In case something happens and you get detained," he said. "You should always have it handy."

From Callao they went to the U.S. Embassy to pick up a new wire transfer, $10,000 from a Defense Fund that had been set up by Cathryn's aunt and uncle. Her parents' wire transfer was still somewhere in limbo. Most of this money from the Defense Fund would go to the court for her bail. Cesar never asked for more money for himself, only for expenses. Cathryn would advance him $500 US and he would keep all his receipts. Sometimes he'd hire a taxi for the day when they had a lot of places to go. Things moved easier with a driver who could wait instead of parking Cesar's car.

At the embassy they were told the cashier's window didn't open for another hour, at 11 a.m. They went across the street to the mall to look at stores and kill time. She was looking at shoes in a window when she heard a man's voice say, "Cathryn?"

She turned to see one of the DEA agents who had interrogated her, Mr. Estrada. He gave her a big hug but his face said he thought he saw a ghost. She told him about her release on bail.

"It would be a great help if the DEA would testify in my case," Cathryn said.

Estrada's face sobered. "You would have to ask the head of the DEA here. His office is in the embassy." He pulled a notebook and pen from his shirt pocket and wrote a name, Sonny Gretcham. As he handed the paper to her he mentioned that Mr. Tjon, the DEA agent in charge of her case, waited in a nearby truck.

Cathryn walked to the truck to say hello. Tjon started when he saw her. "I can't talk to you!" he hissed.

She stepped back in surprise, not knowing what to say. Her eyes welled with tears, and she took a deep breath.

Cesar, who had followed her, was startled, too. What was the matter with Tjon? Did he feel speaking to her was a conflict of interest? Was Tjon surprised that Estrada had been talking to her? They said no more, walked back to Estrada and gave him an awkward *adios*.

Cathryn never spoke to Tjon again. Once she asked David Ryan about it, but all he could—or would—say was that Tjon had been transferred to another country.

Cesar and Cathryn walked back across the street to the embassy and retrieved her wire transfer. At a bank in Miraflores they deposited her security bond, the 20,000 _soles_—$6,800. US—she had to deposit for the court to assure that she would stay in Lima until her trial. She was handed a receipt to present to the judge. From there they hurried to an internet *cabina* where Cesar could type the documents. Cathryn had a photo taken for parolee's ID.

Back at the Palacio de Justicia Cesar learned that the judge's decision to release Cathryn would now be reviewed by a new judge assigned to her case. The prosecutor wanted to see her returned to prison.

"A new judge?" Cathryn said in horror.

"It's just a matter of procedure, but it's unfortunate that the prosecutor wants to send you back." Cesar shrugged his body as if his suit had become a discomfort in the heat. "Cathryn, you must face the fact that you might have to go back to prison."

Cathryn's throat tightened and her limbs went numb.

"You should enroll in a Spanish language school as soon as possible. That might help persuade the judge to maintain your freedom."

Cesar wanted to stop at Dinandro to see Ruben, one of the Peruvian detectives who had investigated her case. Happy to see her out of Santa Monica, Ruben said the judge had come to Dinandro to talk to him and the other detective about her case. Ruben had reported that Cathryn's processed film showed tourist photos—no photos with drug people—and that Hector, her Cusco tour guide, had sworn he'd taken her on a private tour, and had called twice to be sure she was okay.

Cathryn began to cry, her present freedom scarred with this reminder of her arrest and incarceration. The blue shirt she wore that day had been Rosemary's father's, another reminder. She found it impossible to hold back emotions that overpowered her senses. She sobbed through the entire visit.

Their travels that day made Cathryn realize she needed to get used to moving around Lima on her own. It wouldn't be easy, with her lame Spanish. Her throat choked at the thought of being on her own in this strange city. She would have to pay someone to teach her the language.

Just before six in the evening Cesar dropped her at Olivia's. All of a sudden the impact of the day's events slammed into her mind. Would she just get used to life outside prison and have to go back? Why release her in the first place? This was too cruel. In bed at Olivia's Cathryn stared at the wall. But she was seeing the partition wall at the back of her bunk in the cubicle of cellblock B.

That night sleep proved elusive as she lay alert with nervous tension.

Chapter 40

On Friday morning the 13th Cathryn enrolled in Spanish classes at Euroidiomas, a school within walking distance of Olivia's. Euroidiomas was a language school for Peruvians to learn English, French or German. As a foreigner, Cathryn would have to pay for private lessons to learn Spanish. She would go to two-hour sessions several times a week. It wasn't cheap—$1,500 US and she had to pay in advance.

Olivia had a guest arriving on the 24th, so Cathryn would have to move out of the house. She had known she couldn't live there forever, but to have to move so soon!

Cathryn already counted each *sole*. She tried not to worry that her only source for money was her parents or the Defense Fund. She had no idea what to budget for living expenses. How could she live on her own in Lima? Where would money to live come from? How long could the money she had last? Not knowing when her trial would be, it was impossible to speculate. She worried more about money than whether the judge would find out she no longer lived at the address authorized by her parole.

Olivia took her to a market and introduced her to wonderful South American fruits—*cherimoya, granadilla, sauco, maracuya, platanitos* and *carambola*—and Cathryn fell in love. The weather, hot and humid, made it all in season. From the market they went for ceviche to a restaurant that happened to be near the Santa Monica Women's Prison. When they drove by sweat broke out on the back of her neck, and memories flooded her mind. It was visiting day for women, and at the entrance a line of people waited to get in. Cathryn thought of Susan and Felda and Alice and Phan and the others, and felt like a traitor. She had just eaten ceviche while they ate gruel.

Olivia offered her an extra cell phone that her son didn't use. Cathryn could receive calls without cost, but would have to buy phone cards to call out. Still, this would be cheaper than using pay phones to call the U.S. It would also make it easier to communicate around Lima. She felt so grateful to Olivia, she couldn't find words enough to thank her.

At Euroidiomas Cathryn began her Spanish lessons. She felt like a dopy *gringa* when she tried to speak. At least she no longer said *muy gracias* instead of *muchas gracias,* as she had in prison. But when she meant to say a million dollars—*millones dolares*—she said *millones dolores*—a million pains. She said *tengo hombre*—I have a man—instead of *tengo hambre*—I'm hungry. And consistently confused *peine*—comb—for *pene*—penis. But she was trying, and could report that to the judge.

The morning after dining on ceviche with Olivia near the prison Cathryn had called Susan. How wonderful to hear her voice. Calls were limited to two minutes, so she just had time enough to tell her how much she missed her.

When she mentioned this to Cesar, he became angry and abrupt. "You can't have any contact with the prisoners in Santa Monica!"

"Why not?"

"If the judge finds out, it will look bad. Part of your parole is that you cannot have any contact with drug people."

"Susan isn't a drug person."

"Doesn't make any difference. She's in prison with drug people."

The next day Susan's daughter, Elena, came to Olivia's. Tall like her mother, dark-haired Elena had a job in magazine publishing. She didn't speak any English. She had a note for Cathryn from Susan. Cathryn wrote a note back explaining that she couldn't call her anymore at the prison, that they would have to communicate by secret notes, and gave it to Elena.

Cathryn had four days left to find a new place to live. She and Olivia looked at a place two blocks from Olivia's house, $170 US per month. It contained a little kitchenette with ugly formica, a tiny refrigerator and sink. Cathryn didn't like the place, called a *pensione*, but the walls were white, it seemed clean and quiet, and there was no alternative.

The first time she tried to use her keys to get in the front gate, she had trouble. A neighbor, Uberto, tried the key for her, and when it wouldn't work he rang the bell for the landlord's mother to let her in.

Cathryn had seen Uberto before in the neighborhood; a lot of people walked and you got used to seeing your neighbors. In his thirties, Uberto was a Peruvian orthodox Jew. Sometimes he wore his yarmulke openly, and sometimes he hid it under a baseball cap. She liked Uberto and felt grateful for his help.

Again she went to the U.S. embassy to check on the lost wire transfer from her parents. To her relief, the $10,000 had arrived. Now, what to do with it? She couldn't open a bank account since she had no official ID. And she couldn't trust Peru's volatile economy; it had been stabilized in the 90s by Americanizing it with the U.S. dollar, but most Peruvians—if they had any money at all—didn't use Peruvian banks. Olivia had lost $40,000 and her father his entire life savings in the 80s in banking scams, so now they stashed any money they had in U.S. banks.

Cathryn's solution was to stash the money in various hidden spots in her *pensione* apartment. She thought it best because what if the prosecutor decided to freeze her bank account?

The prosecutor wanted her back in jail because of the phony $100 bill they found on her. Cathryn knew it had been switched either at the airport or at Dinandro, but how could she prove it? Both Cesar and Olivia said she couldn't say that in court. It was considered "bad form" to say that the Peruvian system did something scandalous.

While the Peruvian State Prosecutor worked to put Cathryn back in prison. Cesar worked on getting Vargas, the Peruvian DEA officer, to agree to answer any questions the judge might have of him.

The days crept by, filled with walks with Olivia, Spanish lessons, and waiting, waiting, waiting. Cathryn's case seemed to be in a holding pattern. Lonely and bored, she sometimes wished she were back in prison just so she could talk to Susan. Elena came by one evening with a letter from her mother. The nice thing about letters was you could read them over and over, but she still missed their conversations.

The cell phone Olivia had given her sometimes just turned off. Other times it wouldn't recharge. No wonder her son didn't want it. Cathryn would have to find out where to buy a new one, and how much it would cost. Nevertheless she felt grateful to have it on February 26 when she was able to call her mother in the morning and wish her "happy birthday."

Cathryn contemplated running. Yet she knew that if she ran, she would be running for the rest of her life, always looking over her shoulder. If she ran, she'd destroy Olivia's career and credibility because she had put up the personal guarantee. Cathryn decided running wasn't an option. If the prosecutor had his way, she would go back to prison to die.

She didn't want to think of the Mellaril option. She still had her stash of fat, orange pills. But if the prosecutor won, she vowed to take them the night before she went back to prison.

Chapter 41

Uberto planned some kind of celebration and invited Cathryn to come. She gave him a vague answer about other plans, not wanting to commit to anything that she wasn't sure she could attend. But there was more to it than that. She felt afraid to be around people celebrating, people who were happy. Happy people made her aware of what she could lose in an instant. She felt afraid to be happy.

One morning Cathryn and Cesar went to the U.S. embassy to get the letter of reference written by Dwight Meyer, mayor of a city in Washington State. A friend of her family, Dwight had been kind enough to write it for her.

David Ryan was still on vacation and the letter could not be found. Cathryn was informed that since the letter had "been misplaced" she would have to wait until David returned to get it.

Cesar delivered to Sonny Gretcham, head of the DEA, a formal request to Gretcham for a meeting regarding their request for a certified letter from Vargas answering to the judge questions about the night of Cathryn's arrest.

Cesar let her ride with him while he went to Callao Men's Prison on a case. Cathryn didn't want to go back to the *pensione* and be bored, and she was still trying to learn the streets.

More days of waiting passed, marked by trips to Spanish class and the *cabina de internet*. Sonny Gretcham did not answer either her phone calls or Cesar's. Was Gretcham avoiding them? Cathryn hated to get Congressman Weatherman involved in this, but there seemed no other way to deal with the situation. She called his office. They agreed to call Gretcham to find out if he would allow Vargas to answer the judge's questions via letter.

Waiting, waiting, waiting. Cathryn was desperate to know what the fuck they planned to do with her.

Cathryn awakened trembling from a nightmare where Dom had found her and threatened to kill her for "talking." She tossed back the meager blanket, her body wet with sweat. She blinked her eyes to be sure she was in her *pensione* bed, not on the floor with the cockroaches or in her bunk in cellblock B.

Later that day Cesar came to talk to her. "I've been offered a job with the government," he said. It paid a lot, and he'd be tracking down laundered drug money.

"Oh," was all that came out of her mouth.

"I can't work as an attorney anymore," he explained, "It would be a conflict of interest."

She should have felt happy for him, but this new worry frightened her. First a new judge, now a new attorney?

"When do you start?"

"I haven't decided to take the job. It's just something I've been offered. I have to think about it."

Cathryn's instincts told her he'd take it. She tried to tell him about her dream, but the law of diminishing enthusiasm had already begun to set in, and he wasn't interested.

When several days went by with no more word from Cesar, she figured it meant he hadn't heard from Sonny Gretcham about their request for the DEA to testify in her case.

Cathryn took a long walk to shop for groceries. Another day she scoured the mall for a sale on clothes—what she had was raggedy. She couldn't shake her cloud of loneliness. She called her sister and cried more than talked. At the edge of her cloud of loneliness lurked a knife of fear. She didn't want to die, but she couldn't go back to prison.

In the evening Elena came by with a letter from Susan and took one from her. So far, this method of corresponding was working.

Elena had just left when Cesar called. No, he still hadn't decided whether or not he would take the government job. But Gretcham had called. They would meet with him at 8 a.m. Wednesday.

Cathryn took a taxi to the courthouse to do her monthly sign-in. Her use of taxis had to end—she couldn't afford the expense. But public transportation in Lima intimidated her. All the busses were privately owned, with no schedule or maps to show different lines or times. Some busses were like old 1950's school buses, and some were just converted passenger vans that squeeze people in. It looked chaotic but she'd have to figure it out.

She signed in, thinking, had it already been four weeks since she left the women's prison?

On Tuesday Cesar and Cathryn met to discuss their forthcoming meeting with Sonny Gretcham. Cesar had met with the new judge and received in writing eight questions the judge wanted Vargas to answer in the event the DEA wouldn't let Vargas appear in person. Cesar was ebullient. "If the DEA answers these questions, and they don't conflict with your testimony, there is a chance all the charges against you will be dropped and you can go home."

Cathryn couldn't imagine that the DEA would lie, so she allowed herself to feel hopeful that this nightmare might soon end.

Their meeting with Sonny Gretcham went well. A black American from Philly, he seemed nice enough. He didn't see any problem with Vargas answering the questions, but—why is there always a "but"?—the request would have to be presented to Vargas and the DEA on embassy letterhead.

Cathryn's parents had received several strange telephone calls. Always a woman, who asked to speak to Cathryn. When they said she wasn't there, the woman would say, "Tell Cathryn I have a message for her," and hang up. These ominous calls alarmed them.

Did someone want to kill her? Was Cathryn Prentis the target of a drug cartel? It would sound hilarious to anyone who knew her.

Two days later, when she spoke to her parents, they agreed that the next time the woman called, she'd be told to contact Cathryn through her email address, available on the *BringCathrynHome* web site.

Cathryn felt sure the "message" they had for her was that they wanted her dead. In Lima a tall, blonde *Americana* would stand out and not be hard to find. *Well, bring it on,* she thought, *I've got nothing to lose. Come and get me.*

Chapter 42

Cathryn spent an afternoon at the Larco Museum where, though photography was not allowed, she sneaked a few photos of *huacos*, vases made by pre-Columbian cultures, many with animal themes and some quite sexual. Coming out of the museum she wondered with a crazed smile, did taking those surreptitious photos violate the terms of her parole?

On the way back to the *pensione* Cathryn encountered Uberto, just leaving a store with an armload of beer. He invited her to a place around the corner, where he and his friend Carlos were getting shit-faced. She had a beer with them, thinking that there was nothing more pathetic than drunk, unhappy people commiserating.

When she returned to the *pensione*, she called Gretcham's office to ask about the letter and learned he was "out all week at a conference." Cathryn couldn't escape the feeling that he was avoiding her.

Brief meeting with Cesar on March 17th at a corner coffee shop. When Cathryn arrived he had his usual cup of coffee in one hand and cigarette in the other. But all he had to say was that there was no new word on any part of her case.

Waiting was her life.

Cathryn's mother called. When was she coming home? It hurt Cathryn to tell her she didn't know. Her mother became angry. "Why is it taking so long?"

"Mom, it's a legal matter."

"Well, we're running out of money. We can't continue to pay rent on your apartment. There's no more money to send you. This is just taking too long."

Cathryn knew she wasn't angry at her, but she felt responsible just the same. Since little remained in her checking account, she told her mother to empty out her apartment, just throw all her shit in a dumpster. Have a garage sale. If they couldn't find homes for her cats, give them to the SPCA, put them to sleep. It would break her heart, but what could she do?

Her mother responded by saying that she and Cathryn's father were so stressed out they were going to have strokes "over this thing."

Cathryn felt paralyzed, like a dead nerve ending. What could she say to relieve her mother's suffering? She had no answers, no words of encouragement. She couldn't feel anything anymore, not even guilt for being unable to reassure her parents.

After the conversation Cathryn laid on her bed, numb and shaking with exhaustion. Why couldn't she have died in prison? Wouldn't that have been easier for everyone?

She floated through the days on a sea of indifference. Towards the end of March Cesar learned that David Ryan had not returned from his vacation because he'd fallen and punctured a lung. When Cesar told Cathryn this, his manner was curt, dismissive. He still had not said if he planned to take the government job he'd been offered on March 4.

When Cathryn called Sonny Gretcham to ask about the letter of request to Vargas, he was dismissive as well, saying he would get back to Cesar about it. She couldn't believe how long it was taking just to get a fucking answer to eight questions about the night she was arrested—they were putting more thought and effort into that stupid letter than the whole administration did about going to war in Iraq.

If they didn't want to answer the questions, she needed them to say so—did she dare to hope they'd also say *why*?—in a letter so that her trial in the lower court could be closed out.

David tried to explain it to her in "government-speak." The questions and possible answers had to be carefully considered for "potential minefields." What if answers to the questions put the DEA in a compromising position? What if an answer betrayed "means and methods" of their work?

In an email from Karen Mack, District Director for Congressman Weatherman, Cathryn learned that Karen had spoken with Sonny Gretcham and he'd explained how the immunity thing worked. The Peruvian court would send the diplomatic note requesting the limited waiver of immunity to the Peruvian Office of the Foreign Ministry, which would send it to the U.S. Embassy, which in turn would forward it to the U.S. State Department for reply.

Dierdre directed Cathryn to a woman at the State Department in Washington, DC who knew about her case, a U.S.-South American liaison of some kind. Cathryn called her to find out what the delay was on the Vargas letter. The woman said the legal department of the DEA was looking at it, and it could take a long time…at least two weeks to decide whether they would answer the questions or not.

When Cathryn pushed her for more information, she said, "We may never get the letter," explaining something about the DEA legal department being a part of the new Homeland Security and nobody knew who to contact there for more information, blah, blah, blah.

Cathryn thought the President had said the formation of the Homeland Security Department was to streamline things and make information easier to access. Instead, just more bureaucracy.

Cathryn called the office of California U.S. democratic Senator Marion Lockhart. No one there knew anything about her case and the bottom line was that they didn't want to help her with this letter.

All the papers on her case needed to be translated and notarized. Cesar drove Cathryn to downtown Lima to the office of a translator he used.

Cathryn had the impression Cesar planned to take the government job he'd been offered weeks ago and didn't want to tell her. So she wasn't surprised when he admitted he wanted to take the job. They kept offering him more and more money, and he loved analysis and would get to analyze all the information for the money laundering division of the government.

That same day full of strange energy, Cathryn received an email from Senator Carter's office saying there would be no more help from that direction. They could not help her to get the DEA to answer the questions.

Senator Carter's Constituent Services Representative had emailed to Cathryn a copy of an email sent to David Ryan offering a letter of support for her from the Senator. Cesar had emailed back saying he needed the letter to be addressed to the Secretary of State, Colin Powell, like the other letters of support, with a copy to be sent to the Director of the DEA in Washington, DC. He had also requested a notarized copy be sent to David Ryan along with a copy in Spanish.

Now Senator Carter's assistant emailed, so sorry, she was unable to translate the letter, and while she was happy to fax it to David Ryan, it would not be notarized. She added that the Senator's office was legally prohibited from becoming involved in legal cases involving a foreign government, and what they'd already done was the most assistance the office could provide.

Cathryn returned from the *cabina de internet* to find no electricity in the *pensione*. *Señor* Cardoza said they wouldn't have any until the following Monday. No lights, no buzzer, no phone, no refrigerator. *Señor* Cardoza handed her a candle like it was a gracious substitute. She thought, *you cheap motherfucker.*

Chapter 43

Without electricity Cathryn couldn't recharge her cell phone, so Olivia couldn't call her. One morning Olivia came and pushed the buzzer, which, without electricity, didn't work. Cathryn happened to see her driving by on the street and they hailed each other. Olivia invited Cathryn to spend the day with her.

They drove out of Lima to a beautiful beach where they walked and talked for hours. On the way back they stopped at the house of Olivia's friend, Adelina. A duplex apartment, Adelina's home was middle class by Peruvian standards. The place was immaculate, but shabby. In the living room they sat on an old sofa, run down like most of Peru. Adelina, an architect, had never been able to find work in that field in Peru, so she worked as a secretary. Her daughter, Felisa, read Tarot cards. Adelina insisted that Felisa read for Cathryn.

Felisa, a pretty girl in spite of pocked cheeks, said the cards showed that Cathryn had been in a horrible place with unspeakable suffering, but it was "all to meet this man."

"What man?" Cathryn asked.

"A man whose work is important to him. You are compatible. The problem in your relationship will be distance...but you will work this out in the end."

The last card she turned upwards in the deck was the card of lovers. Cathryn asked herself, *who is this mysterious man I'm supposed to meet? Could he show up soon to relieve my loneliness? Do I believe in this stuff?*

In English she whispered to Olivia, "I've given up on romantic love. I'd settle for good sex."

It was official. Cesar Xavier was no longer her attorney. On the last day of March he came to tell her he had accepted the government job. He said he'd take care of the remaining paperwork. What could she say? Cathryn wished him good luck, told him that he deserved it.

They had been through so much together, she felt lost—terrified—at the idea of not having Cesar as her attorney. Who would represent her now? How would she find another attorney? How would this affect her case?

On April 2nd, 2004 Cathryn pleaded her case to the new judge and he agreed to try to delay the prosecutor. But she had to find a new attorney—fast. If only Olivia could be her attorney, but her area of legal expertise was with intellectual properties and copyright law, not much help for an accused drug smuggler. Cesar had said he'd help find her another attorney, but she didn't hold out much hope from that direction. Olivia said she would check around, too, and there was still the list of "recommended" attorneys provided by the U.S. embassy.

When Cathryn again tried to reach Sonny Gretcham about the Vargas letter, she got the royal brush-off. First the secretary said, "He's on the other line" and Cathryn said, "I'll hold for him." The secretary came back on and asked, who's calling? "Cathryn Prentis."

"He's out of the office." *Pulleeeez!*

When Cathryn told Cesar this he shrugged his shoulders. He told her that a new prosecutor, a woman, had been assigned to her case. Oh, and by the way, if she didn't get that letter from Vargas in ten days, she would go back to prison.

Again Cathryn called Gretcham, with the same result. He was on the other line, he found out who was holding for him, he was not in the office. Why not just say he wouldn't talk to her? She was blonde, but did he think she was *that* stupid?

Any other company, Cathryn would have camped out and laid in wait for him to appear. But the U.S. embassy is quite restricted. You go through a thorough search at the front entrance, far from the real offices. If you don't have official business or a documented appointment, you don't pass. If you do get in you walk a long way to the embassy itself and through heavy doors—supposedly bomb proof—and go through a metal/detector/search station. From there you go to a window and explain to a guy behind bulletproof glass why you're there, and he tells you where to go.

If she tried to wait outside for any length of time, she would be arrested.

So Cathryn called Dierdre, her designated family representative, and asked her call him. Gretcham took Dierdre's call. When her sister called back she told her to hang up and call back from a pay phone.

Cathryn had to walk all over the neighborhood to find a pay phone that wasn't broken, and the first thing she asked was, *why the pay phone?* Dierdre said Gretcham had told her to make sure they talked on a "safe phone"—a pay phone, not a cellular. Apparently it's easy to listen in on cell calls in Peru. Was this DEA paranoia? Or could someone be monitoring her cell phone?

"He told me to tell you to get out of the country. Fast. He says you'll never get that letter." He'd also told Diedre that everyone at the embassy expected Cathryn to flee Peru when she had gotten out of prison, so why was she still around? *Uhmmm*, trying to clear her name? Keep her word? Not burn anyone like the asshole who did this to her?

And just how did they think she would get out of the country without a passport? Cathryn guessed they expected her to do it illegally, like everyone else.

"What're you going to do?" Dierdre asked.

"I have to talk to Olivia. She put up a personal guarantee for me, that she would be responsible for me. If I run, the scandal will ruin her career. It would be a reflection of bad judgment on her part, and she would never be able to work again as an attorney or run for any political office. I can't burn her."

Cathryn disconnected without giving her sister any definitive answer. She walked to Olivia's office and told her what Dierdre had said.

"I need that letter for the new prosecutor in order to stay out of prison, and the DEA won't give it to me." Cathryn felt so awful that she couldn't look Olivia in the eye. "I can't think for myself anymore—you have to make the decision if I should run or not." Cathryn felt so frozen she didn't think about how this might put pressure on their friendship, how this might be uncomfortable for Olivia, how heavy this decision would be for her. "I'll do whatever you say, even if it means I go back to prison."

"It looks hopeless for you," Olivia said. "There's no denying that, Cathryn. But we should stand and fight this."

Cathryn raised her head, their eyes met, and they made the decision to ignore the advice of the DEA. To hell with the woman who was the new prosecutor, too.

"You have my word of honor." Cathryn straightened from her slumped position in the chair. "I won't leave Peru unless you convince me to go." If Olivia wanted to stand and fight, they would stand and fight together.

Olivia's smile was gentle. "Something good will happen, Cathryn. We have to believe that."

Chapter 44

Cathryn sent emails to both Senator Lockhart's and Congressman Weatherman's Constituent Services Representatives, explaining that Sonny Gretcham wanted to write the letter answering the judge's questions, but could not until he received an okay from the DEA's legal department in Washington, D.C. She asked them to contact the legal people and find out what was holding things up. She asked them to find out if permission was going to be granted or not—if not, please tell her. She added that each day she didn't have the letter was bad for her case.

Cathryn called her parents to explain her decision.

The DEA had let Dom get away, had told her to plead guilty, had lied to her about getting this letter, and now they were telling her to run. She explained how it would affect Olivia if she ran. How could she enjoy freedom back home knowing she ruined someone's life to get it? That would be life without bars and chains, but it wouldn't be *freedom*. As unhappy as her parents were with this, they said they understood.

Cesar spent a day with Cathryn driving around Lima to pull the loose ends on her case together before he began his new job. But it seemed like everywhere they went, a new wall appeared.

At the U.S. embassy, David Ryan told Cathryn he wouldn't accept any more letters on her behalf. "We're not a post office." Nor could she receive any more wire transfers. "We're not a bank, either."

"But I can't receive wire transfers anywhere without a passport." Cathryn clenched her teeth to curb her trembling frustration. "I need a valid form of ID to get wire transfers. So, can you give me a passport?"

"Sorry. I've got to honor the order from the judge not to issue you one."

It was as if there was a conspiracy designed to force her to run, to take away her choice in the matter, to leave her no alternative. She was *persona non grata* in her own embassy. How could David Ryan have turned on her like that? She suspected he'd already gotten into trouble for doing all he had done for her—the wire transfers, the affidavits for her letters, letting her receive letters at the embassy.

Cathryn loved her country, but she had learned to hate her government. She walked out of the embassy feeling like there was no place she belonged. She felt totally fucking lost. Just before she got to the street security station, David came running after her.

"I understand your predicament, Cathryn," he said. "I'll try to do something about the wire transfers. What's happening with your case? Why's Xavier leaving?"

"He's accepted a job with the Peruvian government, a high level position in the money laundering division. I have to find another attorney."

As they spoke David Ryan seemed like his old self again. *I'm Alice in Peruvian Wonderland,* Cathryn thought. Later she would learn that all conversations, phone calls, etc., at the U.S. Embassy are recorded. David couldn't talk to her freely until he was out of the building.

At the café in the mall across the street Cathryn spotted Sonny Gretcham having coffee with another American DEA agent. She no longer felt shy about approaching them and, to her surprise, Gretcham said that maybe the DEA would answer the eight questions—if the judge subpoenaed them.

Cathryn returned to the table where Cesar and she had settled for coffee and told him what Gretcham had said.

Cesar exhaled a stream of cigarette smoke. "Go back and ask him if he will put that in writing."

Cathryn turned and discovered Gretcham and the other agent had left their table. As fast as she could in skirt and sandals she ran out the door and across the street towards the embassy. She saw him at the entrance and yelled. He stopped at the door, waited for her to catch up to him and catch her breath.

"Would you put that in writing?" She asked without preamble. "What you said about answering the questions if the judge subpoenas you?" Gretcham squinted in the sunlight. She continued in a more forceful voice. "All the DEA has to do is tell the judge the truth. I'm not asking anyone to lie for me. Just tell the truth." What was the big deal about that, anyway? If the DEA refused, at least the fact that she fought to get the questions answered would show the judge that she wasn't afraid the truth would incriminate her.

Gretcham made a deep sigh. "I'll do that for you."

"Thank you. When can I pick up the letter?"

"Call my office tomorrow. I'll try to have it for you on Wednesday."

Shit, Cathryn thought, *here we go again*. "Do you mean that? Or are you just going to have your secretary give me the he's-not-in-the-office routine?"

With a sheepish smile he promised to take her call.

Chapter 45

Meanwhile, life—if you could call it that—went on. Her Spanish language course at Euroidiomas, too expensive to continue, ended.

When Olivia invited her to a spiritual meeting at her brother's clinic, Cathryn discovered she could understand some of the speaker's words. She also discovered that she could relax a little and enjoy the evening. Most evenings she took a long hot shower, watched movies on TV, and tried not to succumb to depression, that dark companion to the boredom of waiting.

On Tuesday when Cathryn went with Cesar to the Palacio de Justicia for her monthly sign-in, he handed in a formal letter of substitution stating he would no longer be her attorney and another attorney would take over her case. Cesar said little , and she felt afraid to say anything to him. He sent her off on her own to get her documents copied and notarized. "It's not my problem anymore," he said. "It's yours."

Late that afternoon Cathryn called Sonny Gretcham. As he'd promised, he took her call and told her he would have the letter for her the following day.

This should have made her feel better, but she had been so disheartened by Cesar's behavior and harsh words that she went back to the *pensione*, threw herself on her bed and cried herself into an exhausted sleep.

The next morning Cathryn went to the embassy and picked up Gretcham's letter.

"Dear Mr. Cesar Xavier,

This is in response to your letters dated March 10 and April 5, 2004, as well as conversations held within that period of time seeking our response to interrogatories concerning your client, Cathryn Prentis. After consulting with our Office of Chief Counsel, Washington DC, it appears that this office is unable to respond in light of the diplomatic immunities that are in place relating to U.S. diplomats testifying or providing evidence in Peruvian Courts. If the Peruvian government or courts make an official request through a diplomatic note for a waiver of this immunity, and the US Department of State subsequently grants a limited waiver of immunity, the Drug Enforcement Administration will, of course, respond fully to the extent allowable by such a limited waiver.

This office also must consider the protection and legal rights of all our employees. Therefore, a formal Peruvian request from the government or courts requesting the appearance of any DEA employee/contractor would be required, thereby affording them all the protections of the law.

Sincerely,

Sonny Gretcham
DEA Country Attaché
Lima Peru."

Cathryn had to take the letter into downtown Lima to get the signature certified and leave it with an official translator. Another single page pimped out to three—at $40 US per page. The translation would have to be notarized, followed by a certification that the notary was legit. It was all at different offices and cost money—the signature certification alone at the *Ministerio* was $50 U.S. Plus, Cathryn had to pay for Cesar's time to do all this. Money fled her hands fast.

The next two days were Easter holidays, celebrated in South America Thursday through Sunday.

On Saturday Olivia invited Cathryn to go with her and her family for the holidays to their vacation home near a river about two hours outside of Lima. But the complications of her case, Cesar leaving, her disastrous financial situation, all crowded her mind. How could she put on a phony smile for several days when what she wanted to do was hide in the bathroom and slash her wrists?

And—though she didn't say this to Olivia—Cathryn wasn't sure her parole restrictions extended that far outside of Lima. So Easter became a long, lonely week-end, but that had been her choice.

Cathryn stared in the little mirror in her bathroom and thought, *no wonder I feel overwhelmed and defeated. I was arrested with 8.7 kilos of cocaine. I shrugged off the advice of two of the most powerful government agencies in the world, the DEA and the U.S. State Department. I have no attorney. I am in a country where I don't speak the language, and on my shoestring budget survival is day-to-day. I have no political clout to protect me, no financial fortune to buy influence, no valid identification papers. And a drug cartel probably would love to see me dead.*

Yet she had decided to stay and fight for her innocence. *Am I a fucking fool?*

Chapter 46

When her cell phone died Cathryn gave it back to Olivia's son. She needed to get a new one, but found herself in another catch 22. Without valid ID, she could not buy a cell phone and could not open a phone account in her name. Again, Olivia saved her. She added Cathryn onto her plan and bought the phone for her in her name. Cathryn now had 200 "anywhere" minutes a month, including to the U.S., and unlimited incoming calls. Communication with her family would be easier and could be more frequent. Olivia and Cathryn had unlimited calls to each other. The phone, the first month, the activation fees and the service contract through her cell phone provider swallowed another two hundred of Cathryn's dwindling dollars.

At the *cabina de internet* she searched online for a job. Alas, nothing posted for an American prison parolee in Lima who spoke broken Spanish.

Back at the *pensione* Cathryn discovered that again they had no hot water. She told *señor* Cardoza that with the shoddy electricity and no hot water, she wanted her security deposit back. She wanted him to feel like the piece of shit he was, but he only spoke Spanish, and in her limited speech she couldn't be sure she'd made herself clear.

Uberto introduced Cathryn to señor Benitez who owned the house next door and rented out rooms. The available room had no light, no air, no shelves, and she would have to share a bathroom. But the cost was $120 U.S. per month, and Cathryn felt she had no alternative—she had to conserve what little remained of her money. She took it. Better than paying $170 to *señor* Cardoza for no hot water and spotty electricity.

This *pensione*, a narrow building with four floors, had an electric thermos-style hot water dispenser and outside the second floor room an old 1940s-style refrigerator that she could use. The fourth floor rooms had lots of light and air, and Benitez said she could move there later when a woman who lived there now moved out.

On April 21 she moved in and arranged her dark, little room as best she could.

Señor Benitez, a sweet, retired Jewish ophthalmologist who spoke English and reminded her of her grandfather, always smiled when he saw Cathryn and said, *"Ahh, la mas linda gringa preciosa de Perú. Como estas gringa?"* Ah, the most beautiful, precious, north American of Peru. How are you?

How was she? Unsettled, paddling on the surface of a sea of uncertainty. With no new attorney yet, Cathryn had no idea what was happening with her case. She still didn't know if the judge had subpoenaed the DEA to answer his questions.

For all she knew, the police could come for her tomorrow.

When Arturo put his hand on her knee Cathryn didn't know whether to slap his hand or his face. Because he was old she decided to just slap his hand…then she realized he liked it.

Arturo, her neighbor on the second floor, had cable TV and invited Cathryn in to watch CNN. In his seventies, Arturo spoke English with a thick Latin accent. With a good sense of humor, Arturo wasn't a bad sort. He could make her laugh. But he had roaming, suction-grip hands. Her best defense was to keep moving. She got good at watching television and anticipating his moves. Sometimes just a quick stand-and-twist maneuver was enough. If she saw his hands move towards her breasts, she rose and went out into the hall to get hot water for her tea.

Cathryn nicknamed Arturo *pulpo*—Spanish for "octopus"— which he thought was a great joke. He could move fast for an old man, but she was faster, and when his attacks were foiled they both would laugh loudly. Cathryn was sure everyone in the *pensione* heard.

She would point to the picture of Jesus he had on the wall and say, "Jesus is watching you, Pulpo." But it was no deterrent—she should have known that from what went on in front of all the religious pictures on the cubicle walls in Santa Monica.

Cathryn spent a day walking all over Lima, window-shopped in Miraflores, splurged on facial soap and an eye pencil. Within 24 hours she developed a raging eye infection. So much for the hypoallergenic eye pencil. Pulpo went with her to Pharmax to get eye medicine. One good thing about Peru, for most medications, you didn't have to spend money to go to a doctor to get a prescription.

In her last conversation with her sister, Dierdre had said she would talk to her mom about another wire transfer. This must be what it's like, Cathryn thought, to be a homeless beggar. She accepted a small loan from Pulpo. Again she was almost out of money.

As her sponsor and a copyright attorney, Olivia was able to find out that the judge hadn't heard anything from the new prosecutor, and there was no word about the status of the subpoena. That was the nature of things—nothing would happen until the last minute, and the shadow of change loomed ominously above Cathryn with no way to anticipate what came next. She wasn't waiting for an axe to fall—she was waiting for a guillotine.

Cathryn kissed off more money taking a taxi to the U.S. embassy. She had to figure out a way to make sense of the chaotic busses. In addition to no signage and no posted fares, the in-a-hurry drivers barked out destinations so fast she couldn't understand them. Tourist guidebooks in English were no help—they all advised to take taxis.

She pressed David Ryan enough that he agreed to write her an identity paper, explaining that her passport was in protective custody by the U.S. embassy. He attached a photo she provided and stamped the paper with the embassy seal. This probably wouldn't fly, but it was better than nothing. The first thing Peruvian officials would say is, "Why is your passport in protective custody?"

Chapter 47

Pulpo—now her connection to CNN, *Larry King*, and *News Night*—gave her tips on dealing with Peruvians.

"They are all crooked and untrustworthy. You must always be on your guard."

He tried to explain to Cathryn Lima's *chama* or bus system. He promised to show her how to negotiate better prices for taxis. "The best way to learn it is to do it." Knowing she was broke, Pulpo bought her dinner in a Chinese place—awful food—which she thought was sweet.

Cesar called to say he needed Cathryn's help and could she see him tomorrow in the afternoon? They met at the Pharmax coffee shop. Cathryn was curious to know what he wanted. Cesar said he needed help writing a formal letter to the U.S. government. Of course. He told her he worked long hours at his new job and needed an assistant. Could she polish her Spanish? If so, he could get her hired.

"I'm on parole for drug smuggling, and you're telling me the Peruvian government would hire me to work in a high-level security office?"

He didn't seem the least surprised at her response. "Do not worry about it. I can handle everything."

Cathryn needed the money desperately. She wanted to believe that he could do this for her.

Olivia called the Palacio de Justicia and learned the judge's subpoena to the DEA to answer his questions had been sent by courier to the U.S. Embassy.

"You'll have to go before the judge on Monday at 2:30 p.m.," she said. Cathryn would also have to give a statement about her case to the judge on Tuesday, and she would have to go before the new prosecutor on Wednesday. Cathryn didn't know how she would have managed without Olivia; she was her contact person, receiving calls or written notices for Cathryn at her office or home. Technically, Cathryn lived with her and they had been stretching it since she had moved into the *pensione*.

At the last minute, in true Peruvian style, Cathryn's Monday meeting with the judge was cancelled. But Olivia saw him on Tuesday, gave him a statement describing how she had met Cathryn, what kind of person she was, what she'd been doing.

"I think it went well," Olivia said, "but you still have to go to court about the fake hundred dollar bill."

She told her the judge had sent someone to look into it, and that most likely it had been planted on Cathryn by one of the people involved in her arrest. But she advised Cathryn to say it must have come with her from the U.S. No Peruvian would be brave enough to confess, which would cost him his job, so it would be better to let that person save face. Cathryn didn't like it, but she understood what Olivia was saying.

At the Palacio de Justicia on Wednesday Cathryn was informed that her trial for counterfeiting had been cancelled because no interpreter was available, and Olivia could not be allowed to do it.

"The judge was impressed with you," Olivia said. "He'll do what he can to keep you from going back to Santa Monica. He said that if you haven't fled the country by now, you probably never would."

Was it a good sign that this new judge felt bold enough to uphold the decision to let her stay out of jail during the remainder of her trial? Was the guillotine on hold?

Mid-May saw winter coming. Constant humidity made Lima bone-numbing cold. Cathryn would have to buy sweaters, a warm coat. She still wasn't used to the reversal of seasons south of the equator.

Soft alpaca was for sale everywhere. It was so cheap that Cathryn couldn't believe it was the same heavenly alpaca that is so expensive in the U.S. If she could get it to the U.S. at Peruvian prices, she'd be a millionaire. Cathryn had been thinking about how to import alpaca textiles from Peru and decided to run the idea by Olivia. She would also talk to Pulpo, who had an entrepreneurial background.

At first Cathryn had thought about alpaca baby blankets, but decided the market was wider. She asked Olivia where she could go to look for *artesania* for the U.S. market. Olivia described a village of artisans called Huancayo, but since it was outside Lima, they would have to ask the judge for permission for her to take Cathryn there.

On Friday, May 14th, 2004 Cathryn went to the Palacio de Justicia courthouse to appear before the new prosecutor. The woman asked two questions about the counterfeit hundred-dollar bill and grilled Cathryn on her prior testimony. She said that Cathryn made conflicting statements. "The prior record shows that you received the call from Dom in Lima."

"I never said that. I said he called me in Cusco."

Cathryn asked the interpreter—the same woman who interpreted twice before—to read over the prior testimony.

"The prior record doesn't say which hotel, either Lima or Cusco," the prosecutor said.

"I received his phone call in Cusco the night before I flew back to Lima."

The prosecutor seemed unhappy with this answer. She snapped something in Spanish at the interpreter.

The new attorney assigned to her case, soft-spoken Segundo Leon, just sat there, unimpressive. She reminded herself that Cesar, who'd recommended him, had said Leon had a stellar reputation. However, Segundo Leon didn't speak English. And right now he wasn't speaking anything. He'd been so quiet that the interpreter asked Cathryn where her attorney was. She pointed to Leon and explained that the man who had represented her before, Cesar Xavier, had left to take a job with the government.

The prosecutor went back over her testimony, repeated that Cathryn had said things she hadn't. The interpreter went back over her testimony and read it to her in English so she could refute it. The prosecutor made no effort to hide her nasty sneer. This had the effect that the woman typing that day's testimony kept giving Cathryn disapproving looks as well.

Though Cathryn felt she faced a lion with no protection, she never looked away from the prosecutor's face.

The prosecutor began questioning her again about the phone call from Dom.

"Look, don't take my word for it. Subpoena the phone records. I never made any phone calls during any of my stays in either Lima or Cusco, and I received one phone call from Dom, and that was in Cusco." Cathryn could feel anger flush her face.

That shut the bitch up, and she tried to conclude things fast. Cathryn asked for the interpreter to read over what she had said because she didn't want erroneous information in her statement.

The prosecutor became indignant, saying she had another appointment, this was a waste of her time.

"I don't want what happened today to happen again," Cathryn said. "So I want to go over it with the interpreter to make sure it's correct."

The prosecutor frowned. "Don't take too long."

"I'll take as long as I need. It's my life on the line, not yours."

The whole experience numbed Cathryn so that for the rest of the day she couldn't repress tears. She had no energy to do anything but cry. She cried so much that again her left ear felt infected. She put her antibiotic eye drops in the ear, and that abated it.

Each time Cathryn thought of how useless Segundo Leon had been in court she wanted to puke. She had given him $1,000 US and couldn't see what he'd done to earn it. Whatever else she would owe him would have to be paid from her bail money when the case was over. When she told Olivia how lame he was, Olivia said she understood how she felt, but they had to stick with him.

That same Friday Cathryn emailed David Ryan to see if they'd received the direct order from the judge to the DEA—addressed to Sonny Gretcham—to answer his eight questions about her case. It had been sent out by courier Wednesday and should have been delivered to the embassy on Thursday.

David emailed right back saying that they couldn't find it. He explained that a standard reply from any embassy—not just American—to a foreign court making such a request would be to please submit this through "diplomatic channels." It all had to do with diplomatic immunity. A diplomatic mission—government-speak for embassy—that answered to a court order would be waiving its diplomatic immunity.

On Tuesday Cathryn emailed again and David emailed back that Gretcham hadn't seen the judge's order, either. The only documents that were logged and tracked at the embassy were actual diplomatic notes. A document such as the one from the judge, just addressed to Gretcham, would, in theory, go through regular inter-office mail. In any case, no one could find it. He said the judge should send it again, this time "with a diplomatic note."

Aauuugh! Cathryn felt like a dog having his tail cut off one inch at a time, never knowing when the next inch would be taken.

She learned that the prosecutor had the woman who had been typing her statement subpoena the rail line and the Cusco Hotel Novotel to find out if she'd been there. Cathryn had thought the detectives in Dinandro had already done that.

Olivia said, "We have to let the prosecutor have the opportunity to prove how bad she is."

So they had to wait this out, meaning it could add months to her trial.

However, the judge said she could go to Huancayo for business.

No problema. He would also issue a new subpoena while she was gone and take care of the necessary protocol to get a diplomatic note attached to it from the *Ministerio Interior Exteriores.* He also overruled the prosecutor's request to return Cathryn to prison—at least until all her subpoenas came back from the railroad and the Cusco Hotel Novotel.

Chapter 48

David Ryan emailed Cathryn to ask if she had replaced Cesar yet and if a trial date had been set. Feeling much like Dorothy in Oz, she emailed back:

"My Beloved Scarecrow (David),

This is Dorothy (Cathryn). It nearly killed me but I got the broomstick (the diplomatic note, #RE/LEG7_4/584) of the Wicked Witch of the West (the new female prosecutor).
It was delivered to the Emerald city (the US Embassy) from Munchkin Land (Ministerio de Relaciones Exteriores) yesterday, June 7th. Please let the Wizard of Oz (Mr. Gretcham) know so that the Lion (Mr. Tjon) and the Tinman (Mr. Vargas) will be prepared to answer the questions once the process is complete.
Let them know there's no time to lose as the Wicked Witch of the West wants to get me and my little dog, Toto (Segundo/Cesar Xavier). When the broomstick leaves the emerald City, can you contact Glenda, Good Witch of the North (Congressman Weatherman's assistant) so she can pave the way for a rapid response?
Hurry Scarecrow! I haven't much time left...I'm trapped in the tower of the haunted castle and the hourglass is running out!"

Cathryn signed it, *"Dorothy Gale of Kansas/ Cathryn Prentis of San Francisco"*

Señor Benitez announced that the girl in the fourth floor room hadn't paid her rent that month, he'd told her to leave before dark, and Cathryn could have the room if she wanted it. Twenty dollars US more per month, and she would have a private bathroom. Three times the size of her dark little closet, there would be privacy, air, and light. *Yes.*

When Cathryn tried to pay him rent for the remainder of the month, he wouldn't accept it. He let her stay for free for the remaining ten days. *Que bueno!*

The road to Huancayo, made of gravel with big potholes, wound upwards through the Andes. At times, Olivia and Cathryn had to stop for long periods because of construction. Cathryn became nauseated and they stopped to drink coca tea, which helped.

They drove into Jauja, a rustic place with a town square and a church and city hall and a *cabina de internet*. In this part of Peru, Cathryn's tall, blonde looks brought open stares.

Here poverty was pandemic. Little three-wheel motorized carts, most sporting Che Guevara bumper stickers, functioned as taxicabs. They checked into a reasonably priced hostel—no hot water, of course. They then drove on dirt roads to a rural township to meet Olivia's friend, Ciro. It was dusk, there were no street signs, and twice they had to stop and knock on doors to ask directions. Dusk had turned to complete darkness by the time they arrived at Ciro's remote home.

A well-educated Peruvian who spoke English, Ciro reminded Cathryn of a middle-aged Desi Arnez complete with charm and compassion. He had worked for a pharmaceutical company traveling all over the globe making big money, then resigned and returned to Peru to help build infrastructure in remote places like Jauja. He raised the funds and equipment to build a *cabina de internet* and an astrological observatory in this little outpost. He also raised the funds to extend electricity to nearby villages.

They discussed with Ciro the kinds of products Cathryn might be able to market back in the States. He described a community nearby with a herd of vicuña. They could drive out there the next day and see if they were making any products with it.

A problem was that by law all products made of vicuña have to be manufactured in Peru. It's illegal to export raw fleece, and the Italian fashion industry had the vicuña market cornered. Most suppliers had signed exclusive contracts, and without competition the Italians owned the industry. However, this little community hadn't yet signed a contract.

In the Andes Cathryn discovered cold days became freezing nights. In addition to no hot water, their hostel lacked heating. That night Cathryn slept with all her clothes on, including her shoes.

The next day Ciro drove them in his Jeep to a small community with no name. Its residents were interested in weaving, but had no samples to buy. The community accumulated ten to twelve kilos of vicuña per year and wanted $400 a kilo, more than Cathryn felt she could spend.

They drove to Pachacayo, a community with 1,000 vicuña and 5,000 alpaca, but were told that the head guy couldn't talk to them because it was Sunday. They dined in a restaurant on chicken so salty Cathryn couldn't eat it, watched people stroll or sit in the town square, saw the inside of the church, and returned to their cold-water hostel.

On Monday Ciro drove them back to Pachacayo, where they learned that the village people didn't weave—were just fleece suppliers—and had signed a contract with the Italians.

Leaving Pachacayo they encountered a police roadblock. Cathryn froze in the backseat, wishing she could shrink into the upholstery. Since her arrest, all police frightened her. They were stopped two more times at roadblocks where police checked their documents.

Since Cathryn hadn't found any artisans with products to sell, discouragement accompanied her all the way back to Lima. Sober and contemplative, she felt like nothing she did had any importance. Again she wondered why she hadn't died in Santa Monica. Again she wondered who she was, what she was doing, and why this thing had happened to her. Was her depression hormonal, or was it from all the poverty she saw along the trip? How could anyone from the First World not be affected by the level of meagerness most people in Peru lived with? Now Cathryn understood why someone would risk their life to travel all the way to the U.S. for a chance at a better life mowing lawns or babysitting *gringitos*.

During the week Cathryn had been gone, nothing had happened with her case. She was told nothing would happen until Friday. Another week lost… In Peru, no one can hear a *gringa* scream.

Pulpo became more aggressive. They were like prey and predator, always evolving new tactics to outsmart each other. What a girl had to do just to watch CNN.

Their *pensione* housemates, knowing Arturo's reputation, laughed when Cathryn called him, *Pulpo*. Jake, a fourth floor, pudgy Peruvian who spoke excellent English said Pulpo, being "an old man in his seventies" probably was impotent and would need Viagra. Jake said her problem with Pulpo was just like his sister had with her boss's father. What she did to stop it was tell him, okay, they could fuck. The father got all freaked out and nervous and stopped bothering her.

"Most guys are all show and no substance," Jake said. "You should try that tactic with Pulpo."

That evening Cathryn tried Jake's advice about calling frisky Pulpo's bluff. "Okay, Pulpo, let's fuck."

When she turned away from the television, Pulpo stood with his pants at his feet, displaying a hard-on. Cathryn screamed and ran the two flights to her room and locked the door. Later she told Jake how shitty his advice was and vowed never to take it again. Pulpo may have been an old man from the waist up, but from the waist down he was still a teenager.

Pulpo never mentioned the incident. Next morning at the hot water thermos he gave Cathryn a hug. She ignored the fact that he still had a hard-on.

Pulpo said he would help her go to select alpaca yarn samples. He thought that in one day they would visit one place, but that fall day in May he and Cathryn visited Mitchell's, a third-generation Peruvian supplier of alpaca, and two places in Miraflores. They took buses and *chamas* and one taxi—and did it all by 3 pm. This amazed Pulpo. Cathryn laughed. "I'm a *gringa*—I can get a lot done in one day because efficiency and productivity are in my blood."

Pulpo sighed. "I've been polluted by the slow pace of things in South America."

Pulpo told her he had done well as a broker reselling everything from toothbrushes to clothes, but had lost all his money during the Alan Garcia presidency. He said Garcia let the *sole* devaluate and did nothing to save the economy. Pulpo proved to be a good businessman. At Mitchell's, while Cathryn talked to the sales guy Pulpo slithered out for a moment to the warehouse. Later he told her all the shipments from Mitchell's were going to Hong Kong, where they manufactured their alpaca clothes.

That evening when they watched TV Cathryn didn't have to do many evasive maneuvers. Running around Lima all day had exhausted Pulpo.

❖

Olivia called Cathryn's attorney and was told "no news until tomorrow." The next day, Friday, she was told she would have to wait until Monday to find out if the diplomatic note had been processed.

More lost days. Cathryn felt so disappointed and bored that she complained to anyone who would listen about how fucking slow things were. The final days of May dragged, the humidity heavy as wet laundry.

Cesar came by, happy. He worked a lot and loved his job. He

asked about her case. Cathryn told him nothing was happening. She thought that at the time he mentioned her job offer he had been sincere in his intention of getting her hired. However, the subject never again arose.

Chapter 49

Cathryn was not good at doing nothing—leisure had never been her forte. She was used to being on the move. She guessed that most people would love to just lounge around and wile away the days and weeks, but it was fucking driving her batty!

She took pastries to sisters Amelia and Luz Maria, and they were eager to know how her case was going. They were all sweet smiles. They took her into their little convent chapel where together they all whispered a prayer.

Sister Amelia took Cathryn to their convent daycare to show her where she could volunteer. Besides orphans, they took care of other people's children as a way to raise money for the convent. The daycare house contained no furniture. In the big living room off the kitchen, they kept the toddlers. Upstairs were three bedrooms, two with cribs for infants, and one with almost wall-to-wall mattresses on the floor. A playground in the backyard had a a tiny plastic slide and swing, some big wheels, some little scooters. Cathryn's heart lurched to see a sweet little girl of eighteen months, abandoned by her mother because she had a harelip.

In the evening, Pulpo took her out to an Italian deli for ravioli. Lots of people there recognized him. It amused Cathryn that people would see her with Pulpo and think, "Is Arturo dating this young girl?" Cathryn guessed that what's important for guys is not who you are fucking, but who people *think* you are fucking.

All morning on Monday, May 31 Olivia and Cathryn sat in the anteroom of the court at the Palacio de Justicia, but the order for the diplomatic note to accompany the second request from the judge for the DEA to answer his eight questions still wasn't ready. Though Cathryn wore a jacket over her shirt and skirt, she felt cold, as if the moisture had seeped into her bones. Her feet felt like ice sculptures in high heels.

"We just have to sit and wait," Olivia said.

When the order came through, they were told they could have it the next day between 10 and 11 a.m. after it was signed by the President of the Superior Court.

When they returned the next day the judge told Olivia that the diplomatic note had all the signatures and would be sent to the *Ministerio Interiores Exteriores* on Wednesday. From there it would be out of their hands. When "processed" it would go to the U.S. Embassy and on to Washington, D.C.

Cathryn had heard it could take one to two months for D.C. to answer a diplomatic note, but if they responded to the judge's questions, this could be over for her soon after. In a good case scenario, she could be home by September or October, a year from her arrest. That would be something to look forward to. She longed for her San Francisco apartment with its American toilet. What efficient suction power! In Peru all the toilets she had used hardly worked. She had learned that you don't flush the toilet paper because it plugged the plumbing. Next to the toilet would be a little open basket in which to put your soiled spaper.

The coldest months approached and the damp winter weather plus the bureaucracy of repetitive trips to court left Cathryn physically exhausted and emotionally drained. She couldn't get warm, even in her *pensione* room. She would crawl into bed in a sweater and wait for the chill of being outdoors to pass.

Through an internet friend Cathryn discovered an SGI center—Soka Gakkai International, a Buddhist lay organization—in Lima, just three blocks from where she lived. It had no sign, and because of terrorism was hidden behind barbed wire and high walls. There she could chant in front of a *gohonzon* for the first time in a year.

Cathryn began to go often to chant at the SGI center. She made new friends—found it comfortable and refreshing to be around upbeat Buddhists who had practiced in the U.S. She must have had someone from almost every religion on the face of the earth saying prayers for her: Buddhists and Muslims and Jews and new age/shamans and Christians of every flavor—Catholic, Baptist, Protestant, Lutheran, Morman, Greek Orthodox, Unitarian. She was on a lot of prayer lists. She liked to think that all that focused energy would somehow make everything turn out for the best.

That evening Pulpo confessed his undying love for her. He apologized for being so touchy feely, but he said he couldn't help himself. When Pulpo was young he had been a handsome man, and Cathryn thought that if she had met him 35 years ago she might have fallen for him. She tried to be as kind as possible. "We have a big age difference, and a sexual relationship is just not possible."

His smile was so sincere. "That is all right, Cathryn. I will wait for you to change your mind."

The rest of the evening they watched TV, laughed, enjoyed each other's company. He could be a well-behaved gentleman when he put his mind to it.

June 4th, 2004—Cathryn's birthday—phone calls from family. She explained how nerve wracking it was to watch the money dwindle without any way for her to generate income. She felt stranded on a deserted island where all she could do was scan the horizon for distant ships. But day after day and week after week and month after month... nothing. Each day Cathryn would awaken and think, "This is the day. This is the day I get the break that'll take me home."

It never rained in Lima; the most that happened was drizzle. Cathryn felt constrained in a winter prison of cold and damp and drizzle. One morning she went to the hot water thermos in the hall and discovered no water in the house—the water shortage had become so severe that it would be only turned on in the afternoons. She would have to remember to take her shower in the evenings now...and pray for rain in the Andes, the supplier of all water to

Lima. Cathryn thought of Santa Monica, how prisoners were the first to suffer from a water shortage.

Wednesday, June 9th Cathryn went to the Palacio de Justicia for the fourth time to sign in and submit to the judge her monthly activities list. Four months since she'd been released from Santa Monica Women's Prison into the greater prison of the city of Lima.

Olivia accompanied her, translating the news that the judge had lifted her travel restrictions—she could go anywhere in Peru without permission. She didn't have to carry papers.

On the way home Cathryn's cell phone rang—David Ryan, saying something about issuing her a passport? What about the judge who issued the order not to give her one? When she asked him about the diplomatic note with the second subpoena from the judge, he said he didn't know anything about it.

Next day when Cathryn called him to ask about the note and the judge's order she had to leave a message. When several hours had passed and he hadn't called back, Olivia called the *Ministerio* and found someone with information. She was told the order wasn't there and should have gone out right away to the US embassy.

The following day David Ryan called Cathryn, his tone breezy and chatty, as if he had no other problems but hers. He told her someone high up at the State Department had called him and instructed him to issue her a passport and encourage her to get out of the country.

"Who? Colin Powell?"

David said he couldn't tell her but that it was someone who took his directions straight from Colin Powell.

"But the Peruvian judge has ordered you not to issue me a passport. What about that?"

"There are laws that will protect me if the judge learns I've issued you a passport." David said he was afraid for her and that everyone wanted her to run. He told her not to worry, he would take the fall for it.

"I can't do it." Cathryn sighed. "I need that passport for ID purposes, but if I get it I still won't run. Believe me, I've given this a lot of thought. So many people here have stood up for me. Olivia's become my best friend. If she hadn't put up that personal guarantee for me, I'd still be wasting away in Santa Monica. I owe her big time."

And, Cathryn thought, *what about the first judge who allowed me to go free?* What about her current judge who lifted her travel restrictions because he believed in her so much and fought the new prosecutor to keep her from going back to prison?

She hit David Ryan with the telling question: "If I got re-arrested leaving the country illegally, would the State Department tell the Peruvian government they told me to leave? That I was acting on their advice?"

Long silence on the phone. "No," David said. "You'd be on your own if you tried to leave Peru."

So. What did that tell her? Cathryn suspected they had received the diplomatic note and didn't want to answer the questions. Those questions must have been causing a big problem if they wanted to see her either leave the country illegally or get rearrested.

"I won't leave Peru unless Olivia tells me to go." David said he understood her position and respected her for it because "no other prisoner in Peru would turn it down."

David hadn't let his government work leach out his humanity. At the same time he suffered because he hadn't yet lost the ability to not give a damn.

"I'm just doing my job by passing along the information," he said. "Your passport will be ready next week."

Their conversation left Cathryn feeling like she was dancing with a king cobra that would remain hypnotized as long as she kept staring into its eyes. If she blinked or stopped moving, *BAM*—she would be stricken by fangs. Sometimes she felt so ground down that she could almost talk herself into blinking or stopping the dance just to let it be over. Then she would think about her parents, brother, sister, friends and all the people rallying for her... and she would keep staring at the cobra.

Back at the *pensione* there was still no water.

Chapter 50

Olivia believed Cathryn would prevail. She told her that when she visited her in prison and all looked bleak, she felt something positive would happen, but she didn't know what it would be. She felt more sure about this than about things in her own life. When Olivia talked like that Cathryn didn't say that the "something positive" would have been that she would die in prison—she had come so close to taking the Mellaril.

And now Olivia helped her with the baby stages of her envisioned textile business. She took a gray, overcast Sunday away from her family to help Cathryn locate and contact weavers. On Monday she drove Cathryn to the American Chamber of Commerce to get information on exporting textiles. This chamber of commerce was all about trade within the three Americas—South, Central and North; it had nothing to do with the United States of America.

They passed through the *serenaznos*—security guards—and waited. While the receptionist sent for someone to come out and talk to them Cathryn remembered that a lot of Latins consider themselves "Americans" because they were born in either South America or Central America, and don't understand why North Americans want to bogart the "American" identity.

Cathryn was going to lose her San Francisco apartment. For eight months her mother had paid the rent out of her personal checking account, thinking any day now Cathryn would be home. The landlord had also let Cathryn use her security deposit, which amounted to about two months' rent.

When her mother called to say she'd used all the money in the checking account Cathryn said, "Give all my stuff away, or just throw it all in a dumpster."

She didn't care so much about her furniture, but who would take her kitties? They'd been living in the apartment, with Jim stopping by to take care of them.

Her world was caving in.

Though she couldn't eat and had no appetite she felt she was entering the last leg of this long, strange journey. In her deadened state, she couldn't imagine how much more would come.

Cathryn asked Diedre to call Sonny Gretcham and clarify whether or not if she ran she could be extradited back to Peru. But could she be sure Gretcham would tell her the truth?

Dierdre reported back that Gretcham stated that if she came back to the U.S. she would need an attorney and, yes, she could be extradited back to Peru, but it was unlikely to happen until after the Iraq war was over.

After the Iraq war was over? How long was this war expected to last? Her entire lifetime?

Cathryn's chosen weaver had completed the replications of the baby alpaca blanket samples, simple designs machine-made in pink and blue and white. But this weaver didn't replicate the designs exactly, and she felt disappointed that he hadn't followed instructions. She had tried another weaver who did a nice design, but had poor quality control so the designs from blanket to blanket weren't consistent. Common problems in Peru.

Her days were filled with visiting the *cabina de internet* and volunteering at the nuns' daycare where she babysat two- and three-year-olds. These places were within walking distance, and Cathryn liked strolling through the quiet neighborhoods.

Evenings she watched TV and laughed with Pulpo. If she chose to run, he vowed to help her get out of Peru through Ecuador.

One morning her cell phone woke her.

"Do you want to go running?" a woman's voice asked.

Susan! To hear her voice after all this time…to hear how they'd let her out on parole after almost three years…to hear how she and her family were overjoyed. Cathryn felt thrilled for her, couldn't wait to see her! Susan had to sign in at the Palacio de Justicia weekly, and they agreed to get together as soon as Susan finished all her family celebrations.

To go from thrill to despair in just under an hour should not have surprised Cathryn.

Olivia had offered to check on the Cusco Hotel Novotel to find out why they were taking so long to answer the prosecutor's order to verify her visit. Now Olivia called to say the hotel had returned the prosecutor's order with a written statement that there was no record of her stay. Again Cathryn saw the guillotine above her head. How could they lie? There'd been a reservation for her when she checked in. Was it because she had paid cash for the room?

Olivia's voice sounded far, far away when she said she would try to talk to the hotel manager.

After the call Cathryn laid in bed a long time, wanting to cry, but no tears came. All day she remained there, staring at the ceiling. She wrapped her body in her aunt's quilt that had survived Santa Monica. What would the judge think when he got the document from the hotel stating there was no record of her being there?

Olivia said that if they couldn't find the receipt the prosecutor would immediately send her back to prison.

Chapter 51

That Sunday, June 27, Olivia called to say the manager of Novotel found a copy of her receipt. They hadn't read the prosecutor's order carefully to check *October 2003*. Instead they had checked current hotel records, going back just three months. The rest of the records, containing her receipt, were stored elsewhere.

Olivia tried to get a copy from the manager, but he said he couldn't give it to her. The judge would have to subpoena the receipt again. Olivia called the judge, who said he'd handle it himself this time. He would re-subpoena the receipt before the prosecutor could jump on this glitch.

It had been a fluke that Olivia had been in Cusco for a seminar and could personally confront the hotel manager. Cathryn felt so faint of heart—how much more of this drama could she take?

From dejection back to exaltation: Cathryn had to deliver passport photos and $80 to the U.S. embassy, and at the bus stop she saw Susan. She had to report there also, so they rode together.

Susan was no longer the woman Cathryn had last seen in prison. Dressed in a skirt and clean, pressed shirt, she looked like an American university professor touring Inca museums. They couldn't stop grinning, they were so happy to see each other. After leaving the embassy they went for a bite at an Italian family café.

They babbled about things as only women can. Susan said things were now worse in Santa Monica. Bars had been installed around the *talleres* and around the place where they had to line up in the mornings for *recuentro* and now they planned to make the inmates buy uniforms. Susan gave her an update on Felda, Alice, Kadlin, et al. She said Phan was scheduled to get out soon. Cathryn exhibited such excitement to hear about the women that Susan ordered a rum and coke to calm her.

Cathryn had wanted to visit the friends she had made in Santa Monica, but the judge's orders specified that she wasn't allowed "to associate with known criminals." Violating these orders would mean an immediate return to Santa Monica.

Karen Mack sent a lengthy email saying the judge's eight questions were now in Washington, D.C. being reviewed by DEA and State Department lawyers. She explained the situation: Vargas' employment status complicated it. If Gretcham granted immunity to Vargas, what would be the consequences for Vargas as a Peruvian citizen working under contract with the U.S. Embassy? Would Vargas be compelled to answer? If he declined, what then? It would be simpler if Gretcham or an embassy employee could answer the questions. But Peru has certain hearsay laws that could affect that.

Cathryn needed to go to court to see the judge, but Tuesday, June 29th was another Peruvian holiday. She heard it was religious, and she heard it was a day commemorating an important historic battle. There were so many legal holidays that none were special, just a reason not to work.

When she arrived at the court on Wednesday the news, though tedious, was encouraging.

The judge had sent another order to the Cusco Hotel Novotel. He had explained to the prosecutor what had happened, putting her on hold. Regarding the diplomatic note—if Mr. Vargas couldn't answer the questions, Mr. Estrada or Mr. Tjon could. Cathryn emailed this new information to the Constituent Services Representative in Congressman Weatherman's office, hoping she could exert pressure on the DEA agents to move.

Olivia's landlord had accused her of paying her rent with two bogus $100 bills and they had a heated argument. She had agreed to pay another $100 toward the rent, but not $200.

"Protect yourself," she warned Cathryn. "Keep a written record of the serial numbers of the bills you hand out."

So Cathryn paid her rent, $100 (AB87776905H) and $20 (EL39043297A). Señor Benitez told her a tenant had paid the rent just last month with a phony $100 bill. He was able to deposit her money, *no problema. Peru: land of scams,* Cathryn thought. *You spend so much energy covering your ass that it wears you out.*

"What if they never let you leave?"

The Fourth of July weekend—not a holiday in Peru—was a long, lonely week-end. When Cathryn spoke to her brother on the phone he sounded depressed. She reassured him as best she could. He had disturbing news: He'd run into an old friend of Cathryn's at Trader Joe's and heard the guy speaking badly about her. Mark was upset that anyone who knew her could believe she was guilty of drug smuggling, could believe she was stupid because this had happened to her.

"Don't let it bother you," Cathryn said, sounding more reassuring than she felt. "Only small-minded people do that." She didn't tell him how teeth-grinding angry she felt that another week had passed with no response from the DEA regarding the eight questions.

On Tuesday, July 6, her parents called, their voices radiating distress.

"We had a conference call with David Ryan at the Embassy and Congressman Weatherman's office," her father said. "They told us to tell you to pick up your passport at the embassy and run."

Sometimes Cathryn thought it would be so much better if her family wasn't involved and knew nothing about this. Other times she felt so grateful for their love and support. It shamed her to hear fear and confusion in their voices, the same fear and confusion she lived with each day.

Now they were telling her to run! She explained that she would be rearrested. "This is a set-up." But they were too freaked to understand.

As soon as she closed her cell phone it rang again. This time it was a man who identified himself as Ernest, calling for Sonny Gretcham, who was out of town. Cathryn broke down in tears.

"Why can't you just answer the judge's questions?" she raged between sobs.

Ernest spoke as if he were in a business meeting, not speaking into a telephone with a hysterical woman. "Mr. Vargas has answered them in a letter which is now on Mr. Gretcham's desk. It will go out to the judge next week when Mr. Gretcham returns."

Then he asked her what the questions were! He worked in Gretcham's office—hadn't he seen the letter?

"I can't remember them exactly, but they're about the night of my arrest. They're questions the judge wants answered. I'm not asking anyone to lie. All I want is for them to answer the questions truthfully. Is that such a big deal?"

This entire issue of the DEA answering these eight simple questions and all the fucking brouhaha about it swirled Cathryn into an uncontrollable frenzy.

Lurking under her hysterics was a rising demon of bitterness. Who was the biggest sham artist, Dom or the DEA?

Chapter 52

On Friday Cathryn went to the Palacio de Justicia and—in her limited Spanish—signed in and submitted her monthly activities list. Afterwards she chanted at the Buddhist culture center and went to the nuns' daycare to entertain the terrible two-year-olds.

The following Monday she went to the embassy to get her passport. Ernest had told David Ryan he never said to Cathryn that Vargas' letter answering the judge's questions would "go out this week." He now said the letter would be *reviewed* this week.

Since the judge Cathryn had now was a Superior Court judge, her case must have moved to the Superior Court. Olivia had heard from an attorney friend that this judge, hoping the letter from the DEA would come through, had put an extension on her case.

"However," Olivia said, "The people who work for the courts are threatening to strike again starting tomorrow. They didn't get the raise they were promised last time they went on strike."

That strike had been right after her arrest and had lasted a month. Who knew how long it would last this time? Nothing happened in court during a strike. All trials postponed indefinitely. On Wednesday the court workers went on strike, with big demonstrations in downtown Lima, all over TV, the radio, the newspapers.

Fucked again, Cathryn thought. *This whole thing could end for me if the DEA would just answer those questions.*

Cathryn had been meeting with weavers, using Olivia's office as the headquarters for her new business, *Enamorata*—in English, "in love." Her market would be high-end retail.

One by one, the weavers disappointed. She would give each one a sample blanket and the baby alpaca yarn and he would reproduce it. One would do a poor job of production, another did good work but asked a ridiculous price, another never came back. Mitchell's made recommendations, and Pulpo helped Cathryn run an ad in the Sunday *Comercio*. She could use his telephone and he would screen calls for her.

Cathryn emailed an LA. advertising designer friend. She had good ideas for Enamorata, and Cathryn promised to send her blanket samples via UPS. At the UPS station she was told she had to have a paper from the *Ministerio de Comercio* before she could send them. Why did something so simple have to be so complicated?

The court strike continued into the following week. Olivia called to say that though the court workers were out, the judges and prosecutors were still working. She had the impression that there might not be a trial for Cathryn's case after all, but all would be determined by the prosecutor.

Olivia felt it would be helpful if David Ryan or the U.S. Ambassador came to court with Cathryn. They wouldn't have to say anything—it would be a sign of support.

Cathryn emailed David and he agreed to go. Diedre said she'd call the State Department to ask if the Ambassador could go. But David explained that an ambassador, because of his high rank, had to be careful of doing anything that might be seen as interfering with a foreign judicial system. Congressman Weatherman also felt it would be "a conflict" to ask the Ambassador to meet the prosecutor in her case.

The U.S. embassy had never before appeared in court in a drug case in Peru, so just the fact that David would be there—even though he couldn't say anything—would make a huge impression.

In the second week of the strike Cathryn wanted to pull out her hair, scream and rant, bang her hands on a wall until it broke into a million pieces. She wanted to smash and break things, to make something happen. She wanted to go home—*now*.

Two days later Olivia called to say the prosecutor could meet with them the following week.

Cathryn had coffee, bread and cheese for breakfast. There was no place to cook food in the *pensione*, so meals had to be ready to eat, and she could keep these items in her room. She kept perishables she bought in the communal fridge on Pulpo's floor. She didn't eat much, and though she had gained weight since prison she remained thin. Besides *gringa*, people called her *flaca*—skinny girl.

Middle and upper class Latinos never cleaned, washed dishes, made beds, laundered or ironed clothes, or cooked for themselves. Hired help did that. A maid in Lima costs $100 US or less per month. Homes were designed with separate places where help could work. Maid quarters had separate entries. The help had their own table because they weren't allowed to eat at the family dining table. It was a regimented class system right down to the architecture.

Cathryn's male neighbors had no clue how to make a bed. The *pensione* maids adored her because she made her own bed and washed her own clothes. Peruvians were astounded when Cathryn told them she didn't have a maid because that's a luxury in the U.S., that they cost much more than $100 a month.

The court strike, like the Energizer Bunny, kept going and going and going.

On Thursday, August 12, at 11 a.m. they all went to court. David Ryan looked impressive in his business suit. Cathryn wore her cleanest skirt and blouse and her only pair of heels. No one could tell that the night before she had cried herself to sleep, cloaked in fear of going back to prison.

While Cathryn waited outside, Olivia and David were admitted to speak to the prosecutor and her assistant. After a long hour they returned, looking pleased. David said he "wasn't authorized to talk", but could say that this case was "of interest to the U.S. government." We would meet with the assistant prosecutor again at 11 a.m. the following Monday.

All Lima rumored about when the court strike would end, but who knew? It'd been 25 days, and her case couldn't move until it ended.

"My brother knows weavers who need representation in the U.S.," Olivia said. She wanted to go meet them. So Olivia and Cathryn and Olivia's brother drove to Huachipa, a nearby town where they found fabulous items of alpaca and llama. Cathryn could imagine selling them to the North American home furnishing market.

The owners of Huachipa's Moreau & Son—a mother and son partnership—welcomed them warmly in good English. The handsome son, Dante, asked if Cathryn wished to have their meeting in English rather than Spanish. Dante and his mother, Sara, appeared professional—rare in Peru—and Cathryn wanted to represent them, but not without a contract. They agreed to meet again the following week.

Back in Lima, Cathryn gave Olivia $300 US, the cost to incorporate Enamorata in Peru.

It never occurred to Cathryn that Dante could be "tarot-card man."

Their next meeting with Dante was at Olivia's office. He said Moreau & Son planned to join with European investors to expand their business up to 1,000 looms. Two mornings later Olivia and Cathryn drove again to Huachipa. When Olivia had to go back to her office, Cathryn stayed to talk with Dante and his mother. Hours passed unnoticed as Dante explained to her all about the textiles. He had such concise accounting records for each piece produced that Cathryn was quite impressed. And such a nice man...

Dante took her to a late lunch at a café/bar in her favorite part of Lima, a neighborhood by the ocean known for beautiful architecture. He ordered for her a tasty *mariscos con arroz*.

Cathryn felt that if they were going to do business together she should tell Dante about her "past." To her surprise, he only shrugged. She told him she felt things would end well, but he needed to understand there was no guarantee.

They drove to visit several antique places. In front of an elegant colonial house he kissed her on the cheek. Her surprise blossomed into a garden of questions. Was he just being friendly, or did he want something more? Was this a kind of exploration on his part to see how she would react? Cathryn could be doing business with Dante. He was also as tall as her and handsome as a Latin movie star. Cultured, educated, sexy. If he did in fact want something more, could she resist?

They walked along the La Punta boardwalk. He told her he was fifty. She thought he looked much younger. He told her about his years handling Costa Rica's diplomatic relations with Peru. As second to the Costa Rican ambassador he had filled in for the role when the embassy had been between ambassadors.

Jeesh—how much sexier could he get?

"Cathryn, you know I am attracted to you," he whispered. "I would like for us to have a more intimate relationship than working together."

It took a minute for her to recover her senses. "That's the thing. We'll be working together. It's never wise to get romantically involved with someone you're in business with." So there, she had made her stand.

Dante kissed her—full, soft, sensual—an incredible sensation after so long without the nearness of an attractive man. Her George Clooney prison fantasy evaporated.

In the car, riding with Dante back to her *pensione*, Cathryn marveled at what had just happened. On the road next to the ocean magnificent fireworks exploded in the distance. The Lima sun had faded into the gray haze of dusk.

Could Dante be the man foretold in the tarot cards?

Chapter 53

Saturday, working in Olivia's office on a post card layout for Enamorata, Dante dominated Cathryn's thoughts. Saturday night at the movies with Susan, watching *Fahrenheit 9-11*, Dante haunted her thoughts. Chanting with Renata on Sunday, Dante teased her thoughts.

Sunday afternoon Dante came to Olivia's house to sign a textile confidentiality agreement. Cathryn was working on her website. While they talked Dante happened to touch her bare knee with a fingertip. Her breath fluttered. Her body's immediate physical response amazed her. She envisioned climbing on top of him and screwing him right there on the couch. While these lusty, lascivious thoughts danced through her head Cathryn remained the subdued professional American businesswoman.

When Dante left she accompanied him to the door. Olivia had gone into another part of the house, and again he kissed her. When her thigh brushed his hard-on, she knew he wanted what she wanted.

Cathryn spent all day Monday with Dante, learning about different weaving styles—she could now tell the difference between llama and alpaca just by touch—and learning about Dante. She noticed wet spots all over the crotch of his jeans—that hard-on was leaking. So intense was the sexual tension between them that Cathryn thought, *if we don't consummate this thing soon, one of us will have an aneurysm.*

Dante took Cathryn to a café for an energy shake. Where time had dragged through Lima for months, it flew by while she was with Dante. By the time he returned her to her *pensione*, they were flirting dirty with each other. Parked in his car in front of the building, they "made out" like teenagers. Afterwards her belly ached from repressed desire.

Cathryn's mind had been distracted completely from the court strike. Susan had said she'd heard the strike would end on Monday, but Monday came and went with no sign of an end.

On Tuesday Dante took Cathryn to the Prince Hotel. Flowers and fruit and champagne and a Jacuzzi in the room. She fed him grapes and champagne with her mouth and they spent the day engulfed in frantic, romantic sex.

The next day Dante called her eight times to say sexy things about how crazy he was about her. Cathryn felt wild with infatuation.

On Thursday they met to look at digital photos for the textile catalog CD they planned to produce. They drove to a little motel in Huachipa, indulged themselves in each other, and talked and laughed all the way back to her *pensione*.

All that incredible sex with Dante threw out Cathryn's back, made it awkward to move. Dante took her to Pharmax for an anti-inflammatory med. In his car in front of her *pensione* they had another heated necking session, like teen-agers who had fallen in love for the first time. But no "private Spanish lesson"—their new code phrase for sex—that night.

The *pensione* was not the place for lovemaking. The cheap dividing room walls had no insulation, with little privacy. An unwritten code existed that the rooms were not to be used for sex or parties, behaviors that were grounds for being thrown out.

Dante did come upstairs to her room to tuck her in and use the bathroom. He sat down on the side of her bed for a mini-monologue about being monogamous.

As a forty-something woman, Cathryn thought she had a pretty realistic assessment of human sexuality. She couldn't imagine a guy as highly-sexed as Dante being monogamous. She couldn't imagine *any* guy being monogamous—that had not been her observational experiences with her father or her brother. Since puberty she had dealt with unwanted sexual attention from best friends' boyfriends and husbands, a friend's dad, her brother's friends, strangers passing her on the street, next door neighbors, bosses and guys at work. She had it now right there with Pulpo in her own *pensione*. Was her view of male sexuality perverted? Or realistic?

Cathryn was willing to give Dante the chance to prove her wrong. She herself found it easy to agree.

Between conversation over romantic dinners and "private Spanish Lessons" Dante and Cathryn became closer. They talked about what it would be like to travel through Tuscany and the Italian Riviera, about how nice it was to sleep next to each other and snuggle in bed, about what they wanted to accomplish with the rest of their lives, about how they wished they'd met each other 25 years earlier.

They talked about how they felt when they saw each other, what it was like when they had to be away from each other, when they would be able to make love again, and the big question: what would happen to their relationship when Cathryn went back to America?

Dante taught Cathryn how to say naughty things in Spanish. They would laugh and talk about sex and become aroused. They agreed there's no passion without the animal aspect of attraction, and there's no fulfillment without the love component. They agreed that the perfect balance of spirit and matter creates a beautiful union. Was she in love, or what?

Pulpo suspected Cathryn was "different", so she told him about Dante. Distressed, Pulpo called Dante, "a Peruvian jerk who will break your heart." Cathryn countered that Dante was Costa Rican, and explained to Pulpo that he was still her friend, that she loved him like a father, but Pulpo was still pissed. On Sunday when Dante picked her up to spend the day, Pulpo, miffed, hid in his room.

Dante and Cathryn walked the La Punta boardwalk and had lunch. In a tiny romantic restaurant, he raised his beer glass to make a toast. "To Edmundo! Without him we never would have met."

Cathryn smiled. "It's Domingo, not Edmundo."

He grinned, and they touched glasses. "Here's to Domingo! What's his last name?"

"Ramos."

Dante's face blanched white as the tablecloth.

"Do you know him?"

He set down his beer glass without taking a swallow. "He is my ex-wife's little cousin."

"You're sure?" A worm of fear squirmed in Cathryn's stomach.

"Cathryn, there are not that many Domingo Ramos out there with his history."

"The DEA told my sister"—Dierdre was the official contact person for her family—"that he'd been arrested in another country for drugs, but it wasn't America or Peru."

"It was Bali, in the mid-eighties. Dom was arrested for smuggling cocaine in surf boards, and the Ramos family had to pay quite a lot of money to get him out of Indonesia."

Stunned, Cathryn listened while Dante described Dom as a manipulative man who used people. She told him how Dom had worked for Angela for six years, but he said Dom always had some game going. Dante, still friends with his ex-wife, said the next time she called he would ask her about Dom.

"Your DEA probably didn't pick him up in Mexico City because they wanted to let the little fish lead them to the bigger fish," Dante said. "Knowing hundreds of kilos went out elsewhere in the airport that night, they wanted to find out where that went by following him. But Dom was smart and ditched them, and they don't want to admit they lost him." ❖ Tuesday, the first of September 2004 with spring in the Peruvian air. Still reeling from Dante's revelation about his family connection to Dom, Cathryn now had a full-blown cold and felt doubly miserable.

Monday had been an official holiday. She couldn't tell what Peruvians were celebrating, and didn't care because the courts were still closed. Forty-eight days on strike. Rumors still abounded, but nothing of substance. *Strike, strike, stroke*, she thought.

Karen Mack emailed a supportive message that she'd been in touch with David Ryan and that Congressman Weatherman's office continued to "hope for a favorable outcome."

Cathryn tried to meditate but couldn't concentrate. Dante brought her cold medicine and for several days she stayed in bed, drifting in and out of sleep. The evening she felt a little better, Dante took her to an outdoor café for beers. Suffering from a cloaking depression, she didn't feel much like talking, and she loved that Dante didn't press. Just to be together gave her comfort.

Often they would go to different little hotels to spend the night. Laughing, they referred to them as *"Las casitas de joder"*—the little houses for fucking. Cathryn loved having a big bathtub and a beautiful view and waking up together. She and Dante were spending almost every day together now, but not every night.

When Cathryn went to pay *señor* Benitez her rent, he told her that he'd rented her room to someone else.

Chapter 54

Benitez explained that a long time ago he had taken this reservation for September 14th. Cathryn had six days to vacate her room.

When she went for *chifa*—Chinese food—with Dante, he told her she could live in his hacienda in Huachipa with his mother Sara. But Huachipa was outside Lima and Cathryn needed to stay close to Olivia because by court order she technically lived with her.

Cathryn returned to the *pensione* and Benitez said she could stay after all.

"I will give the man another room," he said, "and if he doesn't like it, he can find another place to stay."

She handed him two bills. $100 (CC 83381586A) and $20 (CE 02380268B).

The court strike entered into its fifty-fifth day. Cathryn couldn't comprehend this standstill. What frightened her most was that since the strike had begun she hadn't been able to do her monthly sign-in, as required by the terms of her probation. What if the prosecutor found a way to use that against her?

"Do not worry," Olivia said, "Just keep recording your list of activities so you can submit them when the strike ends."

If it ever ends.

One evening when Dante came to take Cathryn out she introduced him to Pulpo. Dante graciously called him, "Don Arturo."

Later Pulpo admitted that he liked Dante. "I am happy for you, Cathryn. I am glad you fell in love with a nice man. After all you have been through, you deserve it."

The workers in Dante's company produced excellent samples for Cathryn in different styles of alpaca and llama. To celebrate, she and Dante and Sara went to dinner in a café in Hauchipa.

The next morning Cathryn's cell phone awakened her. Babbling in Spanish and English, Pulpo was so excited that at first she found it difficult to understand him.

"Cathryn, the strike is over! It's officially *over*!"

Friday, September 10th, 2004. The strike had lasted 58 days—almost three months. Pulpo said everyone would return to work on Monday or be fired.

The backlog of work in the courts created during the strike pushed her case back several months. She felt devastated—to think she had expected to be home by September or October!

Wednesday, September 15, she went to Palacio de Justicia to sign in and found hoards of people waiting. For what seemed like hours she stood in line.

Cathryn worried that her distribution agreement with Moreau & Son would be in jeopardy if she couldn't return soon to the U.S. And she felt desperate to see her elderly parents. Her lawyer had hinted that there was a possibility the judge would let her return to the U.S. before her trial, if Olivia would make another guarantee. It wouldn't require money, just Olivia's word that she believed Cathryn would return. Olivia would again be putting her career on the line for Cathryn just as she had when she had been released from Santa Monica. If this arrangement could be made, it would be another legal precedent in Peru.

Friday afternoon Olivia called with encouraging news. The judge would allow Cathryn to go to the U.S. for 21 days.

Cathryn called David Ryan. "No way," David said in disbelief.

"The judge will send you a letter to issue me a passport." They shared a laugh over that.

"This is a precedent for sure," he said.

The judge also wanted a letter—written in Spanish—from the U.S. Embassy saying that a) they knew Cathryn would be gone 21 days and would call upon her return, b) they would issue her a passport to travel, c) they knew she was going for business to lay the groundwork for Enamorata, and d) her exact travel dates and Lan Airlines flight numbers.

Thrilled for her, Olivia agreed to provide another guarantee. Pulpo and Dante, stunned at this news, were happy for her as well.

Monday Cathryn waited all day to hear from David that she could pick up the official embassy letter. When she couldn't wait one more minute, she called the embassy. The phone rang and rang with no answer. On her second try, when she got through, no one knew when it would be ready. David was out of town for the day.

The good part of that Monday was that Cathryn went with Dante to a little motel in Huachipa for a "private Spanish lesson." Sex—the best drug of all.

Tuesday morning she chanted at the culture center, concentrating on sending energy through the universe to take her safely home for 21 days. At the U.S. embassy she received her letter from David and delivered it to Olivia, who would present it to the judge Wednesday morning.

Thursday morning Cathryn received a letter from the judge acknowledging that the U.S. embassy had permission to give her a passport, and that they knew she was allowed to return to the U.S. for only 21 days. Unable to get from Callao back to the embassy before it closed, Friday morning Cathryn rose early to take the letter to David Ryan.

An entire week swallowed by simple paperwork. The following Tuesday she would receive the formal court paper that would allow her to travel to the U.S.

Lunch with Dante on Friday was almost hilarious. He behaved like a 17-year-old who is afraid that while his girlfriend is on vacation she might find someone else. They were like such teenagers. After lunch Dante took her to buy her airline ticket, a happy/sad event. Such strange feelings about going home. She would miss Olivia, Dante, Susan, Pulpo, everyone. But they all believed she would return to Peru. It felt surreal to think that this time next week she would be in San Francisco.

Four days until her scheduled departure on Thursday, September 30th, 2004. Monday Cathryn went with Olivia to Huachipa to check out Mon Repos, a manufacturer of alpaca goods. Dante took her for a long, romantic drive around the outskirts of Lima. They dined at an outdoor café, talked about how they would deal with their first separation. Cathryn promised again not to have sex with another guy.

They never discussed the possibility that she might not return. It was always her intention to keep her word to return.

Three days before Cathryn's departure Marge called to say she would meet her at the airport in San Francisco. Cathryn began serious packing. She chanted for two hours at the Buddhist culture center. She and Dante worked on textile patterns. She went to the *cabina de internet.* Through all these activities, she thought, *in three days I'll be home.*

Tuesday morning, two days before her departure, Cathryn went to the judge to get the final Peruvian paper that stated she could travel out of the country.

"The paper is not ready. Come back tomorrow."

Tomorrow? She was leaving the day after tomorrow! What if it wasn't ready tomorrow, either?

Chapter 55

Thursday, September 30, the day of Cathryn's scheduled departure—bags in the car, ready to go—Dante drove her all over Lima getting documents finalized so she could clear immigration to leave the country.

A lot of money passed out of her hands that day. Money for translations and money for the notary and money for verifying the notary signatures and—of course—extra bribe money to get things expedited.

Afterwards they went to Dante's Huachipa hacienda to make frantic love one more time. Cathryn knew her bags were clean of drugs, but felt so paranoid that she checked them one more time.

At dusk Dante and Cathryn and Olivia headed for the airport.

Where the unthinkable happened. Rapid Spanish conversation. Swirling memories of the night Cathryn had been arrested—that raw, helpless feeling.

Immigration would not let her pass.

"They want five hundred dollars," Olivia said.

Cathryn's voice was hollow. "What for? I don't have it?"

"I believe there is an overstay fee of three hundred dollars."

"And the other two hundred?"

In corrupt Peru, people in authority could do whatever they wanted. There was no official explanation for the two hundred dollar difference. Cathryn would have to pay $500 US and that was that.

Because between the three of them at that moment they did not possess $500 in cash, Cathryn was not allowed to depart.

She thought of Dierdre and Marge waiting to welcome her at the San Francisco airport. Her stomach roiled. Her fingers trembled as she punched the numbers on her cell phone to call to say she wasn't coming tonight, she didn't know when she would be coming, she had to go back to the Ministry of Immigration and do this all over again.

Cathryn closed her cell phone and Dante held her as she fought back tears of disappointment and frustration. They spoke little as they waited for her luggage to be unloaded from the plane.

In the back seat of the car, Cathryn cried. Though it was late she walked to the *cabina de internet* to send emails. Dierdre would have to mail her more money to pay the overstay fee to Immigration.

The next morning—a morning she should have been awakening in San Francisco—Dante took her to the Palacio de Justicia to talk to the judge. The judge said David Ryan would need to write another letter saying the same thing all over again but with a different date. She would have to give David her new dates of travel and flight numbers.

Cathryn returned to her *pensione* and collapsed on her bed, weak from tension. She slept through the entire afternoon and into Friday night.

Saturday she went to Chorrillos to have lunch with Dante and Sara. Sunday morning she meditated. In the afternoon she stayed in at the *pensione* and watched old movies with Pulpo. Again, waiting, waiting.

Early Monday morning, October 4 Cathryn went to the travel agent to rebook her flight for October 9 at noon, returning to Lima on October 30th. The penalty with the airlines for changing her ticket was $150 US.

On Tuesday the judge submitted her new papers to the Ministry of Immigration. He confirmed that Cathryn could fly out on Saturday.

Wednesday: back to the Palacio de Justicia for more papers and back to the Ministry of Immigration. Her new passport must be stamped, more papers filled out. Fees here, fees there, everywhere money out of her pocket. Back to the Ministry of Immigration for one more signature...

Thursday: back to the Ministry of Immigration to pick up signed papers. This was the last possible minute, as Cathryn had just learned that the next day was another holiday—immigration would be closed. She paid $300 US for staying in Peru too long. She was now down to $50 US in her pocket, just enough to pay a cabbie from SFX to her apartment.

Friday she stayed overnight with Olivia's.

"You're scratching your head a lot," Olivia said. "You might have head lice."

Cathryn froze in disgust. "I used stuff from the *farmacia* when I got out of Santa Monica!"

"Let me see."

Cathryn lowered her head in her direction. Olivia separated strands of hair, close to the scalp. Cathryn remembered the Peruvians in prison grooming each other like monkeys, and wanted to disappear from embarrassment.

"Yep. You've got 'em. I see eggs."

"But I used the shampoo..." Cathryn wailed.

"They're hard to get rid of. In the morning, we'll go get you more lice medicine."

That night Cathryn dreamed that she put the medicine on her head, big bugs with big legs ran out, and a stern Peruvian airport guard said, "Oh, it is not allowed for you fly with lice in your hair, but maybe for two hundred dollars something can be arranged."

The lice shampoo they bought at Pharmax stank like diesel oil and didn't suds. When it came in contact with the lice, they tumbled out, just like in her dream. Cathryn could feel them in her hair—a creepy, discomfiting, distressing feeling.

While her hair was still wet, Dante arrived to go to the airport with them, so she had to tell him. She asked him not to tell anyone else. The thought of those bugs in her hair sickened her.

Nine a.m.—Cathryn had to be at the airport three hours before her noon flight. Terrified, she stood in line to clear Immigration. The attendant checked his computer and checked her passport and again the computer and again her passport. Her trembling nerves were frightened rabbits poised to flee. He stamped her passport. Next she had to go through the X-ray check point. Her heartbeat thudded and sweat stickied her skin. In her head danced the image of a stranger planting drugs on her.

Chapter 56

She passed and walked into the terminal and called Olivia and Dante.

"I'm through! See you on the 30th."

In San Francisco she sailed through customs, *no problema*. She spent the last of her cash on a cab home. Walking into her apartment, after almost a year of absence, felt surreal. She knew it would be empty—Jim had taken her cats to his loft—but she hadn't been prepared for how quiet it was. On any given day San Francisco could be as noisy as Lima, but the inside of her apartment felt like a catacomb. For a long time before she went to bed she wandered from room to room, touching things, remembering what it had been like to live here, reminding herself this was home.

Cathryn felt so grateful that her temporary release had come about before her parents had been able to figure out logistically how to empty her apartment and where to store her stuff. But she still had to figure out how to continue to pay the rent.

On Monday, October 11, Cathryn sent a mass email to all her friends:

"Greetings,First of all, I want to thank everyone for all their kindness and concern for me during this last year, which has been one of the strangest of my life. I am deeply touched by all the cards and letters I have received. However, all the terrible stuff that happened to me turned out to have a platinum lining as I have made good friends in Peru and built the foundation for a business. None of this would have happened had this terrible incident not occurred.

"I recently returned to California—I set another legal precedent by being the first foreign prisoner in US history ever allowed to return home with the consent of the host country before my trial is over. The courts allowed me to return home to do crucial work on the business that I incorporated in Lima. My time here is limited, but

I believe I am well on my way to being acquitted in the near future when I return to Peru.

"I don't believe this would have been possible without all the kind thoughts and prayers sent to me by you. I am writing to everyone on my mailing list, but if I have accidentally overlooked anyone, please feel free to forward this on because I have been advised not to put this information on the website for security reasons. Again, many thanks, Cathryn"

Peruvian friends who had seen her website cautioned her not to put any information there that could make her a target, such as the address where she was staying. They reminded her that in Peru people get killed all the time.

Cathryn's aunt and uncle—who designed and paid for the website—didn't have a criminal mentality, so they didn't know that they were providing information to people who could harm her. For instance, they had posted the name of the city where her parents lived, and that they were listed in the phone book. That's how her parents had received sinister phone calls on her behalf.

Putting on the website that she was back in the States would be dangerous. People back home wanted specific information —too reckless to give out. Cathryn had been told by everyone in Peru to junk the website

As the only person who could testify against Dom, Cathryn's murder would be clearly a drug-related crime.

The twenty-one days in San Francisco passed in flashes of activity, most with her family. Silly things overwhelmed Cathryn, like being able to drive on roads that weren't falling apart and seeing affluence all around her—the homes, the cars, the businesses, the little boutique shops. Reuniting with her laptop overwhelmed her. In Peru in 2004 not many people had computers, so there were *cabinas de internet* in each neighborhood. In San Francisco, in order to email people she had to drive all the way to a coffee shop near Union Square.

What a huge relief, after washing her clothes, to turn the dryer on high heat. Cathryn realized that without clothes dryers in Peru, it would have been hard to kill the lice egg cycle. With her neglected closet to choose from, she threw away most of her Lima clothes. Still, she had to use a lice shampoo product for months before the creepy fiends were entirely gone—but not the psychosomatic urge to scratch her head like crazy when she thought of them. Dante said it would be cheaper to keep using the shampoo than to go to a psychiatrist.

Cathryn tired of answering the same questions over and over and over. *What was it like to be in a Third World prison? Did you think you were going to die? Do you want to kill Dom? Where do you think Dom is?*

And the reaction questions: *What do you mean you plan to return to Peru? Do you want to go back to prison? Are you crazy?*

Cathryn accomplished a lot of work for Enamorata—establishing phone lines, preparing mailing lists, acquiring printing estimates, networking.

The strangest thing was trying to talk to friends who Cathryn realized were avoiding her, frightened to see her. Jim said that these were the people who had been saying nasty things about her—like how stupid she was and how she deserved whatever happened. This surprised her because she'd known many of these people for years, and she'd often commiserated with them about their own problems.

Jim's next words made her mind freeze. "I don't like your family at all. When they came to your apartment I let them in. They were eyeing all your stuff, and started picking out things for themselves. It made me sick. They were laughing and making jokes. Then your brother took your car and they drove away." This was her mother, father, sister, brother, aunt and uncle he was talking about! This was horrifying behavior he described. "It was like when someone dies and people come in and take what they like."

In her car there had been a cigarette lighter that had gone missing. Jim said, "Oh, yeah. Your brother saw it and said, 'hey, I'm taking this.'"

Cathryn didn't want to believe this, but why would Jim make it up?

Afterwards her relationship with her brother was never the same. She suspected he resented that so many people came forward to help her. She heard that he told Dierdre, "Hey, if this happened to us, nobody would come forward to help us." To her uncle he called her "mother's little princess." Did he feel their parents did a lot more for her than they ever would have for him?

Jim shook his head. "I think when they saw how much furniture and stuff you have and the apartment was so cheap, they decided they would end up paying the same amount for storage so they might as well leave it all in the apartment."

Wednesday, October 20th, 2004, almost one year to the day of her arrest, Cathryn drove to Pacific Heights to buy a mailing list from the American Society of Interior Designers. Waiting for a light to change, the windshield wipers did their hypnotic thip-thip-thip thing, keeping the windshield clear of the pelting rain.

Out of nowhere, *KERACK!*

Another car careened into the back of her car, shoving her forward. Her car shot across the intersection and the engine died. The driver's side door wouldn't open. She had to crawl out the passenger's door. Shocked and dazed, she exchanged information with the woman who had hit her.

A tow truck happened by and took her to a repair place, and an hour later Cathryn was driving a brand new Jeep rental car. *Never happen in Lima,* she thought.

The next day her stiffened and aching body reminded her she was lucky she hadn't been injured. But her car had been totaled. The woman's insurance company wanted a fast settlement—an unexpected benefit, giving her money to keep her apartment and to buy a less expensive car. She thought of the saying, "When there's a mistake, go with it because it's a Buddhist gift!"

Chapter 57

Olivia, Dante, and Pulpo occupied her thoughts. After being with them so much for so long she missed being in constant touch. The unanswerable question haunted her: How could she give up these dear friends to return permanently to the affluence of America?

Then it was Friday, October 29, time for Marge to drive her—with one last plea to stay in America—to SFX for her return flight to Lima. Where Dante waited.

The first week back in Lima, Cathryn plunged into work on Enamorata—writing a textile marketing plan, creating a website, getting printing estimates, laying out a brochure.

She dutifully checked in with David Ryan who said he couldn't decide if he was relieved or dismayed to see her back in Lima. Dutifully she checked in with the court, where the judge smiled, pleased to see her back.

Wednesday evening, November 24, Cathryn and Dante went out for pizza and wine to celebrate their three-month anniversary.

Dante suggested they take a bus to Cajamarca to see weavers and fleece providers. They got the two front seats on the top of a double-decker bus. From there, riding through impoverished little towns for thirteen hours, Cathryn watched Peru pass by. Such a strange contrast from what she'd just come from. They watched a terrible movie and cuddled and talked and slept.

Even in cold weather Cajamarca enchanted—much like Cusco—a central square filled with old, colonial buildings built on the ruins of pre-Columbian cultures. They climbed the steps to the highest part of the city to look down upon it. They went to the museum where Atalhualpa had been held hostage by the conquistadores. They met with potential suppliers, assessing their products and workmanship. A week later they returned to Lima.

As for her legal case, the entire month of November was wasted. Cathryn submitted her activities to the judge as required. She heard that while she had been gone people had said she wouldn't return to Peru, so he was quite surprised. Olivia said her case would be reviewed by the President of the Superior Court, but the strike had backlogged everything, taxing an already slow judicial process.

The days blurred together. Another cold combined with stress sapped Cathryn's immune system, and she fought a urinary tract infection.

By the middle of the month she had new worries: People were beginning to talk about the holiday season during which, due to the nature of the Peruvian work ethic, nothing much was ever accomplished. She had to tell her parents she wouldn't be home for Christmas, and the disappointment in their voices sickened her soul.

That evening Cathryn went with Dante to Huachipa. Dante spent Christmas Day with his kids. Cathryn took a long walk through the town, decorated with religious Christmas lights.. Because all the telephone circuits were busy, she couldn't call home. She chanted and went to bed early. It didn't feel like Christmas. It felt like just another day.

The long New Year's week-end loomed. Olivia invited Cathryn to Lunajuana with her family, but weeks before she'd made plans with Dante.

New Year's Eve Dante was depressed. Moreau & Son had a financial problem, he said. Money from a textile sale hadn't come through in time for New Year's. He felt depressed about business, so how could he go out and enjoy himself? On New Year's Day, Cathryn waited all day for him to pick her up, re-reading *Adrift*. He never showed up.

Dante didn't call until Monday morning, with some bullshit excuse for standing her up on New Year's Day. Later Cathryn learned he'd gotten an invitation to go surfing on New Year's Day, so she suspected he'd gone surfing with his kids. It hurt to think that he'd lie to her.

Chapter 58

The Superior Court had told Olivia they would decide Cathryn's case in "early January", 2005. Olivia suggested they have David Ryan ask to move the process along, but Cathryn didn't want to pressure him. She suspected he wasn't authorized to do that sort of thing.

Olivia made an appointment with the President of the Superior Court for Wednesday, January 5 at 11:00 a.m., and Cathryn called David to see if he could attend. He would "get back" to her. Nerve-wracking days went by with no word.

David emailed to say he had an appointment at 10:30 a.m. on Wednesday, could they move the meeting to 1 p.m.? She called Olivia, who called the court, who told her they would "get back" to her.

Maddening.

Tuesday afternoon at 4:30 a court representative called to say the meeting could be on Wednesday at 1:30 p.m.

Olivia and Cathryn met David in front of the Palacio de Justicia. Together they climbed the stairs to the top floor. Cathryn wasn't allowed to go in, just Olivia and David Ryan. They were inside the courtroom for 45 minutes while Cathryn sat outside thinking about how hungry she was—she had lost a lot of weight, and Dante said she was too skinny. How long could her body cope with all this stress before breaking down completely?

When they came out, the President of the Superior Court came with them to meet Cathryn. Dressed in a well-fitted suit, white shirt and tie, he looked like any successful businessman. He shook her hand, said "Hello" in English, and that was it.

"It went well," Olivia said. David agreed. "We have to go see the prosecutor on Monday."

The appointment with the prosecutor on Monday, January 10, 2005 was cancelled—rescheduled for a week and a half later. Olivia said the prosecutor was considering whether or not to continue on with a trial or to exonerate Cathryn. On Wednesday, the meeting was again cancelled—her file had been "misplaced"—and rescheduled for Friday. Friday they went to court and were told to come back the following Thursday. *Grrrrr*...

On Monday morning Olivia called with alarming news: the assistant prosecutor, Dr. Hugo Gonzalo, had been refused attendance to a money-laundering conference at the U.S. Embassy, a conference sponsored by the U.S. Treasury Department and the Peruvian Government.

David Ryan said that no one at the embassy had the authority to refuse attendance to the man. David himself called Dr. Gonzalo to tell him he could attend. David went to the embassy guard post to ask why the assistant prosecutor had been denied entrance. The guard said he'd been told by the Peruvian division to deny entrance to Dr. Gonzalo.

The next day Olivia and Cathryn went to talk to Segundo Leon. He told them not to worry, that he would explain to the prosecutor and her assistant.

Their appointment with the prosecutor on Thursday was cancelled indefinitely.

A few days later, Dr. Gonzalo told Olivia that after reviewing Cathryn's file, he didn't see anything to support her guilt. He would recommend an exoneration but he didn't know if the prosecutor would support it. She was still angry that her assistant prosecutor couldn't attend the seminar at the US embassy and had written a letter asking them to explain. Dr. Gonzalo said he understood, but she didn't.

Why should she punish me for some oversight by the US embassy? Cathryn thought. *The two aren't related. But,* she reminded herself, *this was Peru and she was the American.* Olivia called David Ryan who agreed to do an investigation and call the prosecutor on Monday.

All this day-to-day angst rubber-banded Cathryn's emotions. She felt ready to snap. She found it impossible to laugh and joke with Pulpo, to chant, to make love to Dante, to take her mind—just for a moment—off her plight.

She was down to her last *soles* and had to ask her sister to send more money. Dierdre would send three hundred dollars in twenty-dollar bills, this time via priority mail to Olivia's office. When it came Cathryn went grocery shopping—she would again have *café con leche* in the morning.

At court Monday, January 31st, Cathryn waited all day to talk to the assistant prosecutor. The embassy money-laundering conference bullshit still hadn't been straightened out. David hadn't been able to call the prosecutor that day because he didn't have her telephone number. Two days later Cathryn was able to get it for him. He spoke to the prosecutor the same day and reported back that all had been smoothed out.

The following Monday morning, February 7th, they again went to see the assistant prosecutor. Dr. Gonzalo said he was preparing the paperwork for an exoneration. "I've gone over it all again and I don't think there is anything here to support her guilt," Dr. Gonzalo told Leon. "But the prosecutor could override me."

Susan drove Cathryn to the Ministry of Immigration so she could pay another overstay fine. She would be good until March 1st, 2005. She dared to hope that by then she'd be home.

Chapter 59

Cathryn discovered that a pair of *gallinazos*—vultures—had built a nest in a cubbyhole on the roof of a house on the next block. From her window she had an excellent view of them. *They make relationships look so easy,* she thought.

In the morning, the father arrived and watched the nest while the mother went for food. Cathryn saw real beauty in these vultures. It was inspiring to see them work as a team, and she couldn't wait to see the little *gallinazitos* fledge. She wished she could see the eggs, but the nest had been built in a recessed area, out of her sight line. Her neighbor Fidel, who could also see them from his window, said he thought they just built their nest so it might be a month before the babies hatched.

Cathryn began to think of them as Mr. and Mrs. Gallinazo and spent all of one Friday night watching them. When he flew in, she jumped off the nest, they had a special moment together, and she flew off. Cathryn imagined they could communicate in a way humans couldn't hear. She imagined he must be telling Mrs. Gallinazo where all the good food was. She imagined she must be telling him if there was any movement in the eggs. She imagined they were in love.

Besides waiting for something eventful to happen with her court case, Cathryn was doing a circus money-balancing act, planning each small purchase, budgeting each *sole*. As a result, she spent time in her room thinking before she left about how much it would cost her. She had lots of time to watch the Gallinazo family.

In the mornings she had coffee with them and said, "*Buenas noches*" to them before she went to bed at night. She waited to catch sight of the *gallinazo* babies, figuring she would know the eggs had hatched when the parents brought them food.

All night the mother sat on the nest. In the morning, the father came to watch over the nest while she flew away to eat. Sometimes the father would go into the recess to check on the eggs. He seemed to care about the eggs as much as the mother. She would return and sit on the eggs all day. Right after her return the father would hang out for a while before flying off.

In the late afternoon when he returned she got off the nest, and they perched on the house together and flapped their wings. They seemed to communicate with their heads. Such proud parents. When the mother got back on her nest for the night, the father flew off. Cathryn worried that Mrs. Gallinazo was getting enough to eat.

Her days were so uneventful that she found herself noting in her journal if Mr. Gallinazo hung out longer than usual one day.

On Valentine's Day, after having coffee with her *gallinazos*, Cathryn went with Olivia to the Palacio de Justicia to sign in and submit her activities to the judge. They saw the prosecutor, who had received the paperwork from Dr. Gonzalo. The prosecutor said she would review Cathryn's file in the next few days and make a decision.

The afternoon after Valentine's Day Cathryn watched in horror as her *gallinazos*, agitated and frenzied, thrashed their wings about their perch. Someone had covered the roof's recess with a piece of wood. The *gallinazos* couldn't get to their eggs.

How could anyone be so fucking cruel? It killed Cathryn to see these parents so distressed about their babies and unable to get to them. She felt devastated, her nerves unstrung.

She banged on Fidel's door, crying, "Did you see?"

"The Quechua maid. I didn't have the heart to tell you. She put the wood there."

"The fucking bitch! How could she do that?"

Jake heard Cathryn shouting and came into the hallway. "This is the mentality of Peruvians here," he said.

Fidel nodded. "When I first moved in there was a dove who built a nest in my window and I used to feed her bread." He choked on his words. "When one of the maids discovered it, she took the nest with the babies and threw it away like a piece of garbage. I was angry when I found out, but it was too late."

Late in the day, the father *gallinazo* flew away but the mother stayed, unable to abandon her eggs. All night she stayed there, confused and distraught.

Cathryn laid on her bed and cried and cried for Mr. and Mrs. Gallinazo and their doomed family. The following day Olivia came by. They took a long walk, and Olivia listened while Cathryn waved her arms and wailed about "the mentality of some people."

The mother *gallinazo* stayed by her nest for another long day, moving only to stay in the shade. Her instinct was so strong to be with her eggs. That night Mrs. Gallinazo died. Her body lay on the roof. Cathryn thought the poor thing must have died of grief, but Jake and Fidel thought the maid fed her poisoned meat.

"That's what Peruvians do. They think *gallinazos* are bad luck," Jake said.

The unnecessary cruelty of life will destroy me, Cathryn thought. For days she was inconsolable, just wanting to be alone. Not even Pulpo could cheer her.

Still numb over the destruction of her *gallinazo* family, Cathryn listened as Olivia related the latest snag in her court case. She sat on her bed holding her cell phone to her ear, picking with her fingers at a fraying edge of her aunt's quilt.

The prosecutor was dragging her feet, refusing to sign the paperwork submitted by her assistant, Dr. Gonzalo, for Cathryn's exoneration. Leon had told Olivia the paperwork for her exoneration would be ready on Friday, February 18. Then it would go to the President of the Superior Court. Olivia thought they should go to the Palacio de Justicia and push in person for it to get done.

Friday morning Cathryn was all ready to go, dressed in her uniform—skirt and jacket—when Olivia called to say it was the prosecutor's birthday. No use going to the courthouse to wait for paperwork when the office would be partying instead of working.

Cathryn remembered that Cesar had said Peruvian people don't want to work. "'Any-excuse-to-get-out-of-work' is their motto. As a result, productivity is low and the infrastructure is crippled. It's why there's not much foreign investment in Peru." Peruvians got pissed if you mentioned how far their country lagged behind the rest of the world in terms of economy and living conditions. They wanted to blame the capitalists because they thought socialism to be an easier ride.

Cathryn felt angry with Dante because he didn't see why she should be upset over the death of some vultures. How could she ever have sex again with such a heartless asshole? She didn't care if she ever saw him again.

Pulpo, who hated Dante when he first heard about him, now became his champion.

"You shouldn't be so hard on him, Cathryn. People in Peru don't have the same relationship to animals as *gringos* in the U.S. do."

They were in his room watching CNN and Cathryn glared at the television. "I don't care."

"Peru is the land of dog eat dog, and the U.S. is the land of dog eat steak."

Cathryn couldn't believe he was trying to keep Dante and her together—a month ago he'd wanted to kill him.

Dante came by to say he was leaving later in the day for Cajamarca and wanted to spend time with her. He knew she was mad at him, and he tried to be nice.

Cathryn told him she was still depressed over her *gallinazos*. She showed him where the nest had been, and he saw the body of the dead mother.

"For me the *gallinazo* family was a symbol of love and life and hope," Cathryn explained. "There was something special about them when you took the time to see them… if you saw the way they took care of each other and how they nurtured their eggs… maybe a person could learn something from them."

At last Dante realized how affected she felt. She told him Fidel said the Quechua maid put the wood over the nest. "The Quechua of today are corrupted spiritually." Dante's voice quiet. "And not in touch with their ancestors. The pre-Columbian cultures venerated the vulture and the condor." He turned away from the window, from the sight of the dead mother. "They're both vultures—one that lives in the mountains and one that lives in the jungle or near the sea. Ancient cultures realized the special powers of these birds, and this is why they appear in their textiles and carvings."

Dante put his arms around her. She breathed in his familiar maleness and felt grateful for the warmth of his hug. "Only ignorant people think the *gallinazo* is bad luck," he whispered.

She pulled away from him and looked out the window towards the rooftop of the house. "Karma's gonna drop a rotten egg on the bitch who killed my *gallinazos*."

Chapter 60

February was almost over and Cathryn suffered from *mañana, mañana, mañana*. Her papers still hadn't been signed by the prosecutor. Why was the woman dragging her feet? Was she still angry about the conference at the embassy? Did she secretly think Cathryn was guilty?

Cathryn caught another cold that kept her room-bound, drinking tea. Again she was running out of money. Thinking that her exoneration had to come through any time now, she'd been paying her rent in two-week increments, still recording the numbers on the bills she gave *señor* Benitez.

Her case file was back in Dr. Gonzalo's office. She had to be there on Monday, February 28th, 2005 at 9 a.m. Olivia had a conflicting appointment. "Dante can take you," she said.

They arrived to discover Dr. Gonzalo's recommendation for her exoneration wouldn't be signed that day, after all. Cathryn also learned that the President of the Superior Court would be going on vacation the next day, not to return until April 1st!

The next day Cathryn returned to the Palacio de Justicia. She waited an hour for Leon and by the time he showed up, Gonzalo had left for the day. Leon couldn't find out if the papers were completed. On Wednesday, both Dante and Olivia had appointments so Cathryn took the bus.

Pulpo went with her and interpreted. The hang up, he said, on getting her papers signed was that although the prosecutor said she believed Cathryn was innocent, she was afraid to sign the papers, and did not intend to do so!

But now it was a moot point because an amazing thing had happened. The woman was being transferred to another court.

"This is a normal procedure since she has been in this court for two years," Pulpo said. "Hugo Gonzalo will be promoted to prosecutor, and he has already written his decision and signed it."

After so long with her papers in *mañana* land, a stroke of luck. As prosecutor, Dr. Gonzalo could forward them with his signature to the President of the Superior Court.

Pulpo crossed himself three times. "This is a miracle!" He called Cathryn the luckiest person he had ever met, and felt surely an angel looked over her.

"See, Pulpo, I'll meet you in heaven even though I'm a Buddhist."

He crossed himself again. "You might be right."

Though the papers now could go to the President of the Superior Court, he would not decide on her case until a month later when he returned from vacation. This was like another strike.

Cathryn's funds were critically low. She went to Citibank to see if she could withdraw money from her personal Citibank account back in the States.

"Lo siento, señora. No."

Cathryn hated making begging calls to her sister. Afterwards she felt small, dependent, vulnerable, like she was on the edge of a precipice where someone could pass by and without thinking push her into financial oblivion.

Dierdre again sent money to Olivia's office. With it Cathryn went straight to the market for food.

Friday morning, March 11, Cathryn took a bus to the Palacio de Justicia to meet with her attorney. With her still-limited Spanish and no one to translate for her, she asked Leon to speak slowly. He said the President of the Superior Court was still expected back on April 1st from his vacation. Leon said he believed this process would end by April 20th, 2005, just five or six weeks away!

All the way back on the bus Cathryn wondered, *did I understood correctly everything he said?*

The following Tuesday, March 15th, 2005 Cathryn paid rent for two more weeks, $50 US (CB 13012815A).

Pulpo took her to lunch in a dumpy bakery/café. Cathryn said, "Something's in the air, but I don't know what it was."

"What do you think it is?"

Cathryn picked at her limp chicken salad. "I'm not sure, but I can feel there's a change in the energy."

"You have an energy feeling?" She could tell Pulpo thought she was crazy. His eyes seemed to laugh at her as he took a bite of his sandwich.

She would not be deterred. "Something's moving to a different frequency. We just have to wait to find out what it is." She laughed. "And I know you know there's a truth to my craziness."

That night Cathryn lay awake, noting the patterns of mold stain on her ceiling, thinking. *What if I wrote the DEA and gave them the names of all the people I planned to work with in Peru? If they reported that someone was suspicious, I would know to worry. Otherwise, I could feel more confident about who I'm doing business with.*

The following morning Cathryn drafted her letter to the DEA. When she went to Chorrillos in the afternoon to work with Dante, she told him her plan.

"It's a good idea, Cathryn." *No problema* if she gave his, Sara's or any of the weavers' names to the DEA.

That evening Cathryn went upstairs to watch TV and talk to Pulpo.

"Look *gringa*, you were right," he said. "You said there was a change in the energy, that something would happen. This is it. You can submit my name because I'd be happy to work with you." If after Cathryn returned to San Francisco she needed anything in Lima pertaining to the business, just say the word and Pulpo would take care of it.

Chapter 61

Hoping her legal process would end soon and needing to conserve the little money she had left, Cathryn decided to move to Huachipa and stay with Dante. She gave Olivia her contact numbers in Huachipa.

When Cathryn began to pack, she discovered mold on most of her clothes. Lima was so damned humid. She'd have to wash everything before she left—by hand of course—and hope it all dried in time.

The morning of her move, Dante arrived at 7 a.m., but no one heard the front door bell ring. He came back in the afternoon, and they crammed her suitcases into his little car and drove to Huachipa.

A high fence surrounded Dante's hacienda, its buildings and charming garden. Whenever someone visited, the gardener or one of the maids had to open the huge entrance gates. Quite pleasant inside but unbelievable poverty outside.

The first thing Cathryn discovered was that the computer was achingly slow. To download a simple page took forever. She would have to find a *cabina de internet* somewhere. Achingly quiet in Huachipa, at least she was saving money, and she had cable TV.

For a week Cathryn busied herself working on animal print patterns for baby alpaca blankets. She found Huachipa uncomfortably remote, but she continued to be hopeful that her legal process would soon end.

Wednesday, April 6, Dante drove her to Callao for her sign-in. She learned that a court date for her had been set for April 20th. At that time the President of the Superior Court would sign her exoneration papers. But they wanted David Ryan to appear, and he would be attending a seminar in the U.S. from April 16th to the 30th. Cathryn worried that his absence might affect her case.

Cathryn wandered around Dante's estate cursing the Peruvian court system, cursing the lost time, cursing the isolation of

Huachipa. She missed going to the culture center to chant. She missed meditating by the sea with Olivia. She missed bullshitting with Pulpo. She wanted to make plans to go see him, but travel was difficult from Huachipa.

Cathryn occupied her time feeding the chickens and playing with the brown dog, Lucas. She played with the maid's little girl. She helped Cathryn with Spanish, and Cathryn helped her with English, which she was studying in first grade.

She worked with Sara on weaving patterns, but most of the time she watched TV and waited for Dante. He spent a lot of time with his kids in Lima, and she didn't get to see him much. His work in Huachipa consisted of bookkeeping activities that didn't include her.

Wednesday, April 20th, 2005—her big court day, or so she thought. Segundo Leon had told Olivia it was okay if David couldn't appear. They arrived at the Palacio de Justicia, and were told the appointment had been pushed back, so they went across the street for coffee. When they returned, Cathryn was told to wait outside while Olivia went in to meet with the President of the Superior Court.

Cathryn sat on a hard bench and leaned against the wall. Was it going to be over? Was he going to sign the papers exonerating her, releasing her from this Peruvian nightmare? She tried to imagine what it would be like to go home, but she felt so tense she couldn't focus her mind, couldn't summon the images.

Olivia appeared, a wide smile on her face. "It's over." The President had agreed to the exoneration. "We just have to wait for his part of the paperwork to get typed and all the signatures completed."

So, she didn't have to make a court appearance after all. She didn't get to meet the President of the Superior Court. But still she had to wait...paperwork typed...signatures completed...Olivia had said. Cathryn still couldn't announce to her family what day she'd be coming home.

From Callao Olivia drove her to the *pensione* so she could visit Pulpo. Afterwards she walked to the Buddhist Culture Center to chant for an hour. Dante picked her up there, and they drove back to Huachipa.

Cathryn called her sister and parents, dreading having to tell them she still didn't know what day she would be home. As she'd feared, her mother broke down crying, and she had to ask Dante to talk to her, to calm her, to reassure her everything was good.

In the bedroom Cathryn began going through her clothes to decide what she would take home. A lot of things she would just give to the maids. But not yet...not until she knew for sure she was really going home...

Eight times the sun rose and set and Cathryn was still at Huachipa. No call from Olivia, no word from Segundo Leon, no signed paperwork from the Superior Court.

Cathryn realized she couldn't turn her head without excruciating pain, She took two pain pills, but couldn't relax, couldn't sleep. Stress insidiously attacked her body. A rash broke out across her stomach and the right lymph node of her groin had swollen.

When she called her attorney, begging in her broken Spanish for news, she heard *mañana* ...always *mañana*.

Mañana was Saturday, May 7th. Cathryn could not wait one minute longer without screaming, destroying, killing something. She grabbed a sweater—winter was coming—had a gardener open the front gate for her, and left the hacienda compound. She walked to the corner where a man coordinated the *chamas*. He showed her what bus to take to the town of Callao. The ride took two hours, but Cathryn got to see her attorney.

"*Lo siento, señora. Nada,*" Leon said. Nothing.

Another long boring weekend—Dante off with his kids. Cathryn watched so much TV that she felt her soul was being sucked into the set. Her neck pain had now moved to the other side, making it painful to move her head in any direction. She swallowed more pain pills, still couldn't relax.

Monday morning, May 9th Olivia called to say they had to go to court again on Wednesday. Wednesday she called to say they didn't have to go to court after all.

Over two weeks since her "big court appearance"—and still her exoneration papers had not been typed and signed by the President of the Superior Court.

Was this the Peruvian version of a Chinese torture? Wouldn't it have been more merciful to let her die in Santa Monica?

For the rest of May and almost all of June 2005, Cathryn worked in Hauchipa and waited for the paperwork that would mean she could go home. Time passed so slowly and she was so stressed that she had bouts of diarrhea and vomiting.

During this time millions of counterfeit U.S. $100 bills were dumped in South America, bills made in Pakistan complete with hologram and anti-counterfeit strip. After Peruvian banks realized the bills were fakes, they continued to circulate them until the US Treasury put their big American foot down. Scandal fired through Lima, and Peruvian banks were forced to pay $70 US for each phony bill turned in during the following 72 hours. After that, anyone holding bad bills was out of luck.

All this talk brought back to Cathryn the horror of the counterfeit bill switch that happened to her the night of her airport arrest. No doubt Peruvians would dispose of the remaining fakes in a similar fashion. Now, no one would accept any American $100 bills.

Chapter 62

Cathryn's exoneration was signed in mid-June, 2005 by the President of the Superior Court, only to be vetoed by the State Prosecutor. This meant that her case rose immediately to the Supreme Court of Peru for review, but now Cathryn was not barred from leaving the country.

In an email to David Ryan she wrote:

"My Beloved Scarecrow,

I hope you never think you haven't made a difference in someone else's life. You made a difference in mine. Thanks for being the best scarecrow any girl so far from Kansas could ask for.

Thank you, David, with all my heart.

It seems bittersweet to finally go home after all this time and so many obstacles. It's hard to believe that "mañana" has arrived.

I will never forget you. Ever. Please take good care of yourself.

Dorothy"

Cathryn was able to book her flight home to San Francisco for Saturday, July 2nd, 2005. Dante took her to Immigration to pay the overstay fine from March 1st.

Four days before she left, she went to a celebration lunch with David Ryan, Segundo Leon, Dante, Olivia and the President of the Superior Court.

David beamed over the outcome of her case. Together they walked back to the embassy, stopping to have their picture taken so they would have a memento of the day. At the embassy Cathryn gave him her letter for the DEA listing the names of the people she was working with for Enamorata.

David read the letter. "Cathryn, this is a smart thing for you to do."

It killed Cathryn to say goodbye to Pulpo, to see his eyes well with tears. Would she ever see him again? Taking her hand, he told her how privileged he felt to know her. "You are a genuinely rare human being and I have learned much about goodness from knowing you."

Though Cathryn knew soon he'd come to San Francisco, it was hard to say goodbye to Dante.

She felt like Dorothy leaving Oz, so happy to go back to Kansas, but torn by leaving people she had come to love so profoundly in such a short period of time. She remembered Dorothy had said something like, "Most of it was terrifying, but some of it was very beautiful."

The day of her flight Cathryn felt fearful from the moment she awoke. Again and again she made Dante go through her bags looking for drugs.

"I'm terrified someone will plant something on me." She locked what she could on her suitcases, but there were side pockets that closed with Velcro. How could she lock those? Should she cut them off? She needed them for stuff. Dante did his best to convince her that it would be all right, that she just had to be diligent in watching her suitcases, not leaving them unattended for any reason.

Since her flight wasn't until evening, he drove her to Miraflores to say goodbye to Susan. Cathryn felt so anxious that Dante stopped at a pharmacy and bought her a tranquilizer. They went to the convent to give the nuns little white, candy-stuffed purses she had made for them. They were so happy to receive the gifts, happy that Cathryn was finally going home. When Dante went to use the bathroom, sister Luz Maria asked Cathryn if he was her boyfriend.

"*Sì.*"

She said he was a nice man and that she approved of him. Coming from a nun, Cathryn thought that was quite a commendation.

Dante drives to the airport....people everywhere...threads of dread crawl through her skin... say goodbye to Dante...the long, slow-moving line through Immigration... remember not to say she has a business in Peru because that requires a business visa, which she doesn't have...they could arrest and detain her for that.

The immigration attendant asked Cathryn if she had come to Peru for business.

"No, mi novio." My boyfriend.

He gave her a long look and stamped her passport. In a numb fog, Cathryn passed through the X-ray machine, walked to the gate, boarded the plane.

She's on the plane...moving down the aisle in a dream... settle in the seat and take the pill and sleep through the direct flight—eight and a half hours... she wakes up...they're serving breakfast...

The plane begins its descent into San Francisco, where a new Hell awaits her.

Twenty months and about $62,000 after her vacation to Machu Picchu, at 7:45 a.m., Sunday, July 3, Cathryn arrived for the second time in San Francisco. She stood in the entry line for U.S. Citizens. The Customs agent swiped her passport, frowned at his screen and called airport police.

I'm in America, I'm in America, I'm in America, Cathryn repeated to herself. *I came in last October, no problema.*

The customs agent gave the airport policemen her passport. They isolated her from other people. Cathryn tried to explain to the female police officer that if this had anything to do with her arrest for drugs, she had her exoneration papers with her. Then she remembered the papers were in Spanish—maybe the woman couldn't read Spanish. But she didn't care about the papers—she told Cathryn to shut up.

I'm in America. I'm in America...

Her bags were the last to come off the carousel. They took Cathryn and her luggage to a special room where they rifled through all her things, looking for drugs. Cathryn told the airport police they didn't have to believe her about the exoneration—call the U.S. Consul in Lima or call Congressman Weatherman's office.

They ignored her. Now her breath came in shallow gasps. Eels of sweat slithered down her spine, and she feared she would have a panic attack. What if they found something Dante and she had missed each time they went through her luggage? *Could something have been planted on me? How? On the plane? When?*

When they didn't find anything, the policewoman called her supervisor who arrived and went through all Cathryn's things one more time. Cathryn pointed to all her legal documents and tried to show her exoneration papers. The supervisor sneered at her, said nothing.

At last they stuffed everything back into her bags and handed her her passport. Their faces told her they were irritated to have spent so much time and found nothing illegal. The policewoman snapped, "Get out of here."

Welcome home to the United States of America…

Cathryn gathered her bags and put them on a cart and headed out of the airport to where Marge waited. Cathryn apologized for the long delay and explained what had happened. Marge said she was just happy to see her alive and well.

Cathryn's emotions were thin, taught wires, her legs rubbery and unsteady. She feared that if someone bumped into her, she would collapse to the concrete.

Fourth of July morning, 2005 Cathryn awoke in her own bed, ready to celebrate her personal Independence Day. The first thing she did was to throw away her Noxema jar with its hidden stash of Mellaril. She was alone, in her apartment, and it felt all right.

EPILOGUE

In Cathryn's words:

In late January 2006 my exoneration was upheld by the Supreme Court of Peru. This put the entire case to rest. My attorney says all this is behind me as Peru uses double jeopardy in its legal system.

Along the way to full exoneration, my case set two foreign legal precedents: I was the first American to be released from a foreign prison on my own recognizance and the first American allowed to return to the U.S. before my trial.

People ask me if I'm afraid to go back to Peru, and I think of Peter Lorre in *Casablanca* with those Letters of Transit. I tell them what he told Humphrey Bogart: "It can't be rescinded—not even by the Fuhrer himself."

It still amazes me that a little vacation to Machu Picchu would take so much time from my life, turn me on my head, point me in such a new direction. I still cherish that white toothbrush Cesar brought me before I arrived at Santa Monica. I can't bring myself to throw it away. That's how much it meant to me at the time. I still treasure the big, white fluffy feather, which I managed to protect from being stolen and still keep by me today.

I have been told that the night of my arrest Dom must have moved several hundred kilos of cocaine through the Lima airport. Apparently making millions drowned any doubt or guilt he might have felt about what he was doing to me. The fact that it was his friend, Cathryn, was irrelevant. I meant nothing to him. He could have done it to anyone.

It never occurred to me not to trust Dom. Not only did I work with him, I laughed with him, I commiserated with him. He was not a stranger, but a coworker and close friend. He never came on to me—this was not a man trying to take me to bed so he could get something from me. We were friends in that wonderful way of camaraderie you can have with a man you don't sleep with. I "knew" him. This is why his betrayal is so difficult for me to fathom.

I've been ridiculed and made to feel stupid by so many people in the United States that, at times, I've felt ashamed to talk about what happened to me in Peru. It is the man who did this to me who should be harangued and made to feel shame. Why should the victim of the crime be condemned?

One thing mystifies me. People who ridiculed me never did it in front of me; they always did it behind my back. Others reported it to me. Those people who ridiculed me can't look me in the eyes now. And that's a good thing, because it means they still have the capacity to feel shame.

I wonder if Dom still has that capacity? If I ever see him again and can ask why he did this to me, I doubt I will be satisfied by his answer. It would be just the last page in this chapter in my life, and I would be able to finally move beyond it.

I'm not sorry that I was friends with Dom. Would any of us want to live in a mental place where we look at each and every one of our friends and wonder if we can trust them?

I don't think so.

Today Cathryn Prentis lives incognito. She has a PO Box and never has mail delivered to her house. Her phone is in another name. One day the DEA could find and catch Dom—they call periodically to tell her they are "very close."

— The end —

If you enjoyed reading *Dare to Survive*, I would really appreciate a rating and a short review at amazon.com.

Just a few sentences saying what you liked about the book would be enough, and really helpful to me as an author.

Thanks for reading **Dare to Survive**!

GROUP GUIDE

I'd be thrilled if you would recommend **Dare to Survive** to your fiction reading group.

Here are some questions you might want to discuss:

1 - What do you think was the most powerful scene in the story?

2 – How much did you know about international drug trafficking before you read the book?

3 - What do you think about Cathryn's friendship with Dom?

4 - Have you ever had a travel situation where you suspected something
"just wasn't right?"

5 - If so, how did you handle it?

6 - What do you think about the U.S. position on helping Americans in foreign prisons?

7 – Have you ever been the victim of a counterfeit bill switch?

8 – What part of the story did you think was most bizarre?

9 – What part of the story did you find to be the most scary?

10 – Have you ever been to Peru?

* * *

Carolyn
www.carolynvhamilton.com

Other books by Carolyn V. Hamilton:

FICTION

IMPLOSION

Time is running out.

With the pending implosion of the grand old Las Vegas hotel/casino, the Desert Palace, an eleven-year-old mystery of stolen money remains unsolved.

Newspaper reporter Nedra Dean feels the pressure to use every means she can to make this dramatic moment in Las Vegas history her biggest scoop, one she hopes will catapult her to big-time journalism at CNN.

Celebrity maitre d' Eduardo only wants to reconcile his estranged family before his forced retirement.

Hotel/casino manager John Cusamano schemes to find the money and run away with the love of his life, his boss's wife.

Elvis impersonator Hector Deatle and star showgirl Candy Bybee are also hot on the trail of the stolen millions.

No one seems to care that the money is rumored to be cursed—everyone who has touched it has died a horrible death. Now cocktail waitress Linda Mayo's nine-year-old daughter—after secretly finding the money—suffers from a terminal, flesh-eating disease.

And somewhere within the walls of the Desert Palace is hidden that six million dollars, which owner "Crazy" Foxy Craig will do anything to find before the walls come tumbling down.

MAGICIDE

Maxwell Beacham-Jones, the world's most famous magician, has reached the zenith of his success. Now he's planned the most daring, outrageous trick of his career.

But when Maxwell dies in a Las Vegas roller coaster escape stunt before a national television audience, it's no accident. He was hated by his contemporaries, and all of the suspects are magicians—with plenty of secret motives for murder.

MAGICIDE introduces Las Vegas Metro Police detective and single mom, Cheri Raymer, and her vegetarian partner, Tony Pizzarelli. Together they follow a trail through the world of magic and show business that leads to intrigue and shocking revelations.

Raymer will face the most devastating personal threat in her career when her teen-aged son, Tom, fascinated by magic, becomes the protégé of a suspected killer.

HARD AMAZON RAIN
(An eco-adventure romance)

Burned-out art therapist Dianti Robertson dreams of building a library for an Amerindian village on the upper Amazon in Peru. She's searching for a feeling of completion, and the library is a project completely different from her ongoing work with troubled children in America.

Roaming the Amazon River, English eco-activist Christian St. Cloud sails his trimaran, the *Rio Vida*, wherever he perceives a threat to the Amerindian way of life, opposing those whose greed would strip the people of all their natural resources. Christian is haunted by having been unable to save nine indigenous villages from being destroyed by a dam project in Venezuela.

Dianti and Christian strongly disagree on how best to aid indigenous people. Complicating their outspoken differences is the intensity of their unspoken physical attraction.

Dutch soldier-of-fortune Kees Wijntuin and a ruthless gold consortium threaten the area where Dianti lives. When two young Amerindians are kidnapped by the Dutchman and sold into slavery at the mining camp of Santo Ignacio, Dianti and Christian must join forces to rescue them.

ELIZABETH SAMSON, FORBIDDEN BRIDE
(a historical fiction based on a true story)

In the 18th century Dutch plantation colony of Suriname, where wealth is measured by the number of slaves one owns, the Free Negress Elisabeth Samson, educated and wealthy owner of several flourishing coffee plantations, wants only to marry her true love, a white man.

But can she overcome the strict Dutch laws forbidding marriage between black and white against the powerful forces of the colonial Governor, the white planters who make up the Court of Justice, and the Society of Suriname, who call her whore, covet her property, and accuse her of treason?

Carolyn V. Hamilton

MEMOIR

COMING TO LAS VEGAS

A true tale of sex, drugs and Las Vegas in the 70s, Carolyn V. Hamilton tells how she arrived in Las Vegas in 1973 to join a circus, and opened the new MGM Grand Hotel/Casino as a cocktail waitress.

How one young woman arrived in Las Vegas in 1973 to join a circus, opened the new MGM Grand Hotel/Casino as a cocktail waitress and, among other adventures, experienced a city-wide Culinary Union strike that shut down the famous Las Vegas Strip.

In 1973 Carolyn Hamilton arrives in Las Vegas with boyfriend Del to join the business side of the newly-formed Las Vegas International Circus. When they run out of money Carolyn gets a job as a cocktail waitress in the soon-to-open MGM Grand Hotel/Casino. Through nefarious means, Del gets the position as bailiff for District Court Judge Paul Goldman. Carolyn and Del marry, but Dale's ex-wife surfaces, and he is revealed as a bigamist.

Working cocktails at the MGM turns out to be more involved than a nice Lutheran girl from Seattle would think: rumors, parties, stealing, sex, drinking and drugs are the main entertainment for a bored crew of cocktail waitresses, bartenders, dealers and floormen. Some waitresses date culinary union bosses, who have their own high drama of payoffs, fights for control, fire bombings and an 18-day culinary union strike.

After a ménage a quatre with two other waitresses and a casino floorman, Carolyn decides this is not the kind of life she wants for herself. After three years she leaves the MGM to rediscover her personal values and commitment to her marriage.

Each story told in this memoir—of the Martin Scorsese *"Casino"* era of Las Vegas—is true, and many of them are humorous as well as outrageous.

AUTOBIOGRAPHY

MY MIND IS AN OPEN MOUTH

With his outlandish, machine-gun rapid-fire humor, comedian Cork Proctor has been knockin' 'em dead for sixty years ... literally. From his first attempt at stand-up comedy as a gravedigger entertaining his co-worker to lounges and showrooms around the world — on land and sea — this left-handed, dyslexic, two-time high school dropout has not only seen it all, he tells it all.

PRAISE FOR MY MIND IS AN OPEN MOUTH:

Sit up, take a deep breath, pat down your hair, and straighten your tie. Cork Proctor is known for playing with the audience.
—Dick Clark, Television Host

Roastmaster General of the United States.
—Tip O'Neill, former Speaker of the House

Cork Proctor has been one of the funniest men in Las Vegas for many glowing years. Read his book: Giggle and laugh!
—Phyllis Diller, Comedienne

The fastest, funniest comedic mind and mouth in town.
— Las Vegas Sun

His observations are intelligent, his delivery original. He is in command at all times, and like the drums he plays, his mind works in a double paradiddle beat. In other words, I like him: Brash, bright, and brilliant!
—Shecky Greene, Comedian

NON-FICTION

POWER EDITING FOR FICTION WRITERS

Finished writing your memoir? Get ready for EDITING, where your major work begins. This short guide covers everything you need to know to edit your book like a pro, and take your story and your writing from good to POWERFUL!

Professional editing for any book is not cheap. But by editing as well as possible yourself, you can drastically reduce, or even eliminate, professional editing costs.

Power Editing For Memoir Writers helps you look at every aspect of your writing—from your initial story concept, through the telling of your story, to how you craft your sentences.

Now you can feel confident in your writing, and impress your reader with your storytelling *and* the professional presentation of the words on each page.

This short, concise, no-nonsense guide makes the editing process easy. It introduces you to a fantastically easy editing system, shows you how to use powerful word arrangements called "rhetorical devices", and how to use the NUMBER ONE SECRET to power up your writing today!

Power Editing For Memoir Writers is arranged in two sections: Part One addresses the elements of your story, and how you have used them. Part Two addresses your sentence structure, grammar and word usage, with tips and tricks professional writers and editors use every day to write and market best-sellers.

The author has purposefully kept this book as simple and concise as possible—under three hours to read—with practical information you can APPLY RIGHT NOW to your manuscript.

In her private coaching program, ***Memoir to Legacy,*** Carolyn V. Hamilton helps aspiring memoir writers share their stories of adventure, adversity, personal challenges, trauma and redemption.

www.carolynvhamilton.com

* * *